Talisman of the Winds

by
JP Wagner

For Carol,
who still has a
horn on her nose.

J P WAGNER

Introduction
by
Beth Wagner

If you are taking the time to read this introduction, thank you. I put it here for a reason. (I mean aside from introducing the book of course!)

My dad was a man who loved learning and he instilled this love for learning in me, often to my detriment. He was a linguist who knew many languages (living, oral and dead). He also studied anthropology as part of this, which included history. All of this fed back into his writing, along with a love of military history.

Get to the point? My point is that when editing his stories, I find myself having to do research to try to find out where his inspiration was coming from. I know that he wanted to make things fairly accurate, but where does accuracy end and imagination begin?

For example, there is the use of the word wootz. My dad was a bit of a prankster so at first I thought, what is this? This isn't a word. But just to be fair I began looking it up. Lo and behold:

Wootz steel is a crucible steel characterized by a pattern of bands and high carbon content. These bands are formed by sheets of microscopic carbides within a tempered martensite or pearlite matrix in higher carbon steel, or by ferrite and pearlite banding in lower carbon steels. It was a pioneering steel alloy invented in Southern India in the mid-1st millennium BC and exported globally.

I then fell down a rabbit hole researching more about this steel. But it's things like this that make editing his books so challenging. Are they real things that I am altering to fit a narrative or was it all just made up?

I hope that you enjoy this story, the first in the Talisman Trilogy.

SINCERELY;
Beth Wagner
November 1st, 2020

Chapter I
City of Suragos

What might have happened, Thotgol wondered later, if the storyteller had been better at his craft? An old man, and one would assume an experienced man, yet he was making the Tale of the Uncouth Peasant sound mundane. How could a storyteller live to earn those wrinkles? That sparse hair around the bald crown? The grey beard, and yet cannot communicate the excitement the story demanded?

The market Square of Suragos swirled around them, tradesmen, stall-keepers, watersellers, beggars. In an eddy beneath the majestic statue of Thogor Peacemaker, the storyteller stood and chanted. Now and then, one of the crowd tossed a small coin toward the bowl at his feet.

There was even, Wardesh guard and guide, a silver coin among the coppers. Thotgol guessed that the storyteller himself had put it in the bowl as a suggestion that he actually could tell a story to someone's satisfaction.

Thotgol pushed through the crowd. As befit a major trading city such as Suragos, the people were a varied lot. Local men tended to slenderness and often wore trousers and tunic and round cloth hat. There were black-bearded Tarrakins, hooded Kondellini, and bandy-legged Zhotani. The Zhotani, looking out of place without their ponies under them. There were others, too, that Thotgol could not place.

There were even a few Batan, his own folk, distinguishable by the long dark hair pulled back and tied at the back of their heads. He knew none of them, of course. Batan-ji was a large country. None carried an ox-goad such as his, either. The ox-goad was four feet long, thrust through two loops that hung from his sash, point upward, with a thumb-sized hook just below the point.

He slid through the crowd and approached a stall. There he bought a skewer of spiced roast pork. His first taste revealed the food to be not worth the exorbitant price he'd paid for it.

He continued to wander around the Market Square. Young N'daan had paid the whole train off, and it would be at least another week before Thotgol had to look for work somewhere else. Longer, if he had good luck with the Dwarves' bones. Or maybe less, he was honest enough to admit, if the bones nipped his fingers.

As he approached an alley-mouth, he heard blows striking flesh, along with nasty laughter and what sounded like jeering. Though he couldn't understand the language.

Intent on avoiding trouble, he stepped wide around the alley-mouth, glancing down to make sure the trouble wouldn't spill over. The fuss was caused by three Zhotani kicking a lame beggar around.

He knew a bit about Zhotani customs and beliefs. according to them, any person with a disability or disfigurement was under the gods' curse, and therefore fair game for any abuse.

He also knew that, while philosophers in many lands declared the need for those who were better off to help the poor and downtrodden, there was little justice anywhere for them.

'*Three to one. Best stay out of it.*' He thought to himself.

Even as he admonished himself, he stepped into the alley and delivered a healthy boot to a loose-trousered Zhotani. Thotgol's foot landed squarely on the Zhotani's tailbone. The plainsman staggered forward, tripped over the cripple in front of him, and sprawled in the alley muck. The other two turned shaggy faces on him, one demanding, "*What do you think you're doing, stink-house dwelling horse-dropping?*"

Thotgol shrugged, holding his arms wide, "I thought we were playing kick-in-the-butt. Was it a private game, then?"

"Are you making a mock of real people, ox-offal?"

"No, don't call me that, I'm not your mother."

He observed as the plainsman translated his response, realized what had been said and reached for his sword.

"Oh, the game's changed to swinging-sharp-pieces-of-metal, then?" He pulled the ox-goad from its loops, and held it up in an awkward angle.

"*You're fighting me with pointed stick?*" the Zhotani demanded, disgust heavy in his voice.

"All I've got at the moment. If you're afraid, we can call it off."

The Zhotani snarled and charged.

The awkwardly held stick suddenly danced lightly in Thotgol's hand. Whipping up and over, it slapped the downswinging Zhotani sword aside. Then continued its circular motion up to a point by Thotgol's left shoulder. From there he struck backhand as the off-balance plainsman staggered by.

The man dropped and lay still. The man Thotgol had first kicked was up now. He and his companion advanced side by side. They moved carefully, having seen the ox-goad in action against someone who was too enraged to remember any skill.

Thotgol took a step sidewise, as if to deal with one of the plainsmen first and slipped in the alley muck, almost going down on one knee.

The nearest Zhotani shouted in triumph, lifting his sword, but his shout turned to a groan as the sharpened ox-goad took him in the stomach.

Thotgol came to his feet with a speed revealing his stumble for a ruse, and batted aside the third man's tentative sword-cut.

Then something blunt hit him behind the left knee, causing him to stumble for real. But the Zhotani was prevented from taking any advantage by two spearpoints hovering six inches from his chest.

"Fierce flying pig-guts!" Thotgol swore. He checked his wild backswing reflex, stopped for a moment, then he took a breath and said, "I'm getting up. No trouble."

"Better not be trouble," said a horribly accented voice from behind him, verifying what the spearhead shape told him. It was the City Watch.

Carefully Thotgol regained his feet and looked around, "I'll put this stick away. All right?"

Only a suicidal fool would do anything else, with two spearpoints poised for a thrust that would be quicker than any move he could make. Carefully, he slipped the ox-goad in its loops. Now he could have a more careful look.

'*Wardesh guard and guide! A short one!*' he thought to himself. Yes, the Patrol Chief, smacking his ivory-sheathed baton into the palm of his left hand, barely came up to Thotgol's shoulder. While some short people seemed to rise above their lack of height, he'd found altogether too many of them holding minor authority and using it as a club. That habitual gesture with the baton did not bode well, either.

The Patrol Chief glared at the Zhotani, who was still standing, *"I'll say that you can take anything valuable off friends corpses and go."*

"Willigo is still living."

The chief cast a brief look at the downed plainsman, "Willigo has a gut wound, it will be a long hard death. Or maybe you have shaman close by can do something?"

After a short staring match with the Patrol Chief, the last Zhotani knelt by the bodies. He removed several things from their bodies: a copper bracelet, a few coins, and two strange objects, apparently made of leather, wood, and feathers, tied into a small bundle with a leather cord.

These he tucked into his sash, then knelt beside Willigo once more and, in a quick movement, pulled a small knife from his boot and cut Willigo's throat. He wiped the knife off on his friend's shirt, and returned it to his boot, then stood, glaring defiantly at the Patrol Chief.

The Chief only grunted, *"Huh! Off with you, now."*

The Zhotani stepped toward Thotgol, to find two spearpoints blocking his way. He stared at the Batan and said, *"We've seen your face, we've seen your tracks."*

He moved carefully past the watch and out of the alley.

The Patrol Chief turned his attention to Thotgol.

"The Most Noble Magistrate, he does not like people brawling and killing each other in alleys of his fine city. He likes murderers to hang from the rope."

Thotgol had had a fair notion how things would likely go from the time the Watch first intervened. The crippled beggar who had caused Thotgol's involvement, disappeared around the corner while Thotgol and the Zhotani concentrated on each other. His staying or going didn't matter; the Watch were not looking for anyone to bring before the magistrates, otherwise they'd have brought the Zhotani as well.

Thotgol couldn't be too blunt about things, otherwise the little Patrol Chief might just decide to save the Magistrate the rope and all that bother.

"Is it really necessary to trouble the Magistrate?"

The Patrol Chief thumped his baton against his own chest, *"I'll be the one to say what goes to the Magistrate and what does not! ME! Do you understand, foreign cow-chaser?"*

"Perfectly, Captain." To give the Chief a slightly inflated rank might help, or it might make things worse.

The Chief smiled a twisted little smile, "Is it worth something to you, not go to the Magistrate?"

"Suppose we say a copper laba to each of your men, and three to yourself, Captain?"

The Chief stiffened, *"For that much, we can gut-stab you and leave you beside friends here! Maybe you say five silver rinda for me, one for each man!"*

In any other bargaining session, Thotgol would use gesticulations and insults, but it was clear the little Patrol Chief would need little incentive to kill him here and rob his body. Finally, at one silver rinda to the Chief and two copper labas to each man, the agreement was made. The Watch went off with their money, leaving Thotgol's purse so light he would need to find a hire fairly soon.

Of course, they hadn't let the Zhotani go from any love for the bandy-legged oaf. It was well-known that no Zhotani, save a chief was allowed more than a few coppers to spend in town. A Batan ox-driver, though, would probably still possess some portion of his pay.

"If I eat small and drink small, and the bones don't nip my fingers too badly, I might just have time for a rest," he muttered at his flattened purse.

Someone behind him cleared their throat; in an instant Thotgol had whirled, and the ox-goad was in his hand.

The man stood a discreet distance away, flat fur hat, grey trousers and tunic, with a Thawrd Wizard's amulet round his neck.

Thotgol relaxed, but only a bit. Thawrd Wizards were not known to be dangerous, save in one of their causes. But he had not reached this age by taking things at face value.

"You handle yourself well," declared the magician, "Not only with your weapon, but knowing when the odds are against you, too."

"Flatter me all you want, wizard, I can't afford even the smallest charm you might have for sale."

He just wanted to get away and drink something. Thawrd Wizards were not like the bazaar-wizards, dealing in love-charms and such.

The wizard refused to be insulted. He continued to smile, and said, "I saw the whole thing, and the reason for it. The Watch, being the Watch, would not care if they had seen. I, however, appreciated what you did and why you did it."

Still only wanting to get away and do some serious drinking, Thotgol demanded, "Do you appreciate it enough to pay back what the Watch took from me?"

"I do have a proposition for you. If you would allow me to buy you a cup of wine while I explain it?"

Thotgol gave him a suspicious look, "A proposition, is it? And what does this proposition require of me?"

The wizard clucked his tongue, "I'd rather not talk my business out here in an alley. If we go to a wineshop, I can at least promise you a cup of wine, whether or not you accept my offer."

THE LAUGHING GOOSE was a wineshop like any other. It had a low-ceiling and smoky from the oil lamps flickered in the corners.

Wine, cooked meat, crowded human bodies, and other more nefarious things, added to the smells. Some parts, between the lamps, were dark enough for any conspirator to feel safe. The wizard picked a place, not dark, but not well-lit.

"Now," he said, once they were seated in the wineshop with cups of fairly good wine before them, "I am known as Hrezorio. And before you answer that you have never heard of me, let me assure you I prefer few people to know about me."

"My name is Thotgol, an Ox-driver by trade, and I still fail to see what a Thawrd Wizard might want to do with me."

"Ah, you know something of Thawrd Wizards, then? What is it you think you know?"

"It seems, from what I've heard, you've involved yourselves in one cause or another, mostly to do with what you call 'natural justice,' and woe to the person who stands between you and that end."

Hrezorio frowned, leaned back, took a sip of wine and said, "A somewhat simplified view, and we not are all so ruthless as you make us out. Though I'm not entirely surprised that we have such a reputation.

"The definition of 'natural justice,' for instance, tends to be a slippery one, and too often the man judging the situation has insufficient data to work from, and even with the most thorough information, the most thoroughly experienced wizard is still a man, prone to making judgements according to his own experience.

"Rather than any philosophical abstractions, mostly we try to do the best for the greatest number. And I would hope that, overall, we do more good than ill."

Thotgol nodded. "Well, I just got finished dispensing some natural justice back there. All it got me was the honour of paying a supreme bribe to a little Patrol Chief, and the further distinction of having a Zhotani clan swear vengeance on me.

"That last means I must leave Suragos by day after tomorrow, putting some pressure on my hiring on. I may need to take a hire from someone I'd otherwise prefer not to know. No, I think I'll leave justice, natural or otherwise, to other people for a while."

"You still haven't finished your wine," Hrezorio stared over his cup of wine towards Thotgol, "Do me the favour of listening to my proposal. After that, if it is still not to your liking, you can go, with no ill feelings on either side."

Thotgol smiled. "As you say, there's still wine in my cup. Go ahead."

"The truth is," Hrezorio said, "we of the Thawrd sect have a reputation which puts us at odds with nearly every ruler in the world. As a matter of fact, I am using a great deal of my energy at the moment purely to prevent anyone else from seeing me as you see me.

"But there are certain despots that do well to fear us. What do you know about Wennz-Askos?"

"That it's said to be Hell on Earth."

"Indeed. Unless you happen to be pure-blood Wennz."

Memories of rumours and campfire tales shook free in Thotgol's mind, "You want me to go up against Bloody Narnash's heirs?"

He began to stand.

Hrezorio waved him back to his seat again, "Don't be a fool! I admire your skill, but I have no desire to make a heroic battle leader out of you. I only desire you to make a delivery for me."

"How simply he puts it! *'Make a delivery,'* he says, as though making a delivery will not put me in the same position as one who raises a war-banner against Narnash III!"

The wizard's brow wrinkled in a slight frown, "You insist that I intend to send you into the jaws of Morkerr Deathlord. You will have all the help I can give you to deliver the item and remain unnoticed, leaving Wennz-Askos as unmarked as you came. Depending on how you move, you could be halfway across the continent before the King discovers you had delivered anything. By which time, he would be much too busy to send agents after you.

"And it's Narnash IV, by the way."

"Sorry, whatever the number, be it Four or Four hundred, I'm determined not to be drawn into other people's quarrels, for at least a year or two," Thotgol stood.

"One moment," The wizard pushed a silver coin across the table toward him, "For your time. Go ahead, take it, it has no spells to turn you into my mindless slave or anything such."

Slowly, Thotgol picked up the coin. It was a little old, bearing the features of Thogor Peacemaker, but still legal coinage. He bounced it in his hand, "You pay well for my time."

"If it changes your mind, the offer's still open."

"No, but thank you."

It wasn't that he disbelieved the wizard about spells on the coin, but just to be on the safe side, before he left, he took it to the counter of the wine-shop and had it exchanged for its equivalent in copper.

When he looked back at the table he had vacated, it was empty, but he knew he had not seen Hrezorio walk past him. He shrugged. *'Wizards!'*

Chapter II
Dwarves' Bones, Daggers, and Zhotani

Thotgol kept his expression blank as the bones spilled from his fingers. They were small, four-faced oblongs of bone, somewhat resembling joints of small fingers, hence the colloquial name. Each of the four had patterns painted on their faces, and bets were made on the combination of patterns which showed.

In this case, what they showed was not good. *'Broken pattern! Fierce flying pig-guts!'*

Aloud, he said only, "Well, I'm done for the night. Bed for me, and me for bed."

Khinnidaiv, the gambler from some place unknown to Thotgol, grinned his horrible snag-toothed grin. "Rushing off so soon? Stay awhile! Your luck's sure to change!"

"Change! The way things are going, the only change I could expect is from bad luck to worse."

He'd learned long ago you made no friends griping about your bad luck. Even when, as tonight, the Dwarves had pretty well nipped your fingers to the bone. Hrezorio's silver piece—or at least, the coppers which replaced it—was gone. Along with a bit more than he could afford to lose. It would be thin meals for him the next day, and worse the day after if he couldn't find a hire. He looked around the common room of the inn.

It was low, lit with torches, whose smoke mostly went out the smoke-hole in the roof, leaving a slight haze over the whole room. Rough wood walls, rough wood furniture, rough wine and rough clientele to match. A lot of people still remained. Even this late at night, most of them somewhere over two-thirds drunk and making up with volume for the facts and logic their opinions lacked.

The wine that had accompanied the gambling pushed him out into the alley to relieve himself. Nor was he alone; at this time of night, there was constant traffic back and forth to the alley.

The cripple with the crutch under his right arm, considering all today's doings, caught his eye. He saw immediately it was a different cripple, different size, different dress, different crutch, if it came to that. And he was taking quite a risk, too. Men in the state of most of the people in this alley could be as bad or worse than a crew of Zhotani. And, Wardesh guard and guide, Thotgol wasn't going to jump to the rescue again!

The cripple moved lithely for a man on a crutch, slipping smoothly between the drunks and semi-drunks, with never a jostled elbow. This nimbleness was just impressing itself on Thotgol's wine-fogged mind when the cripple twisted the handgrip of his crutch and a dagger was in his hand. All trace of lameness gone, he lunged at Thotgol.

Years spent in dangerous places had trained reactions into Thotgol's muscles. His left-hand slapped the knife-hand away, grabbing it at the same time to gain control of the knife. The killer instinctively pulled his hand back. Thotgol at the same time released the knife-hand throwing the killer off-balance and kicked him hard in the knee.

The killer's knee collapsed. Thotgol then struck a hammer-blow with the bottom of his fist at the killer's temple, dropping him in his tracks. Thotgol flung himself at the killer, pulled the knife out of his hand and stabbed the killer in the throat.

He wiped a bloody hand on a clean part of the dead man's tunic, then stood. Not everyone in the alley had noticed the attack, and in this part of town few people would pay attention to it.

He wondered, walking back inside, who was behind this attempt on his life. There were people in the city who would knife you for less than he had in his wallet. But this was not the part of town they usually worked in. They also usually picked people who were drunker, or further out of their usual habitats.

And further, this man had not seemed like that sort at all. He was more like the sort who'd already been paid, and tracked Thotgol to this alley simply to kill him. But who had hired him?

'Zhotani don't hire their killing done; it's a clan-pride thing with them, and they go to great lengths to make sure it's a Zhotani hand on the knife.'

And he'd turned Hrezorio down. Surely Narnash IV wouldn't have everyone killed who'd talked to the Thawrd Wizard? Thotgol considered the possible trail of corpses, winesellers, merchants, innkeepers, all sorts of people Hrezorio might have contacted.

'But you're the different one. All the others he might have had a harmless reason for talking to, but you're just an ox-drover, not even a caravan-master.'

He shook his head. Giving Narnash credit for every bad thing was silly. Might as well suggest he'd put a bad-luck curse on Thotgol to make things miserable for him.

He went to sleep.

AVALSIN'TI WAS A SMALL, thick-set Gafrod. His hairy arms showing out of a black sleeveless vest, equally hairy legs below once fawn-coloured shorts and thinning brown hair lying sweat-plastered on his round head. His reputation as a Master was bad. He was a man Thotgol would have preferred not to know, let alone work for. But he was headed southwest to Kwandel, land of the Kondellini. Away from the Zhotani lands, and he was leaving next day. The soonest caravan after that was not leaving for four days, so this was it.

An ox bawled in the distance, and the sound and smell of caravan yards was familiar in Thotgol's nostrils. Grain, hay, straw, sweat, and various sorts of animal dung all mixed round.

Avalsin'ti scowled at him. "Thotgol, eh? You've got as reputation as a fighter."

"But nobody will say I cause trouble on the trail. In towns, I defend myself as anyone would, and if bandits attack, I don't lie under a cart hoping for someone to save me."

"Huh! All right, then, I'll give you a place if you're here when we leave tomorrow. But no fighting on the trail, or I pitch you out there and then." He might as well not have heard Thotgol's denial of being a troublemaker on the trail.

It occurred to Thotgol that perhaps Avalsin'ti was having trouble finding people to work for him, and, in his own estimation, was forced to take the best of a bad lot.

"I'll be here." But the Gafrod had already turned away.

"You! Yes, you with the stupid look and the load of hay! You just come on back with me to where you made your delivery! You lot have been shorting me for years! Yes, come on, or I wrap a whip round your neck and drag you!"

"And happy to be working with you too," Thotgol muttered to the sweaty back in front of him.

He wandered off, intent on finding a place to lie low until the next day. He'd come back and sleep with the oxen, if necessary.

Thotgol was in a bad mood. He'd spent a half-day or so constantly looking over his shoulders and looking in every shadow for Zhotani wearing the Half-face. Searching for the Zhotani with the right side painted white, left either bare or black, brown, or blue. All depending on the relationship to the one being avenged. He had well-nigh decided that going back and sitting with the oxen for the rest of the day and the night was the best notion.

It was about this time Hrezorio appeared in front of him. "I need to talk to you," the wizard said. "Matters have become urgent."

Thotgol forced himself to relax slightly. "You almost got my goad in your gizzard, popping out of nowhere like that."

"Too late." He noticed the wizard was holding his side, where blood was staining the garment. "You'd think that a wizard of my age would be too wary to allow even a cripple to come close enough to stick a knife in him."

"He got you? He tried me and I killed him. You can't be hurt that bad if you've lasted all night."

"No time for chitchat. There was a spell on that coin, a little thing to allow me to track the first person to touch it after me. When I was stabbed, I brought myself to today, here, in front of you.

"But that's used up more of myself than I can afford. I'm leaving the talisman in your hands, to be delivered to Dalthorio h'Anevoto in Wennz-Askos. I'm laying a spell on you to make you go. I'm sorry, if there were any alternative, I wouldn't do this. As a bonus for yourself, the spell gives you good luck as long as you go the right way.

"Fortune be with you."

Hrezorio disappeared, leaving Thotgol holding a small leather bag with along loop of leather cord attached.

He stared at where Hrezorio had been standing. "Sorry, I have no intention of going to Wennz-Askos." He tossed the bag aside.

"Ox-crap!" The bag refused to leave his hand. He tried to shake it free, but all he achieved was a flailing of the attached cord.

'If this is going to stick to my right hand, then I'm in trouble.' He jerked at it with his left hand, and almost flung himself on his back when it came with no difficulty.

He looked at it. *'So, it just won't leave me. I wonder...?'* He slipped the loop around his neck, and tucked the bag inside the neck of his tunic, leaving it to hang on his chest, out of sight.

Yes, it went there readily.

'So, I can carry the Morrkerr-eaten thing around until I have the funds to look up some wizard to get it removed. But I'm not going to Wennz-Askos.'

He looked around, half expecting to hear some ominous noise or see a vision, but there was nothing.

AVALSIN'TI LIVED UP to his reputation. He rode Thotgol a little harder than he rode anyone else, chewing him out for things which were hardly part of an ox-drover's work. Thotgol had a feeling the only reason he he didn't receive more of the Master's ire was that the Master felt it only fair to spread his nastiness over the whole train.

The food was poor, the bread hard, the stew which came with it was watery and over-seasoned. *'Probably trying to disguise the fact that the two old ox-ears used for stock were rotten.'*

But they were moving away from Zhotani lands, and not in the direction of Wennz-Askos. So, Thotgol figured he could hold on until they reached their destination, where he'd see if he could find someone reasonable to work for.

They travelled through a country of rolling grassy plains which spanned off into the horizon seeming to go on forever. Every so often it was broken up by a clump of brush here and there, or with an occasional rise, which was not hardly enough to be called a hill.

Midway during the second day, his normally sure feet failed him. He stepped on a rounded pebble he was sure hadn't been there an instant ago. He twisted his ankle. It wasn't quite a sprain, but bad enough to make him limp. Which, in turn, made Avalsin'ti gripe about not babying cripples.

And if that weren't enough, a wiry little man on a wiry pony, wearing a scale-shirt and carrying a bow, rode in that evening. It was one of the outriders. Thotgol was near enough to here him say, "Zhotani shadowing us, sir. Wearing the Half-face."

"Shadowing us?" Avalsin'ti sounded personally affronted. "You're sure it's us they're shadowing?"

Thotgol caught a glimpse of the outrider's face. The expression was that of an expert scout whose expertise had been challenged by a know-nothing amateur.

"Yes, sir, it's us," he said in a voice lacking any emotion, leading Thotgol to suspect he wasn't the only one with the train on sufferance of some kind.

Thotgol knew it would be too great a coincidence for Zhotani to be after someone else in the train. Which meant he hadn't gotten away as unnoticed as he'd hoped. It also meant some night along the way, they'd try for him. They might try to slip inside the guards and look for him. Or they might, depending on their numbers, make a sudden raid.

Something gripped his guts, should he tell the Master that it was he the Zhotani were after? Not doing so was leaving them fighting in the dark, but he was almost certain what Avalsin'ti would do.

He was still undecided when Avalsin'ti called the whole group, save for those who were on guard duty, and said. "We've got Zhotani following us, all painted up like they do. Means they're after somebody in this train. Which one of you is it?" His eyes fell on Thotgol. "You, cripple! You seemed awful anxious to get out of Suragos. They after you?"

Thotgol was faced with a direct demand. He found himself at a loss for any kind of slippery answer which wouldn't quite be a lie but might mislead sufficiently. With the train, he was in trouble. Alone, he was pretty much dead.

But all he could find to say was, "I had a bit of trouble with some Zhotani back in Suragos."

"Hah! And you want to bring your trouble on me?" He turned to one of the guards. "Run this fellow out of the camp. If he gives you any trouble, spear him in the leg and leave him for those horse-humpers to find."

As the guard advanced on him, the rest of the men pulled away from him as from someone suffering from a loathsome disease. It didn't take much weighing to see what his best chances were. With one leg lame as it was at present, he was at a disadvantage, probably fatal. If the guard speared him, he'd be nothing but a present for the Zhotani.

He walked out of the camp.

HE HAD A ROUGH IDEA of the geography of these parts. He could head for the coast, maybe hope for a boat, but with nothing in his pocket, how would he pay his way? Tempt the Dwarves again? Best head inland, where at the very least he could do manual labour for meals until something better came along. He felt his mouth twist into a sour expression at the thought he was now moving in the direction Hrezorio had wanted him to go.

'Only for a while, though!'

He was trying his best to slip from one bush to another. He knew the Zhotani were out there. But he wasn't sure exactly how spread out they might be. A root caught his foot and he went down with a thump. *'Fierce flying pig guts!'* he thought, having no breath for speaking out loud.

In that moment, he heard soft horse-hooves trotting up the reverse slope of the little hillock where he had tripped. He held still, hardly even daring to breath. Surely they'd have heard him fall? But perhaps not, the wind, a light breeze, was blowing this direction. If he got up and ran he'd be seen for sure. If he lay here under this bush, he might be missed in the twilight. Bad choices, both.

Then the pony and rider were over the hill and coming down, and movement was no longer an option. Straining to look up without turning his face any further, he saw a Zhotani go by. One side of the Zhotani's face was painted white, the other, magenta.

The man was not looking down, but off into the distance.

'Just keep on looking that way!' Thotgol pleaded silently.

The painted plainsman continually swept his eyes over the ground, somehow missing Thotgol's hiding place. In this light he was hardly likely to be seeing tracks. Neither was it likely they'd miss his traces in the morning. Knowing the Zhotani were wearing the Half-face, he was willing to bet all the contents of his nigh-empty wallet they'd at least send someone to check out who'd left the train here in the middle of nowhere.

He waited until he was sure the Zhotani had gone well beyond earshot. Then got up carefully and continued to move in the direction he had been going. This time he went very carefully. Moving from one bit of cover to another. Stepping as quietly as he knew how. Ox-goad in his hand.

The way he figured it, he'd be best to keep on going as much of the night as he could. Then lie up somewhere during the day. Preferably somewhere where he could lose his trail. He had no idea where he'd find a place like that. His knowledge of the country was limited to the narrow strips of the caravan trails.

HE WASN'T AWARE OF the camp until he was in the middle of it. There was no campfire, just a tethered mule cropping the grass, and the mule's pack set down nearby. Thotgol stopped suddenly, looking around; where was the mule's owner? It seemed as if he had just left, leaving the mule and the pack there. But, in this kind of country, even if one wasn't aware of Zhotani on the prowl, one didn't leave one's things alone.

And that meant the owner was—-

"Over here, O lame wandering soul, with a crossbow cocked and aimed."

Thotgol spread his arms out from his body. "I'm very harmless. Even more harmless, if I can beg a bite of food."

"Oh, so harmless you are, indeed. But what of that thing you carry in your hand? It looks not at all like a bouquet of flowers for a lonely merchant."

"It's an ox-goad, and I'll not deny that it's been used as a weapon when the necessity arose. But with the exception of a few Zhotani, I have no enemies around."

"A very nice speech, and yet I've grown to my present age by being very cautious. If you would be so good as to sit down, crosslegged, against that tree over there."

There wasn't really a good deal of choice to be had. Diving back into the brush would get him a crossbow-bolt in the back before he'd gone more than a step. He sat down, still holding the ox-goad. he hoped he was guessing right that the man didn't intend to kill him, since he might have done that without speaking.

Then his host, if host he should prove, moved into view. It was a little man, standing with his chin about the level of Thotgol's waist, if Thotgol were standing. He was stocky, though, his shoulders little less wide than Thotgol's, and his face, still in shadow, seemed broad and square.

He leaned against a boulder and said, "Now, then, O lame wanderer with the ox-goad, tell me your tale of how you come to be wandering here in the wild, far from any oxen. And should your tale amuse me sufficiently, I will not only leave you unpunctured, but perhaps feed you as well."

So Thotgol told the tale, "I came on three Zhotani bullying a cripple in an alley in Suragos, and just took a hand to straighten things out. Ended up killing two of them, with the other alive and wanting vengeance. And about that time the Watch showed up. They sent the Zhotani off, and let me go, on the understanding that I pay them more than I could afford. That left me with a whole lot of Zhotani wearing the Half-face for me.

"So I took a hire with a caravan to get out of town fast. Unfortunately, the Zhotani were following, and when the caravan master found out they wanted me, he chased me out. So I went wandering across country, and came on you."

He left out Hrezorio and the amulet. The man might not want the amulet for himself, but Narnash might pay well for knowledge of its whereabouts.

Every so often during the course of the tale, the little man would look down at his own hands, then back up at Thotgol again. Finally, when Thotgol was done, the little man nodded. "I've a little magical stone on my wrist here, which glows when someone is lying. A very handy device, in some situations. Of course, when a person is talking of themselves, the ring will glow frequently. For what person can speak of themselves and their doings without occasionally making themselves a bit better than they are?

"This being so, one has then to fall back on one's own feeling regarding the story and the storyteller. Is he likely to rise in the night and ram that sharp ox-goad through one's brisket?

"And, since I have not revealed all my protective devices, I feel that all-in-all, I can safely trust you. Come over here, I will give you a bite to eat and something to drink.

"My name, by the way, is Shapak-ailesh."

"And I am Thotgol of Batan-ji."

Thotgol got up carefully, and giving the matter careful consideration, left the ox-goad where he had been seated. Shapak-ailesh gave him a piece of dried beef and a biscuit, along with a good-sized cup of water.

"Thank you very much."

The little man nodded his head. "You're quite welcome. There are those of philosophical bent who say that good manners is the mark of civilization. Those of us who wander from place to place, however, will say that manners depend on the neighbourhood. Good manners in Suragos, for instance, is very different from good manners among the Zhotani. Though your experiences with them may tend to make you wish to deny that they have anything that could equate to manners."

Thotgol shrugged. "Perhaps the difference is that they feel that their manners and customs should be automatically accepted wherever they are."

"And yet, no one else in Suragos came to the crippled man's aid. Would not this mean that in Suragos, Zhotani manners and customs are allowed?"

"No, it merely means that no one else in that particular place and time wanted to have trouble with three armed Zhotani."

"Ah, so in your own land, the customs require you to jump to the defence of the weaker?"

"Not necessarily. And I don't think I'd do it again, given the trouble it's gotten me into."

"So, then, you have been in the wrong, interfering with the Zhotani and their amusements when no one in that part of Suragos was willing to do so, and when admittedly not everyone in your own country would do so.

"Which means that, even by your definition, you are unmannerly?"

"Which means that you are one of those philosophical persons who can turn and twist one's words to make them mean what you wish!" Thotgol said, chuckling. "You say you are a merchant; if this is the way you talk to your customers, I wonder you do not starve."

"No, you have not thought it through; with my customers, I merely convince them that they really need what I am selling. And do not let that convince you that I sell worthless merchandise. For sure, some there are who will complain of what I have sold them. But there are those who will complain that Zarad sends the rain to water the crops and the sun to make them grow."

Thotgol sighed. "I'm sure travelling with you for a while would be amusing to the both of us, but by morning, the Zhotani will have picked up my tracks and will be following me. If they catch me in your company, you would likely suffer for it. So it would be best for me to leave you early in the morning. It isn't right that my trouble should wear off on you."

The little man chuckled. "And how is it, do you think, that I have managed to travel so far by myself, without being attacked by bandits or the like? I travel by the Hidden Ways."

"Hidden Ways? I've never heard of the Hidden Ways."

"Of course not. If everyone knew of them, they would not long be hidden, would they? They have their own dangers, of course, but they are safer, in general. The Zhotani will not track you through them."

Thotgol was not completely convinced, but he told himself that, if necessary, he could strike out across country tomorrow on his own.

"Right, then, I will travel with you tomorrow for a while at least."

IN THE MORNING, THOTGOL woke up from dreams that disappeared immediately, leaving only a brief sense of peace. He could hear the little man talking. "Now, now! I know the pack irks you, but is it not in the nature of things that beasts shall bear the burdens for people? And for sure, the pack is nowhere near so heavy as you would have me believe. Come, now, or I shall very philosophically break a stick across your hindquarters. For that, too, is the nature of things, that people shall punish beasts that insist in being recalcitrant beyond all reason.

"Ah, now, that's much better. You would not like to give our guest a bad notion of me as a person who cannot control his own pack-mule, would you? For sure, he has been watching us these last few minutes, though pretending he was asleep."

Thotgol sat up and smiled, noticing his blanket smelled somewhat of mule, "If you'd given me a poke in the ribs, I'd have been willing to help you with the animal."

Shapak-ailesh glanced over at the mule, who was now patiently grazing again, waiting for the command to start moving.

"Ach, no, there was no help needed there. This mule is a very philosophical creature, and requires a philosophical discussion before going to work in the morning.

"Now, about yourself, are you near ready to move? I'd like to get a good start, without rushing us.

In the light Thotgol could get a better view of the little man. He was indeed broad and well-muscled, with a round flat face and snub nose, wearing leather tunic and trousers suitable for travelling, and a leather cap embroidered with flowers.

"I can be ready in a moment."

"Very good. Do so, then and we'll have a little bite while travelling."

Thotgol was just tucking his blanket into the ropes on the mule's pack when Shapak-ailesh called to him. "Quick, lad! I hear running hoofbeats, and I think it may well be your old acquaintances, the Zhotani, faces freshly painted and looking for someone to stick a knife into."

"Fierce flying pig-guts! Look, I'll go on, no reason they should stop for you!"

"No, young fool, just step around this boulder after me and we will be on the Hidden Ways! Come on, follow!"

So he followed the mule round the boulder into strangeness.

Chapter III
Old Palace of Askos, Wennz-Askos

The room was rather dingy. It had, at one time, been a Chief Servant's room. But it was one of the rooms which was in decent repair, so it was used by the future Lady of Askos. They had managed some careful repairs to the main audience hall. They were now repairing other parts, carefully. As time and materials were available.

Lusommi h'Askevoto, prospective Lady of Askos, opened the container for the second time in one week. *'Admirable restraint!'* She mocked herself.

The box had the appearance of an ordinary compact for face-powder or the like. Something which would disguise its real use in an extremely cursory search. Any search that went beyond that, a mere test for magic, for instance, would reveal its true nature.

The small mirror, which would ordinarily show her round face, snub nose, and something of her black curls, showed the face of the

Thawrd Wizard, who repeated the message she had memorized by now.

"By the time you are reading this, my dear girl, I shall be dead."

Lusommi's face scrunched up in mild annoyance at first, *'I always hated it when he used to call me "my dear child",'* but then turned into one of wistfulness, *'Why do I seem to be missing it now?'*

"I have, however, arranged for the delivery of the talisman. Dragooning into our service a very unlikely sort, an ox-drover by the name of Thotgol. I apologize for the delay, but necessity was upon me, and there was no other choice at hand.

"The ox-drover is unwilling, but will certainly find himself having to move in that direction. How long it will be before he discovers he is much better off going straight to Wennz-Askos, I cannot say for sure.

"If you open this item in the starlit evening, over the map in the study you have so graciously furnished, a small figure will appear on the map, giving you some notion as to where he is at present.

"Do not do it too often or for too long, lest the magic be detected and traced to you.

"Wardesh guard and guide you, my dear girl, and all those dedicated to our cause."

The picture winked out. However, on the map below her, there was a tiny figure of a man. He was no taller than the breadth of her thumb, but carefully depicted. A Batan, wasn't he, by the way he wore his hair? And yes, he did seem to be headed off in a direction to take him south of Wennz-Askos.

'Destroyer's teeth! Are you sure you he really is going to come this way, Hrezorio?'

She debated whether or not she should share this latest information with the leaders of the Askos Loyalists.

'And isn't that a fine title for a little band of hopefuls waiting for the Wondrous Weapon to arrive and let them overthrow the man who, it

seems, has eyes and ears everywhere? Not to mention having wizards of consummate power to deal death in fashions calculated to shake all but the most hardy soul,' She recalled the sight of poor Zahheron, being strangled to death. Invisible hands squeezing his throat, invisible hands that had no substance and could not be pried loose.

She finally decided not to pass on the information, for that same reason. Narnash had eyes everywhere. The fewer who knew precise times and places and people, the better. No, Dalthorio would have to know; the talisman was coming to him.

Ah, dapper little Dalthorio h'Anevoto, whose aspirations to the crown were so strong as to be practically visible when he was present. But to wear the crown, he would have to marry her. And she, to attain the crown, would need the help of all the force that could be mustered. She had put off making specific promises, but the time was going to come when she must do what had to be done for her people. If only it were someone more personable-—*'Stop it, Lusi! You know what has to be done!'*

She closed the compact and tucked it away in a pocket carefully hidden in the folds of her pale green gown. All her gowns had a pocket or two in them, for tucking away light little things which would not pull the garment out of line.

She also contemplated the thought of sending some trusted person to find this ox-drover and lead him the rest of the way. But from what she understood, and from what she had seen with her own eyes, the man was terrifically stubborn. Sending someone to guide him along the way would probably be just the thing to set him into a heel-dragging mood.

IT WAS BY NO MEANS an uncommon sight in the high-vaulted halls of the palace of the King of Wennz-Askos. Narnash Skalsland, fourth of that name. Ruler of the Dual Kingdom of Wennz-Askos, breathed deeply and controlled his anger. Anger could be displayed later when it would better suit his purposes.

Those present saw a sturdy man of middle years, blocky face, square-cut beard, wearing a leather corselet over green trousers and strong leather military boots.

He glanced again at the small roll of paper in his hand. "Lusommi h'Askevoto. A connection of the so-called Old Royal Family of Askos. How is it anyone of the name survives?"

His very quietness was warning of his anger, and any other of his servants who stood before him would have quailed. Doctor Gobnash merely looked back at him. The doctor was a slight man, in sand-coloured robes, and even his eyes were a sand-brown colour. His thinning grey hair was covered by a skull-cap of maroon, or sometimes black. If he delighted in anything other than his studies, it was his ability to remain unseen in a background while people were making foolish talk about the king. Then to make his presence known to the consternation of all.

Nor was camouflage his sole ability. When the wizard first came to work for Narnash, the king had attempted to discover what sort of pressure would make the wizard afraid. All he had achieved, as he recalled, was a pair of picked guards so broken in mind and spirit they were no longer fit for anything but stable chores, following the simplest of instructions with blank eyes.

"My understanding, Highness," The doctor was always polite, "is most of the aristocratic families had made for them talismans of greater or lesser powers, the kinds of things that confer a general good luck.

"In the nature of things, however, not everyone can have good luck all the time. And before you ask, the battlefield, with all the blood and death and heartfelt desires to live and to kill, is a place where magic does not work reliably, not even talismans. Indeed, a cast spell may well have an effect quite different, even opposite, to what was intended.

"However, the talisman is for the family, not usually for any particular individual in the family. This means while a family may be "whittled down" it is very difficult to totally extirpate one. By the time a family is cut down to five to ten in number, the magic of the talisman is quite concentrated. If one thinks of the way a container of wine can be distilled to a smaller amount with the quality of the original wine increased in it, the matter is much the same. This is not a perfect analogy, but it will do.

"Thus, any move against such families results in incredible good fortune for the family involved. Assassins actually wound themselves by accident with their own poisoned weapons. The whole family may be out riding, hunting, or the like when troops descend on the household to arrest them.

"Fortunately, the effects of the talisman rarely spread to friends, retainers, and so on, so with persistence we may well end with a few members of the last families creeping about the wilderness, staying alive through good fortune, but of no danger to us.

"The matter of concern," the doctor concluded, "is not the woman and her family, but the actual message which was intercepted."

"Someone, ostensibly and ox-drover, is coming to deliver a talisman to someone in the service of the group with which she is working. All terribly vague, and you have claimed to me that the Thawrd Wizard is dead."

"He is, but he would not have used the last of his strength sending along the talisman if it were something none of the recipients could use. He was able to conceal his movements from me, not perfectly, but sufficiently that I do not know which of the wizards in Suragos he consulted. There are some whose works I would consider negligible, and some who might well produce something that could challenge me quite considerably."

"But not defeat you?" Narnash was smiling, almost as though he had caught the wizard out in something.

"Defeat me? Unlikely. As long as my master continues to provide for my researches, I shall continue to become stronger."

"Hmm. Why do you not then make a spell or a talisman which will destroy the power of these family talismans?"

The sand-coloured eyes opened only a trifle wider, but nothing that could be considered astonishment.

"No, that is not the best way to go. I told you about the confusions of spells caused by battles? Well, luck is one very chancy thing. Once a good-luck talisman is in place, trying to actually cause bad luck to the bearer or bearers is almost certain to result in numerous unpredictable reactions. It is not a wise notion, Highness."

"I see. Suppose I find another wizard, one willing to make the attempt?"

Still no sign of alarm. "In that case, Highness, would you please let me know when this wizard is about to go to work? I would prefer to be far away when he does so."

King and magician stared at each other for a long while, then the king said, "So, then, Doctor, away to your tower with your herbs and samples and stenches. Perhaps the next time you come here, you will have answers instead of questions."

Doctor Gobnash bowed politely and backed out of the king's presence.

Narnash awaited while his chamberlain escorted the next group in. Four men, dressed as merchants, in sober colours. While the king would not recognize every man in his kingdom, he had seen these four often enough. He frowned at them and spoke, before the chamberlain could introduce them. It was a breach of protocol, but there was none in the kingdom, man, woman, child, or Eshdhe of the deep woods, who would chide king Narnash.

"A request for relief from the port imposts, is it? Well, is it? Will you all stand there like doorposts? Ah, someone has a tongue, though a feeble one. This makes four times, to my recollection, in the past three years this same request has been made. And once again, for the same reasons as before, I must turn it down.

"And you know what these reasons are, don't you? Yes, bob your heads like that, and take care you don't bob them off. You all trade with the Askos, do you not? Oh, don't trouble to deny it, you know and I know better. And you will tell me that without trade to the Askos your businesses will suffer. And I tell you that the Askos have yet to accept the judgment of the battlefield, rendered so long ago. And are sneaking around in the skulking fashion of that lot, making surreptitious sedition against their rightful masters.

"So, all commerce to the lands of the Askos serves to support them. Rather than have customs posts along every trail to the interior, I collect the taxes at the ports, and decorate the harbour fortifications with the heads of any who try to slip cargoes ashore other than through those cities with the appropriate charter.

"I doubt all commerce with the Askos will cease, for all your complaining. But as they discover that goods are more costly, they will be pressed to work harder at earning their bread, and thus have little energy left to attempt to overthrow their true rulers.

"No. The harbour imposts stay as they are. Good day, gentlemen."

It would require a much more hardy constitution than any of the merchants possessed, to even make the attempt to argue farther with Narnash once he had dismissed them. They left, not even attempting to hide their look of defeat.

The king looked at the chamberlain, who gave the signal for the next deputation to come in.

THE FIRST STRANGE THING was the ordinary boulder, on the other side, was silver shot with copper streaks. Thotgol gaped at it, then put a hand to his knife to scrape off a bit. Shapak-ailesh grasped his arm in a grip like steel and said, "Come, O wandering ox-drover with the eye for riches. One does not stop within the Hidden Ways, for time flows strangely in some of these places. No, not even a coin's worth, though it might seem cruel to you. There are worse things than having to pass by riches without extending a hand to make oneself less poor.

"Now come, accept for the moment that I know whereof I speak. Think, why would I, a merchant, pass by such a thing if it were not frightfully dangerous to stop?"

This statement caused Thotgol to think, and to come along grudgingly for the first step. And by the second step, things had altered altogether.

The silver rock was gone.

To their right was thick forest, to their left was a rolling plain, and a large stone building in the distance, tall and turreted. While in the foreground a man and woman, strangely but richly dressed, met in the center of a small bridge and kissed as if this were the last kiss in the world.

A few more steps and, though the forest was still on their right, on the left was a grassy plain where two armies clashed in combat. The distance was about a hundred yards, and the long-speared phalanx on one side was holding the flank firm. While on the other the cavalry were rushing round to deal the final blow to the exposed enemy wing.

Thotgol had never paid much attention to soldiers and their equipment. But one thing he noticed was that the cavalry did not use stirrups. That seemed strange; didn't everyone know stirrups helped one keep their seat on a horse? And yet these men were riding like mad into a fight, nothing holding them on the horses' backs except, it seemed, fervent good wishes.

He was quite happy to take the few steps that changed the scene again. Soldiers in battle were a dangerous thing. They might prove dangerous to anyone. Even a small merchant, his mule, and a bewildered ox-drover.

He immediately found himself wondering if this step were such a wise notion. The forest, somewhat straggly and thin, was still to their right. To their left was a wide expanse of sand. In the sky were a line of what he first thought were ducks. Then suddenly realized they were farther away than he had first thought and that they were not birds.

"Dragons!"

"Oh, yes. For certain. But I will not stop here to discuss with you the whys and wherefores of what may or may not be encountered in the Hidden Ways. I assure you, before we are done, we will see many strange sights, and dragons will be only one among a host of others. Keep walking, if you please."

Thotgol was quite willing to comply.

THAT NIGHT, THOTGOL was still so overwhelmed by the things he had seen that day he was unsure where to begin. When Shapak-ailesh took out a little pyramidal object, and folded down its sides until it glowed with warmth and light. It seemed merely of a piece with the day's travel

"What do you know of the things we've seen today? Do you know anything of any of them, or are they merely things you pass by, unable to guess what they might be or might mean?"

"Ah, my ox-drover friend, you look for meaning, for explanations? Let me tell you bluntly that there are none, or at least very few, regarding what might be in the Hidden Ways.

"I, and others of my sort, know how to pass through them. Some have even developed spells or talismans to enable them to travel there. But because of the way time moves therein, depending on the places travelled to, that it is very difficult to make any study. For by the time you had gathered your data, kingdoms and empires on the outside would have risen and fallen. The city in which you lived, might well have been destroyed. So you would have all this information, but nothing to do with it.

"The wisest say that one goes through other worlds, worlds which have grown up very differently from this one. And when one passes through them, one passes through at different moments in their history. Sometimes even different lands and places."

"But how do you tell where you're going to come out at?"

The broad head nodded. "A good question. For those of us born with the ability to walk the Hidden Ways, it is a matter of having a special sense of *'Direction,'* so that we know if we go this way, we will come out somewhere in this direction from the place in this world where we began. Some of us can even see our way to coming out in a very particular place, as narrow, say, as three feet."

"No fear of coming out within a rock, or a tree, or a wall?"

Shapak-ailesh shook his head. "Certain young persons, for the sheer devilment of it, have attempted such things. They always came out on the surface of the rock, or up in the branches of the tree. It appears there is something in the nature of the Hidden Ways which forbids two objects to be in one place at one time."

"And were you full of devilment when you were a young person?"

"I must admit that I was, until I grew older and more philosophical in habit."

Thotgol was able to muster a small grin over that. "How far have we come? That is, from where we started this morning?"

"Oh, probably a trifle more than a day's travel."

"Ah. And would there be a town or village nearby?"

Shapak-ailesh considered. "Well, yes there is Hodrang, to the south. It is barely a hamlet, filthy inn at a crossroad with a few houses grouped around. The place has a bad reputation. I never go there except when directly commissioned, and at those times I keep a wary eye on myself and my possessions. You'd be better off to accept my company another day or two."

"And what direction have we been travelling? Towards Wennz-Askos?"

"Generally, yes, though I expect to pass through near the interior border, coming nowhere near to the capital itself. You have an errand there?"

This question reminded Thotgol of his determination to avoid Wennz-Askos at all costs and the bad luck that had been dogging his efforts.

"I have no intention of going near the place," he stated. As he spoke he knew he was being wilfully stubborn, sticking to a decision made in the heat of emotion. Why not go there, get rid of the thing round his neck, and go his way from there?

"You're certain?"

The querying of his decision only made the decision more firm. "Very certain! I'll rot before I see that country!"

Shapak-ailesh raised his thick eyebrows. "Best be careful of the things you swear and vow, young Thotgol. One can make trouble for oneself that way.

"If you are intent on going to Hodrang, remember my warnings. Will you at least avail yourself of my company overnight? After dark is scarce the best time to arrive at the most highly-esteemed town."

The sense in that was too much for any stubborn reaction from Thotgol. He grinned again. "So long as the conversation does not stray to extreme philosophical depths."

The little trader took two cakes of flatbread and leaned them against one side of the shining pyramid. Then took two pieces of meat and leaned them against another side.

He looked up at Thotgol. "A useful little device I acquired in my travels. Were they a little easier to produce, I could take a dozen and sell them to various kings and rulers. Then retire from the business of scrambling along the Hidden Ways for a bit of gold here and a bit of silver there, and a handful of coppers elsewhere."

He produced a full skin of ale, and handed it over. "But here, try a bit of this. It's an ale I picked up the other day, no magic in it, save insofar as the craft of a master brewer might be considered magic."

WHEN THOTGOL WOKE THE next morning, he felt pleasantly rested. Then realized, suddenly, that sometime in the middle of the previous day, his ankle had ceased hurting. Because he had been moving toward Wennz-Askos? He scowled. Well, if it started hurting this evening, he would know what was the cause of it. Would he give in and go to Wennz-Askos? Well, that remained to be seen.

He heard his host having his morning discussion with the mule, and got up to lend a hand. Mules were nothing like oxen. But they were both animals, and he'd picked up, here and there, a few tricks for dealing with various sorts of beasts of burden.

When they were done, Shapak-ailesh looked at Thotgol. "The Lady of Praises has spoken to me concerning you. She wishes me to offer you what help I can. Take this." He held out a small silver coin, with a strange inscription on it.

"Of itself, it is of little use. Carry it with you for seven days, and you will no longer need it, for the bond will have been formed. If you need my help, simply say these words: '*Karda-ezusht lovagolni!*'"

It required three attempts for Thotgol to achieve a pronunciation that suited the little man. Once that was done, Shapak-ailesh said, "I do not promise that I shall come hurtling out of thin air to rescue you. But wherever I am, I will endeavour to come to you. I trust you will not use it foolishly. If you are unable to pay your gambling debts, and you call me to the rescue, I shall be annoyed."

"For seven days, you say? And if I get in trouble after that time?"

"No, no, no! Carry the thing for at least seven days. After that, if you lose it or drop it or anything else, the bond is formed. The bond will last for, well, for longer than you are likely to need it.

"And don't attempt to spend it or gamble it away. There is a seeming on it so that to the casual eye. It seems like no more than a lead token, and dropping it on a wineshop counter would only cause trouble for you. The sort that, while I could get you out of it, would leave me very annoyed afterward."

Thotgol looked from the coin to the little merchant with suspicion growing in him. "There is nothing in this that requires me to go to Wennz-Askos, is there?"

Shapak-ailesh shrugged. "Wherever you go, the Lady has asked me to help you. She has set no limit or restriction on it. Get yourself taken by bandits on the far side of the world, and speak the words and I will come when I can."

"Powerful magic, then, those words?"

"Not in themselves. They are merely an adaptation of the first words of an old epic, which goes, as best your language can put it:
*King Silver-sword went riding out,
Upon a sunlit day.*"

He stopped. "Besides philosophy, ancient epics are another field of great interest for me. With little encouragement, I could stand here and recite many epics, in many versions, and give some learned expositions as to how the differences in the versions came about. But you will be wishing to get on your way to the fascinating town of Hodrang, and I have yet many miles to go to make my deliveries, and even the wisest and most philosophical of us must eat. A good day to you, and thank you for helping me make the mule understand the philosophy and nature of things this morning."

Chapter IV
The Hamlet of Hodrang, Brauhan's Waste

As he approached, Thotgol could see, if anything, Shapak-ailesh had understated the decrepit condition of Hodrang. There were several houses, though in fact none of them rated any description better than "hut." There were charred marks on the ground and a few burned out timbers where one building had been burned to the ground within the last year or two. But apparently not replaced.

The inn sat, not like a king among his subjects, but rather like an ill-fortuned bandit-chief among his followers. It was a squat, log-built, thatched-roof affair. A single story, with quarters in the back for the landlord and staff, and a common room where people could drink and where travellers could rest at night. There was a small stable close by, which almost appeared in better condition than the inn.

The whole thing went well with its situation, on the edge of Brauhan's Waste. The soil was sandy, producing clumps of stunted grass and patches of brush which looked as though they'd finally gotten discouraged with trying to grow there. The people, few that they were, made do with goats and sheep. All seeming to grow in accordance with what they grazed on, and plots of vegetables which grew only a little better than the grass.

The story was Brauhan, a wizard back in the days of the Great Kings, long before Thogor Peacemaker, had been dealing with spells of tremendous power. But things had gone dreadfully wrong. The ending was a huge area burned to ash, which remained barren for ages. Only about three generations ago had the land even begun to recover this far.

'You'd have done better to travel with Shapak-ailesh for another day, I think.' He looked at the hamlet doubtfully. Then on the heels of that thought, *'No, too late for that.'*

He strode down the track toward the inn.

The closer he came, the poorer his impression. The doors of the inn were not hung on hinges of metal, but on straps of several thickness of rough leather. This was not something unusual for rustic houses, or even for houses in poorer quarters of a city. But for the inn itself, it boded ill. There were one or two patches in the roof where the thatch had weathered away to practically nothing.

Well, on a caravan trail he could spend nights with only the oxcart for shelter, and Wardesh knew he could stand rough quarters. *'Now, if only they have some chores to be done that can earn me a bit of food.'*

The common room was empty when he stepped inside. It was dim, and the smells were all old beer, old food, rancid grease, and smoke.

Shortly the innkeeper came out of the back. He looked like a wrestler gone badly to seed. But the innkeeper was still in good enough shape that Thotgol hoped he'd never have to go against this man bare-handed. He also wore an unwelcoming expression.

The innkeeper appeared to size up the situation at a glance.

"Ox-driver, then, and from Batanchi? And since I haven't heard any ox-carts arriving, you're out of work. You'll get nothing free here."

At the moment it seemed inappropriate to correct the man's pronunciation of Batan-ji, so Thotgol answered, "I don't look for anything free. If you have any chores I could do, I'd be willing to earn a meal."

The forbidding expression changed marginally. "Lost my stable-man week, week-and-a-half ago. You willing to shovel manure?"

Thotgol grinned. "Most times I insist on shovelling rubies, at least. In this case, however, I'll make an exception. Tools in the stable?"

"They are." The innkeeper started to turn, then stopped. "If you do find any rubies out there, they belong to me."

The innkeeper was not used to jokes. Perhaps, if Thotgol stayed any length of time, he'd attempt to remedy that.

The stable matched the inn in many regards. It soon became apparent the stablehand who'd quit had not kept up to his duties. Only the two stalls nearest the door showed any sign of having being cleaned recently, and with scant attention to detail. As he went further back from the door, matters grew worse. Until in the last stalls there was grass growing in the light which shone through the gaps in the back wall.

"There'll be mushrooms in the dark corners," muttered Thotgol to himself.

There was a wooden wheelbarrow leaning against the back wall. The wheelbarrow had once hung by a hook. But the hook had pulled out several years ago, to judge by the mark on the wall next to where the fork still hung on its own hook. It was clear from its angle that hook would not last much longer, either.

He set to work, beginning with the stalls nearest the door. He finished those quickly and went on to the ones that hadn't been touched recently.

He wondered what sort of inn would leave its stables in such condition. Even if the innkeeper had to deal with them himself. Most people who used pack or draught animals might put up with shoddy conditions for themselves, but insisted their beasts were well cared for.

About midmorning a slatternly and ill-tempered young woman in a shapeless faded brown shift, came out with a full mug of ale. "Says this is for you." she said tersely, her manner showing clearly she thought him not worth it.

"Give him my gracious thanks."

This earned him a snort and a toss of her dark hair as she left.

He raised the mug, and something began to bother him. He'd been in places before where the employer might send out a mug of ale. But this particular innkeeper had been so unwelcoming. Also, the state of his stables, as well as the attitude of his serving-girl, hinted he had not been in the habit of treating his employees so generously. So why the liberal gesture toward a mere chance-hire?

It wasn't that Thotgol would suffer thirst. He'd already made use of the well out front. The water was surprisingly good, in light of the state of everything else about the place.

He looked at the mug, and emptied the liquid into the manure in one of the stables. He held the mug up and looked at it. "And I'm going to feel a like a big fool if it was only good ale," he told it.

He set the mug aside, filled the barrow once more. He took the barrow outside and dumped it on the now considerable manure pile. All the while he was putting together a rough plan.

Hauling manure was not a task to be undertaken with an ox-goad thumping and tangling his legs. He'd taken the ox-goad off his belt and set the goad aside, leaning against a stable next to the manger. He upended the barrow and set it so the barrow provided a seat, with his back resting against the manger, and the ox-goad near to his hand.

He sat quietly, with his head on his chest.

For a long while nothing happened. He was on the verge of deciding he'd been a fool. But he reminded himself they'd be watching, and if anything were to happen, it wouldn't be until they hadn't seen him for a while. He'd stay there a bit longer.

Even so, he was on the edge of giving it up when the door opened quietly. That was one thing about leather hinges, they usually made very little noise.

Somebody muttered "Don't know why you want to bother with this one, Endahun. Nothing on him but the clothes he stands up in."

"If we were in the buying and selling business, Matsin, you'd be right." The voice was that of the innkeeper. "But we get everything he has, resell it for a few coppers, and that's a few coppers straight profit."

Thotgol lifted his head. "My, my," he said. "And here I was just about deciding you were a nicer fellow than you seemed. Sending me out a mug of ale, and me letting my suspicions get the best of me."

They were carrying clubs, not knives, he noticed. Yes, they'd want to be sure he was out, but they wouldn't want to get blood on anything they might be able to sell.

"Bloody Destroyer's teeth!" cursed Endahun. "Get him, Matsin!"

The first thing Thotgol did was to throw the fork. Sending it spinning like a scythe. The fork flew low, catching Matsin under the knees and tripping him onto the floor. The next thing he did was come to his feet with the ox-goad in his hand. Endahun was big and strong, and Thotgol knew he wouldn't like to meet the man without surprise on his side.

Rather than a natural seeming overhand blow, the innkeeper swung a sidewise cut at the side of Thotgol's head. He caught the blow on the ox-goad, which sent a shudder up and down his arm. Then, as Endahun pulled back for another strike, Thotgol thrust the butt of the goad into his stomach, ducking down as the cudgel swept overhead.

Endahun gasped, but managed a backhand that caught Thotgol in the ribs, then began to fall. Matsin, by now, was coming up beside his partner. Seeing the bigger man going down, he struck a hasty blow that passed a good foot in front of the ox-driver. Then Matsin began to flee.

With a quick step forward Thotgol hit Matsin across the back of the neck causing him to stumble and smack his head into the door-jamb.

Thotgol turned back to Endahun who was doubled over still trying to regain his breath. Sneaking up behind him Thotgol slipped his ox-goad around Endahun's throat and began to squeeze. Endahun struggled and tried to fight against Thotgol's tightening grip but soon went limp.

Thotgol hurried out of the stable. Then he walked into the inn. The first thing that happened was the serving-woman attempted to crown him with a water-pot. He caught her wrist with one hand while he hit her in the pit of the stomach with the butt-end of the goad.

Winded, she fell to the floor. He swung the goad around so the sharp point was directed at her eyes. He had no intent of killing her;

she was probably no better than the men, but dispensing justice was not his job.

"Right. The two of them are out cold, so there's just the two of us right now. I don't really have anything against you, so if you'll show me where he keeps the money, I'll save a bit for you."

As he'd expected, she had no loyalty of any sort to her employer, and the thought of a few coins of her own weighed much heavier in her mind.

Still bent over and holding her middle, she staggered to the back where she showed him a small jar. "Right, pour it out over there on the table."

She did so. He was a bit disappointed nothing came out but three silver pieces and four coppers.

He separated out one of the silvers with the point of the goad, nodded at her, and said, "Take it."

She snatched the coin. Looking at him, warily, suspecting some trick. It was not her experience for people to let her have anything of any value.

He swept up the rest.

"Now, go."

"Go where?"

"Anywhere. I'm going to watch at the door to make sure you get out of sight. You might want to take a loaf of bread, too."

"What about you? What are you going to do?"

"Don't you worry about me. Just take care of yourself."

"You don't want some company?"

"No. I won't say I'd as soon have the company of a scorpion, that might be unfair, to the scorpion."

Watching the snarl on her face, he thought it would be a good idea, whatever direction he went from here, not to go in her direction.

With a loaf of bread and the better part of a roast fowl in a sack, she went out the door. As promised, he watched her until she was well out of sight before he turned away.

He knew it was entirely possible she might turn back and find someone in one of the other houses who'd help her to get rid of this stranger in return for the inn. But he had no intention of being around long himself.

He was fairly sure there was more money around. Quite possibly hidden under the fireplace, but he wasn't going to bother searching for it. Following the girl's example, he out a couple of loaves of bread and some roast goat into a bag. He also found an empty wineskin, which he intended to fill at the well as he left.

Looking around, he found a large wooden platter. He took this and dug out a big heap of coals from the fire. These he tossed over into the common room, where they immediately began to smoulder in the rushes on the floor. Tossing the wooden platter after them, he went out the door.

The girl had gone northwest, So he set off southwest. It was not quite in the direction of Wennz-Askos, which was another point in its favour.

He didn't look back for some time, and when he did, there was a thick rising pillar of smoke behind him. *'Perhaps a bit extreme for vengeance, but the next proprietor would probably find himself running the same sort of business, and woe to lone travellers, or even unwary pairs.'*

The road, to his disappointment, curved around in the direction of Wennz-Askos. Fortunately, the road forked later on, and he took the more southerly fork.

THE RE WAS AN OLD ABANDONED lumber camp in the hills. The camp was away from towns and much of civilization, where new trees and old rotted stumps stood side-by-side. The buildings themselves had long ago rotted away, so Lusi and Dalthorio had their meeting in the open. Each with only three attendants. Dalthorio was in his usual peevish state, though his small frame was stylishly dressed in crimson and yellow, topped by a black cap. "I still don't see why the message was left with you, when it is to me that the talisman is to come."

Lusi kept herself from sighing, and managed to smile consolingly. "It had been decided limits should be put on who is to risk, and how much. We determined communications should be through me, so that if messages were intercepted, only I would be at risk."

'And it was decided that the talisman should go to you as a sop to your vanity, to keep you and your forces on our side. But I oughtn't even to think that.'

Dalthorio muttered something to himself. Lusi pulled herself erect. Perhaps it was time to be the Queen again, to bring Dalthorio into line. She couldn't do it too often, she knew, lest it have the opposite effect to what was intended.

Dalthorio looked up, startlement on his face, and before she could speak he said, "Your pardon, Lady. You are, of course, in command."

Lusi was startled in her turn, and a little uneasy that a mere change in posture could elicit such a response. She might have felt gratified, had it not been for a suspicion that this could be the first sign of trouble. Was he, perhaps, anxious to maintain his status at least until the talisman arrived? And something so powerful it might help them cast off the overlordship of Wennz, might it not make the wielder powerful in whatever cause?

Dalthorio had often been assured, sometimes quite bluntly, that his forces were necessary. For all that, though, he still could not convince himself of his indispensability to the cause.

'Might he do something very foolish if he could not feel himself significant?'

She used her most sincere smile. "These are trying times for all, loyal Dalthorio. The talisman may just give us the advantage we need to win our freedom from Bloody Narnash. We are staking a great deal on it, all of us.

"What of our hopes to detach some or any of his nobles, to convince them to be at least dilatory in their service, if not outright throw their lot in with us?"

"Well, Noble Lady, my agents have done all which could be asked of them, though perhaps some of them-—At any rate, there is a great deal of disaffection among the nobility of Wennz, due to Narnash's constant distrust of them. For all that, though, the normal attitude of the Wennz noble is that we of Askos are little better than the beasts of the fields."

Lusi nodded. Yes, any person of Askos felt that intolerance, and the closer to Bloody Narnash's capital one went, the more strongly the intolerance was felt.

But even one aristocrat of moderate status joining the rebellion could make a vital difference. The difference between a victory which allowed them time to rebuild, and a victory so ruinous as to require an equally ruinous race to rebuild before Wennz could recover its strength. The result of the latter case would be a disaffected people in Askos. Straining under the burden of double and triple taxes. With altogether too many men still serving as soldiers when they ought to be at home tilling the fields.

But Dalthorio was waiting for a response, and only one was possible. "You have done well, Dalthorio. Let none fault you for your efforts. Continue with your work, and perhaps an opening will show itself."

LORD DISIKOMIN RUDASHIN'S home was stoutly built of wood and stone. The walls inside in the high-vaulted room, were adorned with hangings representing scenes from events which stretched back along the years from the time of Thogor Peacemaker to the High Kings. This was where most of his business was conducted.

He himself was becoming grey, though he was still lean and fit, his hands and face showing the wear of years of working all weather.

He smiled grimly at the letter in his hand. So, his Royal Lord was requiring of him more drafts of troops? Cavalry, bowmen, slingers, and pikemen to be raised, paid, and supplied by him for his Royal Lord "to help quell the nuisance of disaffection among the Askos."

Disikomin had his agents nosing around carefully—only a fool would trust in a king's unceasing benevolence—and there were some hints Narnash was concerned with more things than keeping the Askos down. At least some part of the reason behind these continual demands was to draw away trained men and treasure from Disikomin. This would in turn make him think long and hard before attempting to unseat his king.

The worst annoyance of all was that Disikomin had no intention of unseating the king. That pale Doctor of his was just a little too watchful. When Narnash died, however, and confusion reined, then indeed the time might be right to step into his place.

There was an heir, of course, but Narnash had made sure he was a nobody; sons had overthrown fathers before.

Disikomin caught himself scowling. He wondered if, these little irritations, demands here, demands there, were intended to goad him into outright rebellion. At which time, of course, Narnash would fall on him like a mountain. Smashing him thoroughly and scattering his possessions among others so nobody would be quite so strong as Disikomin had been.

He handed the letter to his son, that fine young man who mirrored his own lanky height, slender fingers, and long face, just now attempting a copy of Disikomin's own square-cut brown beard. Wardesh guard and guide, had he ever been so young himself?

"What d'you make of this, Folsidon?" He kept few secrets from his son; the young man would be taking his place one day.

Folsidon scanned the letter, "I'm not certain. It would seem he wants to weaken us, but why?"

Disikomin nodded approvingly. "Just so. He rules by force and fear, and is wary of anyone whose force seems to rival his own. Beyond that, what d'you think of the possibility of his trying to push us into revolt just so he can break us once and for all?"

The young man's eyes widened. "Might he really do that?"

Disikomin smiled. "He might attempt to. But if we are aware of the possibility, We can be patient to the point where he slips, where he makes so patent a move against us that all his lords see what is being done.

"Then we would see what we should see."

Folsidon nodded. "I see. And I hope someday I learn to think so far ahead as you do."

"Oh, you will, you will. Now, what tasks have you for this afternoon?"

"First off, I'll be watching the Green-stripe phalanx drill. They've been on extra drill since last week, when I noted some slackness in their parade-ground performance. Nearly fell over themselves performing *'Present pikes, rear.'* I have to see if they've earned a reprieve."

"Ah, Green-stripe. That's Haklormin, the half-breed. Sometimes those sort try extra-hard to measure up."

"Why put a half-breed in such a position, father?"

"Because he's good. Good enough to be more than a phalanx-commander, were it not for the fact that his race would have all my other pure-blood Wennz nobles in fits. No, the unmixed Askos are not worth training, even many of the mixed-race are of little value. But on occasion, there's one or two in whom the Wennz blood comes to the fore, and they can do well indeed."

THE KING FROWNED AT the stack of iron ingots in front of him. "The problem is Doctor, on occasion, we have had ingots of false wootz palmed off on us. Never twice by the same merchant," he smiled grimly, "but I would prefer to have it never happen at all. Now this fellow," he gestured toward a sweating, stocky merchant in clothes which once been bright, "he assures me that he was sold pure wootz. Can you tell if it is indeed wootz, or the trash we've had, worked on the outside to look like wootz, but only poor iron inside?"

"A problem, but not an impossible one." Doctor Gobnash thought for a moment. "Hmm. Have an ingot set here," he gestured toward a side table.

The king made a brusque gesture, and a servant jumped to set the ingot on the table.

The Doctor drew a dagger from his sleeve, a short but well-made knife, with faint glyphs decorating the blade. He drew the blade, flatwise, between his thumb and forefinger, humming a barely audible tune as he did so. Then he stepped forward and tapped the point of the blade on the ingot. Instead of the ringing sound which might be expected, there was a dull tone and the ingot fell into dust.

"Not what it was purported to be, Highness."

The king turned his stare on the merchant, who was now pouring sweat.

"Highness, I swear it was sold to me as pure wootz. The price I paid—-"

"Was not so much as the price you will pay, fool. Think well, as you spend the next week dying, how those are served who attempt to gull me."

"Highness, If I might make a suggestion?"

The king's glare turned on the wizard who, as usual, showed no sign of concern. "Well?"

"Suppose, instead of wasting the services of a merchant, we send him back to bring what was promised. If he returns with it, well and good, though perhaps a fine would be in order."

"And if he does not return at all, but goes to a far country where he can laugh at how he has made the pair of us look like helpless gowks?"

"Highness, I had no thought of allowing him so much freedom." He turned to the merchant. "You, come here!"

There was no question of compliance or refusal. The merchant moved from where the guardsmen had already pinioned his arms, and stepped in front of the Doctor. The little dagger had already disappeared, and from a pocket of his robe Doctor Gobnash drew a square of black cloth. He drew the cloth through his hand, again muttering some sing-song phrases in a voice too quiet to hear. Folding the cloth diagonally, kerchief-wise, he knotted it around the merchant's neck.

"Now, you will go as directed, and return. Do not dawdle, or the thing round your neck will tighten and choke the life out of you. Best you should not become ill, either. I was unable to make the spell tell the difference between illness and dawdling."

The merchant was shivering. "But—but—but how much time do I have?"

Doctor Gobnash smiled, slightly. "You have until that thing round your neck begins to tighten. Best you should waste no time."

The merchant, not waiting for the king's dismissal, began to stumble out. As he reached the door, the Doctor spoke again. "I wouldn't fiddle with it either, if I were you. The cloth dislikes that very much."

When the man had gone, Narnash turned to the Doctor. "Doctor Gobnash, that was well-done. And the word will pass more effectively than if the idiot had disappeared into my dungeon."

The Doctor smiled and bowed. "Highness, there is a particular shrub which grows in the hills north beyond Suragos. Its berries are reputed to have some very interesting properties, when dried and infused. I should like to experiment with them."

"Hah! Even for the King of Wennz-Askos, nothing comes free, does it, Doctor?"

Doctor Gobnash bowed once more. "I never promised that my services were inexpensive, Highness. Only that they were worth the price."

Chapter V
Brauhan's Waste

"Fierce flying pig guts!" Thotgol glowered at the sight before him. The southerly road had dwindled into a trail. Then a path, and then a mere game track. The trail eventually came to an end on the edge of a slough. Reeds waved in smelly green-coated water. Farther out, a few ducks swam around occasionally bobbing their heads down for food below the surface.

"Black bloody Destroyer's teeth! What are you doing to me, wizard?" He recognized, of course, no wizard's magic was responsible for the trail petering out. His own stubbornness had pushed him to take a trail simply because it seemed to be leading to somewhere other than Wennz-Askos.

He considered refilling his skin with water here, but a slough like this was not usually a safe place for water. Unless, of course, one had a Fresh-Water Talisman, such as most caravan-masters carried on long trips.

Which served to remind him of the thing he carried under his shirt. Well, for certain it was no Fresh-water talisman, nor even likely a Fire-starter. Whatever it was, he had no idea of how to make it work.

All this was futile mind-wandering. In this waste, he didn't want to risk cutting off across country. So he had to go back to the fork in the trail, and take the one that at least seemed to lead toward Wennz-Askos. With any luck at all, there'd be another division in the road somewhere further on that would allow him to head southward.

THE DEAD MAN HAD BEEN a halfbreed, though able to pass as a Wennz with the aid of a touch of hair-colouring. The dark roots gave him away at close range. But most of his head had not been visible until the dark cap had been lost in his death-struggles. His clothing was nondescript, greyish brown trousers, and a faded green jacket, helping him to avoid standing out. Only an attempt to open a door warded by one of Doctor Gobnash' talismans had killed him, and painfully at that.

"Your methods are a little final, Doctor. I'd have preferred to have been able to question him about who he is, and why he's spying here."

The slender doctor considered for a moment. "There is a thing I'd wished to try sometime, Highness, compelling a spirit. It requires the previous owner of the spirit to be newly dead. If you would bid a servant or two to fetch some things from my workroom?"

The king made a gesture and two servants stepped forward. It was clear they feared the King just a little more than they feared the Doctor. He took no notice of their reluctance, merely rattled off a list of apparatus and jars to be brought.

When they had gone, the king asked, "You will compel the spirit of that piece of trash to speak to you?"

The doctor shook his head. "A spirit, no matter how fresh, seldom is able to communicate in words. I will merely set out some symbols. By pointing at one or the other, the spirit will answer my questions."

"And if none of the symbols represents anything like the correct answer?"

"Most likely the spirit will then stand, doing nothing."

"I see. This is likely to be a lengthy process, then."

"Indeed. Do you wish to go back to your chamber, and have me call you when the process is complete?"

"No, I will stay. At least for a time."

Shortly thereafter a pair of very nervous servitors appeared, carrying the items they had been sent for. One of the objects was a brazier. Under the doctor's instructions they set up the brazier and lit a charcoal fire. A small brass pot was set on it, and when the brazier was hot, the doctor took some seeds from a jar and tossed them in. As the smoke began to rise, the doctor breathed in the smoke deeply.

Then, on the coals next to the pot, he poured two careful measures of powder, one from each of two jars. As two columns of smoke, one green and one blue, began to rise, he nodded approvingly.

In a high falsetto he began to chant. The two columns continued to rise, but now they twisted round each other, but apparently not mixing at all. As the twisted cord of smoke rose, the chant went on. The smoke soon began to bend over, reaching down to touch the dead man.

When the two columns of smoke had been in contact with the dead man for some time, Doctor Gobnash stopped chanting and shouted a single word, *"Sihse!"*

For a time nothing happened, then a green shimmer showed over the dead man. This shimmer continued, finally it rose and slowly, slowly, took the form of the dead man.

The doctor set out two pale ivory chips with strange glyphs painted on their faces. Still speaking in an unknown language, he indicated these and spoke to the spirit. It was clear he was explaining the process he intended to go through, because from time to time he would point a hand to the symbols, indicating them both separately and together at various points of his talk.

Finally the doctor asked his first question, for the spirit. After a short hesitation, pointed at one of them. The doctor spoke again, and the spirit pointed at the same symbol.

And so it went. It was a boring process but Narnash, having declared his intention to watch, was not about to change his mind. Besides, if he left, there would be rumours going around about how even he had run when Gobnash got down to his business.

The truth was that, aside from the eldritch notion of a man's spirit being questioned after his death, there was nothing exciting about the process at all. The doctor would ask his unintelligible questions, and the spirit would point, now at one symbol, now at the other.

Then, with no warning at all, the spirit's form began to waver, and within moments the spirit dissipated.

The doctor stood for a time breathing deeply, as one who had undergone intense effort. Though the king was anxious to discover what had been found out. He had no desire to rush someone who could not only kill, but deprive a spirit of rest after death. But finally, just as the king's forefinger was tapping on his thigh—the only visible sign of fidgetiness he ever showed—Doctor Gobnash turned.

His pupils had shrunk to small dark spots, and there was no expression on his face as he spoke. "Clearly, it is a trick that takes some learning.

"As you may have guessed, I could only ask 'yes' or 'no.' I have a notion to make matters easier another time. However, for the moment, the man who hired this one was of Wennz, and he was hired from here in the capital. This does not, of course, preclude the both of them from ultimately working for some foreign paymaster. Merely that the immediate paymaster for this man was local.

"He only knows that he is to meet the one who hired him tomorrow, in the Blue Loon Inn."

"With 'yes' or 'no' answers, you could determine the exact place?" protested Narnash.

With a faintly supercilious air, the doctor explained. "I ascertained there was to be a meeting, and the meeting was tomorrow. I also established that the meeting was to be at an inn. Next I asked if the inn was in the northeast quarter or otherwise. Then, I asked if the inn was in the southeast quarter or otherwise, at which point I was fortunate. After which I went by landmarks, established which common landmark the inn was closest to. Then ascertained which street it was on.

"And, while I have not memorized the inns of the city, the specific area allowed for only two inns, and I knew of the Blue Loon, so I asked, and he answered yes."

"Were you able to gather any sort of description of the man?"

The doctor shrugged. "Medium height, medium build, no remarkable features. A perfect spy, in other words. He wore a green jacket and a leather cap."

"You've done well, doctor, and I hesitate to carp. I suppose we could go to the Blue Loon tomorrow and arrest every man wearing a leather cap and green jacket."

The doctor took no umbrage. "As I said, the procedure was new to me, and I did what I could. And a mere dead corpse could scarce give even that much information, no matter what torments you put to it."

LUSI HAD STOLEN AWAY into her chambers to take a break from her duties. But not entirely. Curiosity drove her, she wanted to know how the ox-drive was fairing. She drew the locket out of her robes and snapped it open.

Lusi frowned at the figure standing, just on the edge of the mountain range. "Come on, you stubborn Batan ox-driver! Find a path through the mountains and come this way!"

She snapped the locket closed and snickered at herself for getting into such a temper over someone she didn't even know.

THOTGOL WAS WORN DOWN and vexed. He stood at the edge of the range of mountains. "All right, magician, I'm going! Are you happy? Black bloody Destroyer's teeth! Rivers in spate! forests full of roots that grab my feet and trip me! Bare plain with rocks that suddenly leap up and bash my toes! Next I suppose there'll be a rain of lizards across my path?

"All right, to Wennz-Askos we go, and the sooner I get rid of this Morrkerr-eaten thing, the better!"

THE ROOM WENT QUIET as the Captain looked around. *'Nothing to get their attention like a squad of King's Guards. I'd wager everyone here has something on their conscience. Most of it'll be petty stuff, though. If they think for a minute, they'll realize that swindling someone in a horse-deal wouldn't call for the Guards.'*

He was looking for a plain-looking fellow wearing a green jacket and a leather cap. Should be enough, if the fellow was there. Nobody but the upper-ups could afford more than one set of clothing. Well, just about everybody was wearing a leather cap. Two of them were wearing green jackets. But another pair had cloaks on, making it impossible to tell at a glance what they had on for jackets.

He turned to his file-leader. "Everybody with leather cap and green jacket, get them over by the wall there. Make sure you look under their cloaks."

"Sir!"

He watched as the squad carried out his orders. Well, of the two with green jacket and leather cap showing, one was well over six feet. The other might well have matched the description. Save for the nasty-looking scar down his left cheek, starting below the eye and running down to hide in his beard. Well, he'd been told no scars or distinguishing marks.

Two of the cloak-wearers also had green jackets, and were of average size. The Captain had been in the king's service long enough to show no hesitation. "Take the two of them for questioning!"

One of them immediately started jabbering about not having done anything. Which the Captain took to be a possible sign that he had been up to something. The other maintained a sullen silence.

Several of those left showed obvious relief. Which probably meant they had something to hide. He wouldn't be thanked for arresting anybody he thought might have done something. Only if those were his direct orders. *'Wouldn't thank me then, either. Just ask "You're sure you didn't let anyone get away?" And, depending on who asked it, he couldn't answer back as he'd like to. The king, for instance, or that Doctor Gobnash in his sand-coloured robes and little black cap.'*

He went up to the innkeeper and said, "We keep getting reports about rebels, spies, and seditionists meeting here. You'd be best off reporting all suspicious characters."

The innkeeper was stocky, stolid, and stubborn. "If I report every suspicious character, I'll have a constant stream of messengers heading to the palace."

The captain merely started at him without speaking. The innkeeper wasn't up to staring back, so after a moment he muttered, "All right, I'll do what I can."

The captain rapped his baton of office on the counter. "Do better than that." Without giving the man time to argue, he turned.

"This place is closed for the night, by order of the King. Everyone out!"

The patrons filed out, trying hard not to look like people glad to have escaped the kind of questioning that awaited the two prisoners.

Outside, the man with the scar moved off, not making any particular hurry, but not hanging round either.

He'd been afraid this kind of thing might happen, which was why he'd worn the disguise. His agent had obviously died, and died before being able to give much more than a vague description.

Well, he'd have to try somewhere else; he had a couple of prospects in mind.

THOTGOL FOUND HIMSELF on what looked like a well-worn path leading up into the mountains. Reddish mineral deposits adorned their rocky sides. The mountains didn't look particularly high, but it would certainly be tougher going higher up.

He hadn't lacked for water. Though the ox-goad wasn't intended for a missile, he had already brought down a rabbit. Later he took down a quail, so he wouldn't lack food. At least for a while.

He looked up the path, and continued walking.

THE CAPTAIN WAS SEATED easy in his saddle, plain worn armour and weapons, tanned and weathered face. His men sat a little apart, under the green oak in the Palace courtyard.

"He appears to be coming up Dunthorn Pass," Lusi said. "Meet him if you can, and bring him back here. He's a guest, not an enemy, so don't make any trouble. If, for some reason, he refuses to come with you, don't press the matter. Just come back and let me know."

"Yes, Lady." Tahheron was one of her most trusted and able men. He wouldn't push the fellow into anything, but she had to make the order explicit.

Tahheron nodded his round bearded head once from the saddle. With a quick hand-gesture he gathered his troop and they were away.

"THE MAN I WARNED YOU of, the ox-driver, is crossing over the mountains through the Dunthorn Pass."

The King considered. "Have you some way of getting there and dealing with him?"

"Instant long-distant travel is not among my talents, I fear."

"Hmm. So it isn't likely that we could head him off, no matter how quickly we travel?"

"Very unlikely. Of course, there are certain indications that, either he has no idea where he's going. Or that he is reluctant to actually go there. A fast-moving cavalry troop might just catch him before he reaches his destination."

"And yet, Askos is a wild place so far west. How could our men have any idea where to go?"

"That is a very small difficulty, a problem within the abilities of nearly any hedge-wizard. Summon your force, Highness, and I will have an item for the commander to take."

HAMELDASH REACHED DOWN gingerly from the saddle to take what the magician offered. It was a small polished sphere of marble, white with black streaks, and strung on a chain.

"It will not bite you, Commander. The sphere has no power, save the slight enchantment of finding that I have put on it."

"Yes, sir." Hameldash was not reassured. "And how does it work?"

He was not convinced of the benignity of the little sphere. But his King had commanded him to take it, and he was certainly not going to go against Bloody Narnash.

"It is a simple device, requiring repetition of no charms or the like. It is sensitized to the man you seek, and the range is about a day's ride. You hold it up by the chain, and if one face of the sphere becomes red, that is the direction you have to go. Also, the redder it becomes, the nearer you are.

"This will also serve to reveal the man to you, should he have taken on a disguise. If you ride past a man who does not seem to resemble the fellow you seek, but the ball begins to glow fiercely red on the side facing him, that is the man you seek.

"I wouldn't bother checking it until you are well into Askos. Now, off with you."

"Sir!" Hameldash led his force out. A full three-hundred cavalry, all wearing the Crowned Bear token of Narnash. There was no telling what one might meet up with in Askos. The people, for sure, were not friendly, and a large force should just prevent any outright shows of hostility.

The troops, well-trained men, rode silently. Any noise that (was) made was from creaking leather, horse-hooves clattering on the stone. No, hostility in Askos was not something he feared.

THE SLINGERS PRACTICED their evolutions, advancing, retreating, wheeling right, wheeling left. All the maneuvers they might be expected to need on the battlefield. At some point during each evolution a whistle would sound. Which would prompt them to all cast stones at a roughly phalanx-shaped target. Most of the slingers were small of stature, all of them were lithe and nimble.

"Most of them are Askos." Folsidon observed.

"Yes, we get good slingers from the interior."

"But you said that most Askos weren't worth training."

"Ah, good!" said his father approvingly. "Don't take anyone's word for something if you can see for yourself. But you remember the context in which I said that?"

Folsidon wrinkled his brow. "We were speaking of the Greenstripe Phalanx, and their commander—"

"Who is a halfbreed. Yes, and we were speaking particularly of the phalanx, whose task is different from those of the slingers, for instance. The slingers have to maintain some formation, and the more complex evolutions they can manage, the better. However, while the phalanx needs to be able to maneuver, they mostly require the ability to stand firm and strong on the battlefield. They need to be the rock that anchors the line, while the cavalry look for an opening to make the finishing attack.

"For that sturdiness, you need the blood of the Wennz."

"I see."

HIS BRIGHT SLEEVES flapping, Dalthorio was beyond peeved, into outright, "So you sent your people to bring the ox-driver in? Why was I not informed? Are my people not to be trusted to play guide and bodyguard to this foreigner?"

Lusi maintained her composure and measured her words carefully as she spoke, "No slight was meant to you or your people,

Dalthorio. It was only that I saw an immediate need, and knew that arranging a meeting with you would take time we might not have, so I sent my own people. And you will notice that I took care to tell you about it as the first item in this meeting."

'And I wonder which of my people made it their business to tell you beforehand?', She did not speak this aloud however.

Dalthorio was not mollified. "If we are going to work together, Lady, I require more trust of you!"

"Dalthorio, you are trusted, and you are vital to this task. It is to you that the talisman is coming, remember? You will be wielding it in our service, and leading your troops when we fight against Bloody Narnash. I simply saw a need to act, to bring the messenger safely to you, and I took action. It was meant as no slight to you, only an aid."

But she could tell, even as they prepared to leave, that Dalthorio had not been completely mollified. Wardesh grant that he cool down over time.

Chapter VI

Dunthorn Pass, and a Convergence of Forces

Thotgol frowned at the riders coming up the trail. *'Too much to hope for that this will be that Dalthorio fellow and some friends.'*

His understanding was anyone who rode for any of the aristos of Wennz-Askos wore a particular design on their clothes, saddlecloth, shields, and so on. Which was fine, except his knowledge of Wennz-Askos was mostly third- or fourth-hand. He had no idea whose people wore what. Well, of course everyone knew Narnash's people wore the Bear's Head Crowned.

And of course, Narnash could tell one of his followers who wore—was that a Chained Unicorn—to do his work for him. And they were all armed with bow, sword, and shield, and wearing a light corselet.

Closer inspection revealed the unicorn was actually breaking its chain. Which told him little more than he already knew, and that the leader was smiling. He'd been around on his own long enough to understand that a person could smile while planning, or doing, extremely nasty things.

Well, when he saw them it had already been too late to try to hide in the brush. All it would do would be to arouse their suspicions. He put on a friendly smile of his own.

"Good afternoon. None of you would happen to be Dalthorio h'Anevoto, would you?"

"No, but we'll take you to him."

"He's nearby?"

"Wardesh guard and guide, no, about a week away."

Thotgol became wary, but tried to show no sign of it. Soldiers were going to ride a week out of their way to escort him to where he was going? Not likely!

"No need to bother. Just point me in the right direction."

"No bother. The Lady sent us to see you safe."

"The Lady?"

"Lusommi h'Askevoto. She sent us out to find you and bring you in safely. The talisman is to go to Lord Dalthorio, so we can escort you there."

This casual tossing in a name as though of course Thotgol was aware of her baffled Thotgol and made him even more wary.

"Oh?" Thotgol's smile turned up in the corners with a slight smirk, "And how did the Lady Lusommi know how and where I was coming?"

One of his eyebrows raised slightly, *'Since I haven't spoken to a soul since long before I made the decision to come to Wennz-Askos.'*

The rider shrugged. "I've no idea, only that she knows, and so she sent us. You are from Batan-ji, and you carry an ox-goad, so I'd guess you'd be the one. There shouldn't be more than one Batan ox-driver coming over Dunthorn Pass."

Thotgol considered for a moment. He couldn't duck and run for it, the riders would run him down before he got ten steps. But if he acted willing until they took their eyes off him...

"I'll be glad to accompany you," He looked to each of the riders showing his compliance, "I've had sufficient time in my own society the last few weeks."

'and of course I could always say Karda-ezusht lovagolni and see what happens.'

The commander looked around at his troop. "Moxtarum, you ride the lightest of us. Take him up behind you. Thortum, Pangall, you go ride point. We won't likely see any of Bloody Narnash's men this far west, but keep your eyes open for anything unusual."

"Sir!"

Thotgol tried to convince himself this might be only part of a complex ruse, aimed at allaying any suspicions he might have. This group was too open, too friendly. But he'd learned of too much of the nastiness that went on here in Wennz-Askos. Best restrain his trust, at least for a while.

HAMELDASH LOOKED AT the marble sphere. Yes, one side of it was definitely pink. By his reckoning, they were nearly dead east of that gap the Askos called, Dunthorn Pass.

They'd been lucky, too. Travelling light, they'd had to live off the country. Only one town was reluctant to supply them, claiming poor crops and thin harvest. After Hameldash's men had set fire to a couple of hovels, the locals hurried to gather the supplies.

He put the marble away, and signalled his men to move on.

"DESTROYER'S TEETH!" Lusi crumpled the message paper in her hand. She would have thrown it to the floor in disgust. But paper, even wadded up paper, would not make a satisfactory sound on marble. "Bloody Narnash has three hundred horse riding through our territory. They've burned three houses in Deskargin, and seem to be headed in the direction of Dunthorn Pass."

Aelkoriat h'Kalssdar asked, "How can you be sure where they're headed? At Deskargin, they could still go in any direction. Maybe they're just looking for sign of illicit army-training."

"Well, we have an important person coming through Dunthorn Pass. Do we dare believe a force of King's Men just happen to be riding that way?"

"Put like that, you're right. Do we send more people out to reinforce Tahheron?"

She shook her head. "Dalthorio would burst into flames if he caught wind of it. I'm going to have to ride to him and ask him to lend us some men."

"With the best luck in the world, if he doesn't go into a fit anyway. By the time you convince him of the necessity, you'll have to ride like fiends to reach the pass in time."

"I know. But things have worked in such a way I've had to do too many things that upset Dalthorio. We need him too badly for me to lose him altogether."

'It would be nice if if Dalthorio showed some appreciation,' Lusi reflected. *'This is definitely not what I came for.'*

The small man was stamping back and forth across the room. "If you'd come to me first time around, I would have made sure we sent enough people at the outset. As it is, we'll have to ride hard to get there."

"Yes, it's going to be a near thing." She clamped her teeth firmly around the next words that wanted to come out, *'So let's get moving instead of standing here blustering.'*

Fortunately, by this time her host had begun to get down to the real business. He turned to a servant. "Find Chortanio, tell him to start his Red Wyverns readying for a hard ride to Dunthorn Pass, then report to me."

He turned back to Lusi. "I'll have rooms prepared for you, Lady, to stay until I return."

"Destroyer's teeth, not likely! I'll ride with you!"

"Lady, this is no pleasure ride. We'll be moving fast and travelling light. There'll be no time to wait for stragglers."

All good intentions of avoiding offence to Dalthorio were blown away like a mist on the wind.

"Lord Dalthorio, you and your men may ride as hard as you wish. You will not find me slowing you down. I will come!"

And Dalthorio, of course, quailed at her anger. "Of course, Lady, as you wish. I had only wanted to spare you—"

She raised a hand before he could talk about discomfort and conditions unfitting for a lady. She was beginning to rein in her temper. Such words, once spoken, would certainly inflame her further. "I appreciate your concern, Noble Dalthorio. But if I am to lead in this coming struggle, I must be willing to undergo little less hardship than those who follow me."

IT WAS DIFFICULT, THOTGOL felt, to decide whether he was being watched as a captive or guarded as a guest. No one laid hands on him, no one drew a sword, no one showed any but friendly expressions. But someone was always nearby. Even when he went behind a bush to relieve himself, someone else always felt the need as well. Or pre-empted him, as when Moxtarum said, "Destroyer's teeth, I have to go! Come on, Thotgol, you've been riding as long as I have!"

All that kept Thotgol from seeing it as a companionable gesture was his abiding suspicion of everything in Wennz-Askos.

They set guards around the camp at night, of course. A pair of men, in shifts, watched around the border of the camp. Their obvious intent was to warn of danger approaching. But it involved no extra effort to keep an eye out for anyone attempting to leave.

Thotgol spent the first night sleeping as comfortably as possible, given his concerns and half-suspicions. The scent of horse emanated strongly from the saddle blanket that Moxtarum lent him. It was warm, though, and Thotgol was used to sleeping in quarters that smelled strongly of ox. Overall, it was much better than the shifts he had been put to trying to stay warm higher in the mountains.

Let them warm to the notion he was accepting them for what they claimed to be.

There was another difficulty about escaping. It occurred to him he had only their word for the direction to take to reach Dalthorio. They might well be leading him straight to Bloody Narnash.

He'd like to find someone local and ask a question or two. But he was not likely to receive an honest answer while accompanied by a band of armed men. For they need only lay hands suggestively on sword-hilts to render the average local farmer dumb.

At times he briefly smiled at the thought that perhaps these men were thinking how well they were doing at lulling him into accepting them for what they claimed. But then again, he was trying to make them believe that he thought himself in the company of friends.

On the second night, he slipped out of camp just before dawn, taking the saddle blanket with him. He was a little sorry about the saddle blanket. Moxtarum was a decent sort, after all. It was mostly Thotgol's suspicions that were pushing him to go on alone.

He would have liked to stay nearby to hear the reactions when they realized he was gone. For example, someone saying "Bloody Narnash will have our guts for garters over this," would justify his leaving. Staying nearby meant they'd have a better chance finding him again, though, so he didn't dare take the risk.

He was also going to have to camp off the trail, and keep an eye out for them, both coming up behind him and waiting for him around some corner.

In fact, they never seemed to search for him. They rode the trail, near as he could make out, less than half a day's travel ahead of him. Of course, they might be playing a deep kind of game with him, going ahead to make sure anyone he talked to told the story they wanted told to him. Risky game for them, though. Only miss one person, have one person come up through the woods after they'd passed, and the game would be revealed.

It almost seemed they were escorting him, riding ahead to discover any trouble before it made itself known. He had no desire to go up to them and say, "Sorry, lads, I guess I was mistaken about you."

LUSI TRIED TO RUB HER behind surreptitiously. Dalthorio had set a fierce pace the first day-and-a-half. But her own mount, Kwandrei, had been bred for stamina, not beauty.

By the end of the first day they had left three of Dalthorio's men behind, and by the middle of the second, five more. Having no desire to upset Dalthorio further, Lusi had affected not to notice what had been happening. She made no comment whatsoever. For she realized even an intended complement such as, "Your men show up well," would be heard by Dalthorio as bearing an unspoken "but they can't ride particularly fast."

Wardesh guard and guide, how could she take him on as consort? He would want to wield power, and he would end up using his status to give poorly-thought-out orders. Orders which she would have to countermand to avoid strife in the kingdom.

She forced a smile. There were many steps between here and the crown. Each one of them a conceivable stumble which would see them all dead, and here she was whining about a possible consort!

HAMELDASH HELD UP THE glossy sphere, the forward side of it was bright pink. "We're closing in! Up this fork!"

The rattle and clatter of war-gear followed as his company came up behind him on the road that wound through the brush.

TAHHERON AND HIS MEN went carefully here. It was brush country and the wooded hills were good ambush territory. Thortum came galloping back from riding point. He pulled his horse to a stop, and both he and mount stood gasping for a moment. "Upward of two hundred horse, wearing the Crowned Bear, headed this way, Captain Tahheron!"

"Distance?"

"Be all over us in a half a day. We could scrag their scouts, gain a little time."

"Might be worth it. Moxtarum, Halbennet, go back and try to convince that ox-driver we're friends."

"Knock him on the head if we have to?"

Tahheron paused, then shook his head. "The Lady doesn't want him taking against us. Might be hard to convince him we're friends if we have to conk him and tie him up. Get going."

"The rest of you, pick positions. We're going to pretend to be a massive army. I hope you've been doing your time at the archery butts.

"Horseholders, rear. Be ready for us to fall back fast."

He didn't bother telling the others they were in a pretty hopeless position; they had the sense to work that one out.

THE TWO MEN RODE HARD in Thotgol's direction. He leaped off the trail, dodging through the brush to find a hiding place.

The men didn't follow him. "Thotgol!" It was Moxtarum, but he didn't answer.

"We know you don't trust us; no reason you should. You don't know us, only what we claim to be. But there's over two hundred horse wearing Bloody Narnash's badge, headed this way. Swear and promise it's true!"

Thotgol thought that one over for a moment. Anyone could swear and promise anything, that didn't necessarily make it true. On the other hand, for several days they had ridden ahead of him, not trying to make contact. Now there was this sudden urgency. It could be, of course, that the *real* Dalthorio had sent riders, making it that much more necessary Tahheron's men catch up to him.

He sighed to himself, *'Wennz-Askos is turning you into a distrustful old curmudgeon. You've got to believe someone, sometime!'*

He stepped put, carefully. "Hello again, Moxtarum. I apologize for the saddle blanket, but it's come in handy during the nights."

"Chaos Away the blanket! Get up here behind me. Captain and the rest are delaying Narnash's hordes so we can escape! Let's not stand here nattering about blankets!"

Thotgol took the young warrior's hand and swung up behind him.

"If they're coming up the road, how do we get through?"

"We'll slip through the brush. We'll need to dismount for that, but we'll ride when we can. Hold on!"

THE COMMANDER OF DALTHORIO'S Red Wyverns dropped back to tell Dalthorio, "We're behind 'em, sir. Bloody great lot of horse tracks heading up the trail."

"How old, Chortanio?"

"Day or less, sir."

"Can we go faster?"

"Yes, sir, but we want to temper that. Come up on that bunch with our horses blown, we'd be little or no use."

Dalthorio considered that. "All right, push as hard as you think wise."

He turned to Lusi. "Bad situation, Lady. We may end up trying to take the ox-driver, or at least the talisman, away from Narnash's men."

Lusi was wishing she had sent reinforcements to Tahheron before going on to talk to Dalthorio. She could only nod. "Best be moving, then."

TAHHERON NOTED THE Wennz riding up the trail. There was room for two horses abreast, here. But no commander worth his salt would leave his men strung out from hell to breakfast if he could help it. It would have been nicer of the king to send something other than his own troops. This lot was not likely to be panicked by an ambush. Best he could hope for was a bit of confusion.

He blew a short, sharp blast on his signal-whistle, and was pleased to hear the sound of his men loosing their arrows on order.

They sent out a second flight. Then Tahheron shouted, "Charge," followed by the whistle-signal to withdraw.

His men were well-trained, and in action would follow the whistle-signal rather than the shouted order.

Shouting war-cries, his men loosed another flight of arrows. This ruse worked to the extent that the enemy spent a few seconds rallying themselves to meet a non-existent attack. Their commander then decided Tahheron's people weren't really attacking, and charged themselves.

Tahheron had one small advantage; this wasn't cavalry country. The Bear-crowns would have to dismount their horses to come after him. On the other hand, with the numbers available, it would be entirely too easy for one flock of the Bear-crowns to hold his smaller party at bay while three or four dozen more came around his flanks and rear.

Which meant they had to pull back slow enough to draw the Bear-crowns after them, but not so slow as to be surrounded.

But they weren't following! A small party were packing up the dead and their weapons, while the rest continue along the trail.

'Mother-goddess' belly! He blew the Rally on me! what now? Well, good sense said try to join Moxtarum and the others.' That meant working their way through this brush in the general direction of where he figured they might be.

That gave a third of Askos to choose from. Logic said the three would be working their way south-east toward the Lady's lands. So, now to take a good guess as to the best heading to pick.

He rapidly outlined the situation for his men, then said, "Shrofton, you're from these parts. Any suggestions?"

"Mother-goddess' belly, Captain, I'm from fifty miles east of here. Most I know of these parts is the odd story I recall."

"Better than any of the rest of us. You have any good notions? I won't hold you responsible if you lead us into a bog."

"Well, there's luck, Captain; few bogs in these parts. I'm mostly guessing, but I'd say this way."

"Right. And all of you keep your eyes skinned for tracks."

HAMELDASH LISTENED to the scout. "Lot of coming and going, sir, but two horses went off the trail here. One of 'em's heavy loaded, probably carrying double.

"Good work, man!" He dug the marble sphere out of his belt-pouch and held it up. It spun a bit as the kinks in the chain unwound, but always the south-east face flared crimson.

"Hah! Got you, you bugger!"

MOXTARUM FROWNED. "I'M no expert woodsman, I've got no idea how you go about hiding tracks, except maybe wading in a stream for a bit. I think we'd be best just making for the Lady's country."

"Who's this Lady you keep talking about?"

"You don't know about the Lady? Are you sure you're the man we were sent to find? But no, you know about Dalthorio, you're bringing something for him, you must be the man. But you don't know the Lady?"

"Fierce flying pig guts, all I know is an interfering Thawrd Wizard laid it on me to deliver this Morkerr-Eaten thing to Dalthorio h'Anevoto. I know nothing of this Lady."

"'This Lady' is Lusommi h'Askevoto, who will be our queen one day soon. And you'd best take care how you speak of her; we're all her men."

Thotgol held up a hand. "No offense intended."

"And none taken. Now let's move along."

"DEFINITELY THREE MEN, two horses. One of the men had different shoes than they make in Askos."

"And does he wear his hair long or short?"

The scout, a man with little humour, said, "Can't say, sir. Tracks only tell so much."

"It was a joke, man. Are we catching up, or dropping behind?"

The scout shrugged. "Can't say for sure, sir. I think we're at least keeping even."

"Right, keep going, report anything unusual." Hameldash didn't bother urging the man to go faster. This kind of country allowed for only so much speed when tracking someone.

IT WAS ACTUALLY A SMALL spur off one of the mountains. Though this far down, bare rock had given way to a steep stone-covered ridge. Which bore thin grass and dappled with small scrubby bushes.

"Question is, how far are they behind us? And have they spread out at all? If they've spread out, and we head along the base of the ridge looking for an easier way over, we may run right into them. And how far will we have to go to find a way over?"

Thotgol shrugged. "Not my country."

"Mine either. I think we'd best go over."

The hill was steeper than it looked. Men and horses were breathing hard by the time they'd gotten halfway. As they neared the top, there was a shout from behind. They looked back to see Tahheron and the others coming out of the trees and starting up the slope.

LUSI NOTICED THE DIRECTION of the trail they were following. She hoped Dalthorio didn't suddenly realize Tahheron and his men were headed towards *her* lands.

She frowned at herself. *'Best be concerned with catching up to the Bear-crowns before they catch Tahheron!'*

She thought she heard shouting ahead; should she bring that to Dalthorio's attention? Wardesh guard and guide, where would this concern for his feelings take her?

TAHHERON STOOD, BREATHING hard. "You shouldn't have waited for us, Moxtarum! They're back there, and not far!"

"Sorry, sir, we weren't waiting for you, not at first, anyway. Horses needed a rest. I will admit we waited a bit longer when we saw you."

"Well, move on now. We'll be up behind you in a bit."

"Yes, sir!"

They were cresting the ridge when shouting came up from behind. Masses of men on foot swarmed out of the trees. They were carrying a different badge, and from this distance it looked like the Bear's head crowned.

They turned and went toiling over the ridge and stopped.

"Fierce flying pig guts!"

The far side was more steep, and over time—with the action of wind and the stream that followed the line of the ridge—it had fallen away. About ten feet below them was a sheer drop of about thirty feet into the boulder-pocked stream-bed.

The Bear-crowns were spreading out and moving up the slope. Some of them testing the wind and the range with arrows. Tahheron was also moving, but the situation was grim.

Moxtarum spoke. "We move down along the ridge, look for a place where we can climb down easier."

Tahheron and the rest were coming up, now, and some of the Bear-crowns were racing along the bottom of the slope. Eventually, as the ridge lowered, they would be close enough to pick off Tahheron's party without bothering to come to grips.

When Tahheron finally caught up with them, he said, "Mother-god's toenails, Moxtarum, should have gone the other way! Make it harder for them to catch us, not easier!"

Moxtarum looked back at the pursuit. "Sorry, Captain, I was just looking at getting us over the ridge and away!"

But Tahheron had already turned to Thotgol. "Can you slip over the ridge, move along upslope, while we keep their attention?"

Thotgol hesitated. It was too much like running away from a fight, leaving other people to fight and die on his behalf.

Tahheron read his mind. "Chaos Away your pride, man. We're going to die. You die with us, it's for nothing!"

Thotgol gave a quick glance at the older warrior's face. He nodded once, went over the ridge as far as he dared, then began moving up along the ridge as fast as possible.

TAHHERON MADE THE BEST deployment he could with his men. They made ready to loose their arrows into the advancing crowd.

They had one advantage. It was near impossible for a man to come all the way up that slope and be fit to swing a weapon at the end of it. The Bear-crowns would have to leapfrog their way up. At least the last half, giving Tahheron and his men opportunity to do a good deal of damage.

On the other hand, while they were leapfrogging, some of them would be shooting too. Then Tahheron's men would start to take losses.

They were kneeling, on the forward slope, so as not to present large targets, and no skyline silhouettes. He had them holding their fire as long as possible. Other than that, there wasn't much else to do.

Arrows came whipping up, most missing, though Pangall gave a sort of gasp and fell sidewise. Destroyer's teeth! He'd hoped to participate in the first flight! His men were loosing arrows as he blew his whistle.

Arrows continued to skip and clatter among the stones. There were enough of the Bear-crowns to keep up a continuous fire, while dividing his force wasn't worth the trouble. They were having an effect on the enemy, however little. Well, there could be worse ways to die. If that ox-driver would just find a good hiding place, it might be worth it.

'Then, Wardesh guard and guide, the Bear-crowns were falling back! Destroyer's teeth! We aren't that tough a proposition!' Then Tahheron took in the men deploying out of the woods. *'Red Wyverns! That's one of Dalthorio's lot! Cavalry, too.'*

Hard to tell numbers, with who knew how many still in the woods. But even fifty or so could turn the trick if they knew what they were about.

And now was no time for his men to slacken their fire. Anything that kept the Bear-crowns busy. Hindering their rallying and reforming, would be useful.

"Steady now, lads, Careful aim. Pick your targets. Just like the butts."

He thought he heard Moxtarum mutter something on the lines of "But the butts don't shoot back."

Another time, another circumstance, he would have vowed to keep that in mind for extra duty sometime. Here, however, he just smiled.

Down below, the Bear-crowns were breaking up, right and left, and rushing along the slope looking for a safe place. If—as seemed likely—their horseholders had already been overrun, they'd have to try to make it all the way back across Askos on foot. And if Dalthorio's men were at all on their toes, blessed few would make it.

In the meantime, there were things to be done. "Moxtarum! You look to be unhurt; you receive the pleasure of chasing down Thotgol and letting him know we're rescued. Rest of you, check the wounded, pick up any good arrows to replace yours."

Arrows gleaned off the battlefield wouldn't be as accurate as arrows they'd made and tested themselves. But better than nothing.

Chapter VII
A Crack in The Alliance

Moxtarum brought Thotgol to where Lusi, Dalthorio, and a guard of some two dozen met Tahheron and his men at the bottom of the ridge. Thotgol looked unobtrusively from face to face.

"Lady," Tahheron said, "this is Thotgol, the man we sought."

"He actually comes to you, Lord Dalthorio." She saw it was too late. Dalthorio had once more inferred his part in the whole thing was only by her will, not any ability of his own.

With poor grace, he said to Thotgol, "You have the talisman?"

Thotgol reached under his shirt. "I have, and glad to be shut of it."

Dalthorio swore. "Black bloody Destroyer's teeth! How long have you been carrying it there?"

Thotgol shrugged. "A bit over two weeks."

"Fool! You know nothing of talismans? After seven days next to your heart, this sort will answer to none but you! The Talisman is useless now, you idiot, you stupid ox-loving lump of—urk!"

Thotgol's ox-goad was in his hand, its point resting on Dalthorio's throat. "I did not ask for this chore. A Thawrd Wizard laid the talisman on me in his dying moments. Being on the point of death, he did not give me lessons in the proper handling of the thing. I've brought it to you, and I'm done with it. And while I will accept that you do not thank me, I will not accept insults. You understand?"

"Thotgol!" The Lady Lusi spoke firmly, but not harshly. He didn't look at her; the man in front was the problem.

"Yes, Lady?"

"Accept my apologies. The Lord Dalthorio is overwrought. The talisman you bring is vital to our cause. Please put your weapon away."

He stood still for a moment, then nodded, and put his ox-goad away.

"Chortanio!" Dalthorio commanded, "Have your men seize this—-"

"Tahheron!" Lusi did not shout, but Tahheron and his men moved round Thotgol.

Dalthorio looked at them, then at Lusi.

"Lord Dalthorio, if the talisman is attuned to him, we will need him desperately."

"More than myself, Lady?"

"Certainly not. But you can see that matters presently rest on a knife-edge. Casting away the talisman may well mean casting aside our best hope for victory."

"So he may threaten me and go unpunished?"

"As you insult him and go unpunished. We need the two of you."

'Wrong choice of words,' she realized immediately, *'No insult to an oxdriver is equal to the least threat to Dalthorio h'Anevoto—at least in the eyes of Dalthorio.'*

Dalthorio bowed. "Then nothing more is to be said. Good day to you, Lady."

At that point she realized she should try to mollify him, to convince him to stay, to make the alliance sure. But she had become sick and tired of the mess. She wanted no more of this ruling stuff. Lusi thought how nice it might be to marry some farmer and spend the rest of her life raising his children as he made their living with an acre of barley.

So she stood, stubbornly quiet, while Dalthorio and his men went off, leading their horses through the wood. As they went, Lusi heard Thotgol mutter behind her left shoulder, "And good riddance to you, little Lord Dalthorio."

She whirled on him, swinging a gloved fist that caught him on the jaw. He staggered a step backward where he caught his heel on a stone and sat heavily on the guard.

As he looked up at her in surprise she said, "I saved you from Dalthorio because it seemed hardly fair that you should come so far through such danger only to be killed at the end of the end of your journey. And also because, to be honest, since the talisman answers only to you, we need you living to wield it.

"But in the course of things I have offended the man who can supply the largest force when it comes to fighting. It is possible that, by saying difficult things and making risky promises, I can win him back.

"And you, you can only mutter insults like a boy safe behind his mother's skirts! Please try to be civil until you know who it is you're insulting."

Thotgol was just gathering himself to leap to his feet in anger, when he saw Tahheron's sword in front of him. He knew without looking the rest of them had drawn swords too.

Tahheron spoke. "Think carefully before you speak or act, Thotgol. I would hate to have wasted the time and trouble we went to in saving you, but we are her men."

Thotgol shook his head. "All right, I'll do nothing rash. My promise on it. Allow me to get up."

Carefully, making no sudden movements, he got to his feet. Despite this, Tahheron was standing beside Lusi when Thotgol faced her.

"I've been knocked down before, but that was as good as they come. I'll have a bruised jaw in the morning."

"My knuckles hurt already."

"So, then. Can we consider ourselves to be even?"

She broke into a laugh. "We can consider ourselves even. Poor Dalthorio! "Even" is never good enough for him, he wants to be ahead. He would like to take my place, no matter how impossible that is.

"Well, you will be my guest for a while, and I think we might as well camp here for the night before heading home."

"I'd prefer to leave the talisman and be off." Thotgol frowned.

"Would you? Think about the woods full of Bear-crowns, not to mention Dalthorio's people. Wouldn't you be safer with us?"

"Do I dare turn you down? You might use the other fist."

She chuckled. "I've declared us even. Don't press me too hard."

DOCTOR GOBNASH PRONOUNCED a phrase as he passed his hand through the air over the silver basin of water. The face of the still water showed a swirling pattern of colours, which coalesced into a view of Hameldash, lying against the root of a tree. Three arrows in his chest, his dead eyes staring.

"Producing the bespelled marble to track the ox-driver was, as I said, a thing well within the powers of any hedge-wizard, as was the matter of locating the item on which I had placed the spell. Sharing with others what my scrying-bowl shows is considerably more difficult. But as you see, Captain Hameldash is dead, his quest has failed."

Narnash scowled. "His second may be carrying on."

"Leaving his captain and these others unburied? And leaving the enspelled marble with his dead captain? No, I believe that the talisman, if not delivered, is on the point of being delivered."

"Mother-goddess' toenails! Then the uprising will be coming shortly?"

"Probably so. You will have seen the reports from your garrisons regarding the discovery of secret training grounds?"

The king frowned deeply. "I think it is time to turn Central Askos into a howling wilderness. My rule irks them, does it? They shall see how badly irked they can be!" He turned to a scribe. "Make a note. Message to my Lords, tell them to muster for war!"

LORD DISIKOMIN TOOK the paper from the courier, broke the seal with his thumb, and spread out the paper.

"War, then. The king bids us muster all forces for an attack on Askos."

"War?"

'Ah, the boy was eager. Well, he must see his first real fight, if not this year, then next.'

"Yes. And before you ask, you will come with me."

Folsidon was clearly restraining himself from jumping with glee. But Disikomin could tell he probably would do so when he was alone in his own quarters. With a commendable effort at seriousness, he asked, "What cause was given?"

"An attack on the King's soldiers, and a general lack of respect for the crown."

Now the boy frowned. "For such matters, shouldn't the king demand fines and hostages first?"

"The king is the king, and will do as he sees fit. And we would be best not to speak too loudly about what the king ought and ought not to do."

"Yes, father."

But the boy was right. Narnash must have been seeking a pretext to march on Askos again. Disikomin's own agents reported rumours of some dread talisman being brought to Askos. Something that could sweep whole armies from a battlefield. Perhaps that was the real reason, Narnash wanted to strike before they could bring that weapon into play.

And perhaps the rumour was something started by Doctor Gobnash, to discover where the rumour ended up at. Best for Disikomin he pretend not to know anything about that rumour. Let some other poor fool fall into the trap. In the meantime, he still had the report, and would not be taken by surprise if the report turned out to be true.

"THIS IS THE OLD PALACE of Askos."

It was not a particularly prepossessing spectacle. The walls of the city itself had not been well cared-for. While the palace roof lifted gradually to a peak well above the rest of the city, the building was more worn and battered than the walls had become. That same roof sagged in some places, and there were also obvious holes in it.

As if reading his mind, Lusi said, "It's not so fair and wonderful as it ought to be. It was decided some time ago to do only the most minor repairs, so as not to give Narnash any excuse to attack again. We hold our business in one of the lesser wings, and pretend to be harmless."

"Hm. Wiping out three hundred Bear-Crowns is not going to seem harmless."

She frowned. "I know. But we had little choice. I suspect we shall be getting demands for reparations over that. If we spin out negotiations long enough, we should be ready.

"You'll stay overnight?"

He grinned. "Lady, for the last several days, ever since the fight, you have been working at me. You have convinced me to come here on the grounds you will be better able to supply me with horses and funds to go my way if I come here. I had scarce expected you to have things waiting here so I could ride off again immediately. Yes, I'll stay until morning."

Thotgol was led to his quarters. They consisted of one small room, which was big enough for a man used to sleeping wherever there was shelter. The room had a large window, looking out on a garden, not too well kept, these days, with a clear stream running by just below. It also boasted one rather tattered wall-hanging, portraying some clash of warriors long ago. He suspected that it even predated Thogor Peacemaker, for there was no sign of a phalanx anywhere. There was merely infantry and cavalry in ranks clashing and loosing arrows and hacking away at each other. Thotgol spent the night in a very soft bed. The bed was so soft as to be uncomfortable for a man not used to such luxuries, if truth be told. In the morning, he had another conversation with Lusi.

He noticed from the start she had a different expression today, a firmer one. He surmised she was about to talk him into staying.

"Before you begin," he said, "I've talked to some people and it is clear joining you would be like tossing the Dwarves' bones with one of them missing. I'd be bound to have my fingers badly nipped."

She took a deep breath. "I'm sorry to hear you feel that way. There is another thing you may have overlooked, though."

"And that is?"

"The spell that forced you to bring the talisman here was worded in terms of delivering it to Dalthorio h'Anevoto. But Dalthorio can't use the talisman, so it is left with you. What do you think the spell will do if you leave without delivering it?"

And that rendered Thotgol speechless, because the truth was, he hadn't thought about it. The question also drew out of him a determination to find some way out, and leave these people to their crazy little doomed war.

But Lusi went on. "I'd rather not have you work with us at all than work with us grudgingly. I'm willing to call in people to figure out what can be done about the talisman. Both about having it attuned to you, and about the spell that traps you here, but it will take time. Will you wait, at least a bit more?"

Thotgol realized, for some strange reason, if she had sworn great oaths to make these things happen, he would have accepted. The simple statement she'd try to discover what could be done seemed much more believable.

"What do you plan?"

"There are some wizards in the city. We can ask some of the more reputable ones."

Thotgol felt surprise, followed by anger. "You have wizards here, and you had to send to Suragos for this thing?"

"It's not quite that straightforward. Shortly after the present Narnash came to the throne, a man called Doctor Gobnash came to work for him. You must have heard rumours of him by now; let me tell you, they are probably close to accurate, no matter how horrible.

"He appears to have a method of tracking magic intended to harm the king, and spells to cause such things to go badly awry. Many magicians died terribly before we learned what was being done.

"Hrezorio travelled to Suragos which, he calculated, was beyond the reach of Doctor Gobnash's magic. However, Gobnash was not unaware of his journey, and sent people after him.

"The rest of the story you know."

"Except why Gobnash does not use his spell against me? Or better yet, against you and your followers?

She shrugged. "I know little bits of this and that, but great amounts I know nothing about. My guess is that he can only attack people who are using or making magic. And that Hrezorio, when he built the talisman, added to it a protection against such magic. After all, the most powerful talisman would be of no use if Gobnash could destroy its wielder long before he could use it."

"I see."

"Well, don't take all that and use it to make bets on. Most of it is my guesswork. Guesswork based on what I know, but guesswork all the same."

"So, when do I get to meet the first of these magicians, then? Do you fortuitously have one of them waiting outside just now?"

She laughed. "I wouldn't take you so much for granted! On the other hand, I doubt you'd be surprised to know I had already sent to some of them to have them come in, one at a time. Probably not until this afternoon at the earliest."

He laughed in return. "Probably the sooner the better, for both of us."

TWO OF THE KING'S GUARDS strode into the Blue Loon, causing a ripple of silence to spread out from the doorway. Behind them came Doctor Gobnash, followed by two more Guards holding up a battered and bruised man wearing little more than rags. After them came the remainder of the troop.

Gobnash turned to the battered man. "Now, then, the man you saw here on several occasions, where did he sit."

The man shivered. "I think—-I think there, by the wall."

Doctor Gobnash's voice turned soft. "No rush. We want to get this right. Close your eyes. Think back to the times you were in here when he was. Just let your mind see the interior of the place, the walls, the tables, various people here and there. The man comes in, and he sits down—-where?"

"Yes, over by the wall, there next to the gouge in the wall."

"Ah, good, good! And you never heard a name put to him, did you? Think about that again. Did anyone ever call to him, greet him?"

"They may have, but I never heard it, I swear!"

The Doctor sighed. "Well, if they had, it might have made things a bit easier. Ah, well. Did he have a favourite chair?"

"Well, he always sat with his back to the wall."

"Hmm. I doubt it would do any good to ask our landlord how often chairs shift around. Captain, take all the chairs around that table. Make sure our men handle them as little as possible with their bare hands. Bag them and deliver them to my workroom."

"And the prisoner?"

"To my workroom as well."

"Sir!"

The parade went back through the streets of the city to the palace. People tended to look at them until they saw the slight figure in the sand-coloured robes. Then, they quickly turned their attention elsewhere.

Up the stairs they went. The guard waited while Doctor Gobnash unlocked his workroom. They ushered in the prisoner and brought in the bagged chairs.

"Set the chairs over there."

"And the prisoner? Poor beggar can't stand up at all."

"Ah, there, that armchair. Then you can leave us."

"With the prisoner, sir?"

"Come, now, Captain, you don't think he's going to overcome me and escape, now, do you?"

"No, sir. Of course not, sir."

"Then there is nothing to be worried about, is there? Thank you, Captain, for your assistance."

With a nod the Captain led his men out the door, leaving Gobnash and the prisoner alone.

Doctor Gobnash went to work with a small knife, cutting the bags away from the chairs.

After a moment, the prisoner spoke. "Sir?"

Gobnash looked at him. Desperation had overcome his fear, "Sir, you promised I should go free in return for my assistance."

The Doctor smiled. "And so I did. But freedom in your present condition would do you little good, would it?"

He walked to a sideboard and poured a large cup of wine. "Here, drink this, and relax."

He watched as the man drank it, and nodded approvingly. The doctor went back to his work, and the man slipped sidewise in his chair, breathing slowly. The doctor nodded once more, and continued with his work.

DOCTOR GOBNASH REPORTED to King Narnash in the middle of the day. A close look at the doctor's face showed he was a little more lined than usual.

"You will be happy to know, Highness, I have more information for you on the man who hired the dead spy."

"Indeed? You discovered this information by means of the chairs from the Blue Loon?"

"Exactly, Sir. The man was almost certainly sent from the lands of Lord Disikomin Rudashin."

"And you were able to discover this from chairs?"

"Unlike some things, this was no mere hedge-wizardry, but the short answer is,'Yes, I was.'

"You see, Highness, anything that contacts another thing leaves some trace there, no matter how minute. A living being, touching something. Particularly for so long a period as a night in an inn, will leave definite traces. Even so, separating out the traces we seek from all other traces and contaminations is not an easy matter. Though it can be done, if one has the skill and the ability. I found a man, one who wore a green jacket and leather cap, had sat in one of the chairs. In fact, at some time he had sat in three out of the four, though one of them contained the strongest traces.

"Concentrating some of these traces, I steeped a wooden pendulum in them, then swung the pendulum over a map. The pendulum came to rest pointing to the land of Lord Disikomin."

"So. We know one of my Lords is spying on me. No doubt most of them are, but I shall have to make an example. No arrest and execution, I think, just death by ambush. Something I can decry loudly, though those who matter will know what has happened."

He put his hands on his knees and leaned forward. "What of this talisman? You have no news of its whereabouts?"

"Not really 'news' Highness. The talisman has almost certainly been delivered. Though the shield around the talisman is too powerful for me to detect its exact location. However, given the care that these rebels have been taking, I doubt if it is in the same place as the leader."

"Black Bloody Destroyer's Teeth! You had led me to believe your powers were unmatched. Yet here is this talisman, very dangerous to us, and you still have no idea just what this talisman might do, and no idea where it is!"

Doctor Gobnash seldom showed anger, and in this case he merely raised his brows a trifle. "Highness, I assure you that most would have little or no notion at all that there was a talisman about, much less tell you anything further of where it might be."

Narnash sat tapping a finger on his thigh for a little, then said, "So. You have done as well as you can, now go do even better and let me know what this talisman is before my army and I find out, and to our sorrow."

THE SMALL GATHERING was held in one of the smaller chambers, cleared out for meetings of this sort. The chamber had high ceilings and grey walls. Only a few hangings, faded and worn, hung on the walls, depicting scenes of better times.

The wizard was old, though not exceptionally so. He wore an ordinary tunic and trousers, like any merchant, and their original dark brown had faded to a piebald pattern of brown and lighter brown. He wore a wild nest of a beard on his chin, still brown, with a few wisps of grey. Baldness had bared his head from forehead to crown, with a ruff of grey round it, showing only occasionally the original brown.

His right forefinger was stained from tip to the first joint. The tip being dull black, the region further up showing the black had been made up of a host of colours.

Lusi introduced them. "Thotgol, this is Arnatio."

Arnatio smiled, holding up his hand. "I see you noticing my finger; my speciality is alchemy, and from time to time I touch and test certain things. No, not the most powerful caustics nor acids, of course, but the result is as you see."

Thotgol had little notion what a caustic was, and even less about acids, so he only nodded politely.

The wizard either ignored or didn't notice Thotgol's confusion, for he went on, "The Lady has explained the situation to me. Suppose you do the same, to ensure that we are not working at cross-purposes here."

"Well, the wizard Hrezorio laid it on me, the duty of delivering this talisman to Dalthorio h'Anevoto. Being on the point of death, he did not explain the nature of talismans to me. So that in carrying it under my shirt, I apparently attuned the talisman to myself.

"What I need is to be able to deliver the talisman and be on my way. It seems to me that freeing the talisman from my control would be best. Otherwise, I would like the spell to be removed to allow me to leave Askos."

Arnatio frowned, raking his fingers absently through his beard. "I see," he said, slowly. "Well, I can tell tell you that dying spells are tricky things. I would be particularly loth to tamper with one cast by Hrezorio. Such spells use the power afforded by death, you see. However, given the specific command and circumstances, the effects of the spell will likely fade in time."

He glanced at Lusi and back at Thotgol. "It is highly likely, for instance, that the spell would dissipate if Dalthorio were to die. This is not certain, though.

"Now, attuning the spell anew, this might be possible. It would require you and Dalthorio to be in the same place while a series of spells were cast. The risk would be from Doctor Gobnash, of whom you will certainly have heard. At some point, such an extensive casting will certainly catch his attention, no matter how indirectly it aims at the overthrow of Narnash. And at a particular stage, lasting for hours at least. Perhaps for as long as a day, the shielding aspect of the talisman will be weakened or removed altogether. I'm sure you understand what this means."

Thotgol looked at Lusi, who returned his look steadily. "I assure you, Thotgol, there has been no collusion between us."

"And whatever wizard you find for me would say the same?"

She frowned at him. "You trust nothing and no one, do you? Is there some promise I could make, some oath I could swear, that would convince you I have not suborned Arnatio?"

Thotgol, uncomfortably aware that Arnatio was there watching the argument. He continued to stare at her for a moment, then sighed. "Trust is a difficult thing, and a man living as I have learns to be sparing with it. Perhaps too much so.

"Suppose I accept your word. What next?"

She did not answer immediately, but turned first to Arnatio. "Thank you, Arnatio. My Chancellor will have your payment."

The wizard bowed and left them. When the door closed behind him, she turned back to Thotgol and said. "I would ask you to use the talisman as Dalthorio would have done."

"And join this straw-by-the-fire uprising of yours, to be burned up by the flame of Narnash's rage? I would need a considerable inducement for that."

"Would it be an inducement to consider that, whether you join or reject us, your possession of the talisman will condemn you in the minds of Narnash and his wizard Gobnash?"

"An inducement, indeed. But I was thinking of the kind of inducement that can be used to buy food and lodging."

"You need have no fear for that so long as you are with us."

"And when the fight is done? Will I be kept at your table like an old horse whose usefulness is at an end, but who for sentiment's sake is stabled and fed?"

She pursed her lips as if seeing him for the first time. "No, that would hardly suit you, would it? What then, twenty gold coins?"

"Fifty."

"Hardly possible. Perhaps twenty-five."

"For twenty-five, I would hardly get out of bed in the morning. Forty."

"I can go to thirty-five, and that at the risk of depriving others."

"Thirty-five. Twenty now, and the balance when the job is done."

"One now, with your food and keep."

"Seven, with the food and keep.

"Five. And there is no one who could ever demand such a bargain of me."

"Five." Thotgol was not going to admit it, but he had never in his life had so much as five gold coins at one time. Not so much as the equivalent of silver, which was much safer for one of his status to possess.

"So, what is this talisman? What does it do?"

"I have no idea. I've never looked at the thing, only carried the talisman in its leather bag from there to here."

"Have I bought a shoat in a bag, then? How do we know this thing does what it is supposed to do?"

"I suppose we shall have to look at it."

He fetched the bag from under his shirt, and opened it. Inside was another leather bag, with a leather cord carefully wound around and about the mouth of it. There was also a leather scroll, rolled and tied with a small leather cord. Some words were scorched on one visible corner.

Thotgol put his hand on the bag to begin opening it. "Wait!" Lusi said.

He looked up at her. "Look! The scroll says *'Read this first.'*"

"What?"

"That writing." She pointed at it and looked down at him again. "You can't read, can you?"

Chapter VIII
Mustering for War

"How were you thinking to be able to use the talisman if you can't read?"

Thotgol gave her an embarrassed smile. "To tell the truth, I hadn't thought of it at all. Never had to read, so I never think of it as being necessary. And to be truthful about it, it was you first said I must use the talisman. I suppose we might get someone to read it for me."

"Too inefficient. Best we teach you to read."

"Me? Certainly not!"

"Wardesh guard and guide, why not?"

"It's nothing I've ever done before. The likes of me don't do that sort of thing!"

Lusi shook her head. "That bird won't sing. You can't tell me you've never learned anything new. And before you learned it, it was nothing you've done before. So?"

He shook his head admiringly. "No wonder you're the prospective Queen. People aren't allowed to say no to you. Do you have someone around who could teach me?"

"We have. I think we should get started immediately, don't you?"

VAHHEROD THE SCRIBE came to meet Thotgol in his quarters.

Vahherod the scribe was a man of middle years, with a bent for sarcasm. "So, you are required to learn to read? I suppose it would be too much to ask if you recognize any letters at all?"

"I recognize the name of Narnash when I see it on a coin."

"Hah! Wonderful! Are you aware the name as you see it on the coins is an abbreviated form? That it consists of only the consonants N-R-N-SH, without the vowels?"

"No. I don't know what a consonant is, nor a vowel either, and until very recently I was happy that way."

Vahherod glared. "We shall do better, young sir, if you show more respect."

LUSI WAS FURIOUS. "DO you have any idea what it has cost me to mollify Vahherod? He demanded the lash for you, and appears to have been within his rights. I only interceded on your behalf because I know the lash would have the wrong effect, making you less willing rather than more willing to work with us!

"And you, all you can do is sit there with that smirk on your face!"

She stared at him for a moment, then asked, "What did you do to him?"

Thotgol tried to hide his smirk, "Surely he told you?"

"I asked, but he became incoherent. It involved laying hands on his person. What happened?"

"Why, we had some words, he and I. About respect. It ended with me holding him upside-down by the ankle over that nice little stream that flows by my window, until he asked me politely to put him down."

Lusi, who had herself suffered under the scribe's tutelage at a younger age, found herself hard-put to suppress a giggle. "You didn't!"

"Oh, I assure you that I did."

She pulled herself upright, and hoped her slip had not been too obvious. "Then I must require you not to do so again. Vahherod is not the easiest person to work with, but we have little time to waste. Suppose I put it to you any more such incidents will result in fines, to be taken out of your wages, and the payment going to mollify the scribe?"

"I'll do what I can, But after a time, the loss of a gold piece will seem little enough cost."

She nodded. "I will also ask the scribe to moderate his own behaviour when dealing with someone unused to our ways."

She turned and left the room quickly, almost rushing to her own chambers. Servants who saw her along the way wondered at why she was biting her lip. At least one muttered someone ought to teach that Batan a lesson, upsetting the Lady and all.

They were more mystified to hear from her room first the sound of giggles, then outright laughter.

VAHHEROD, DISPLAYING only a bare touch of wariness, stood once more in Thotgol's quarters.

"Now, you have before you a board, with the letters carved at the top. The first is the sound 'a'. You will please say that."

"A."

"Very good. You will please take the stick of charcoal and write that letter. Hmm. Fair, for a first attempt. The bottom stem must be a little longer. Try once more."

Thotgol would have been amused to know Lusi had assured Vahherod his person would be protected, as much as possible. But it was well-known that Batans were touchy-tempered, and no punishment could bring Vahherod back if the worst happened.

NARNASH SAT ON HIS horse quietly, observing contingents of troops march in. They came in, battalion by battalion, striding along, aware of the King watching. For all their pride, the greater number of them had had little more than a week's training, if that. However, they would do. They would do. He turned to the aide beside him. "The muster appears to be progressing well. How are our numbers?"

"Eight hundred horse, six thousand pikemen, twelve hundred light troops, Highness."

"Archers?"

"Four hundred of the light troops are archers, and we have one unit of horse archers as well. Numbering two hundred."

"Good. Any word from Lord Disikomin?"

"A galloper has come in, saying that he hopes to be with us tomorrow."

"Does he? Good, very good. And what of provisions?"

"Well in hand, Highness. We have sufficient whole grain for seven days. We also have sufficient milled grain for three more, and our ovens are busily turning out bread. We have rounded up sheep and goats locally to provide for us until we come to Askos."

"Good enough. Have we any dependable estimate as to just what numbers the Askos can field against us?"

"Our various sources differ widely, Highness. But we suspect from five to seven hundred horse, four to eight thousand pikemen, and two thousand light troops."

"Who do we have out there gathering intelligence? A pack of knuckleheads who can't count? Perhaps we should require them to explain their estimates, if they differ so widely. One might almost think they were trying to mislead their king."

"Most of our spies are half-breeds, hoping to win acceptance by taking on risks for you, Highness. Then we have other renegade Askos, working simply for pay, and some few Wennz in disguise.

"It appears that there is a rough pattern, when reports overlap. The numbers we receive from the renegades are higher, lower for the Wennz, and in the middle for the half-breeds. The pattern is not so consistent as to be able to make the basis for any real action, without the loss of half our spies or more."

The king nodded absently. "I see. I see, but I am not happy. Pass the word that I should prefer better estimates than I could get by tossing knucklebones."

"Yes, Highness." The aide was already at working though it in his mind. Trying to word the king's demand in a way which would not totally discourage the people who were risking a horrible death to provide intelligence for him.

A PAIR OF GUARDS MARCHED to the door of Doctor Gobnash's workroom, and one of them rapped sharply on it. It was opened, not by the Doctor himself, but by a man of average size and build, who limped when he walked.

"Can I be of service?"

"The king requests the presence of Doctor Gobnash."

"I shall inform him." The door was closed in their faces. At any other door in Wennz-Askos, the guards would have pounded on the door. Perhaps even knocked it down and dragged away the person they sought. But this was not any other door. They traded looks, then in silent agreement went back to tell the king his message had been passed.

The king was not, therefore, a cheerful monarch when Doctor Gobnash appeared.

"I would appreciate prompt response to my summons." the king declared.

The doctor, as though intent on inflaming the situation further, shrugged, "I was involved with a situation that would not permit me to drop it. No matter how important the summons. And I am here now."

The king took a deep breath. *'Sometime,'* he promised himself, *'I will decide I can do without your services.'*

The thought made him smile.

"I suppose it is too much to hope that this important matter had anything to do with the location of the talisman brought to the Askos, and a means to defeat it?"

"No, Highness, it was not that. But my searching and scrying, along with the work of certain spies, have allowed me to discover certain things. The ox-driver who had brought the talisman has been quartered regularly with a scribe. The general story is that the ox-driver is being taught to read.

"It would almost seem that he himself is going to use the talisman."

The king broke in. "You told me first-off that he was merely a messenger, carrying the talisman to the one who would actually wield it. Now you seem to have changed your mind. Was your information not so good as you claimed?"

The elegant beige-covered shoulders shrugged again. "Highness, my information was as good as could be. I cannot be completely certain, given the shielding influence of the talisman. But it would almost seem that sometime during the journey, the talisman became attuned to the ox-driver. This would seem ridiculous, though. Hrezorio would hardly have been so careless with his messenger. Yet this explanation does fit the facts."

"You are saying that the talisman may not be ready for use?"

"I would promise nothing, Highness. How complex are the instructions? How much learning, if any, does the ox-driver already have? All I can say is that, at the time of my latest information, some two days after the event, I do not believe the ox-driver to be capable of using the talisman against us."

"Hmm. My own muster is not complete yet, but..." He turned to his aide. "Pass orders that we will march tomorrow. Some contingents will have to force their march to catch us en route."

He turned back to the doctor. "Thank you, doctor."

'But I will still rejoice to see the day when I can dispense with your services!'

THOTGOL WAS WALKING in the Market of the Old City. Like markets everywhere, it roared and clattered around him. The Market was a little small, after Suragos, but that didn't bother Thotgol. And the usual statue of Thogor Peacemaker stood on a much shorter and plainer column. But it was a market, and in all its boisterous disorder, it was cheery to Thotgol.

Lusi had asked him, though not ordered him, which would have provoked the wrong reaction, to stay out of the less savoury parts of the city. This meant he would probably not find a place to toss the Dwarves' Bones. He drifted into a position where he had promised to use the talisman for Lusi. Which meant staying alive to do so.

He had changed one of his gold pieces, back at the palace, for its equivalent in silver. He did not wish to walk round flashing gold in the market place, no matter how law-abiding the people were.

The market was bright and loud. Voices chattered in both the Common Language and what he had to assume was the local language of Askos. This was interesting, as the Common Language had replaced local languages almost entirely in the major cities. One still found people here and there obstinately holding on to their language. Though not usually where it might have an effect on their livelihood, such as the major Market-places.

Though Market-places in large cities were usually "safe," Thotgol had gotten used to being aware of his surroundings. He was therefore aware of the four men almost as soon as they had taken up their positions. Through the shouting clatter of the bazaar, he first noticed one man who didn't belong. He was about Thotgol's height, though broader, and he bore the look of one who'd seen a lot of fights. His arms were thick and muscular, and his knuckles bore old scars. His face was unmarked save for a small scar that bisected his left eyebrow. He was looking over a produce stall, but it was obvious, he wasn't planning on making a purchase.

Taking a trinket from the stall in front of him, Thotgol held it up. He turned the trinket around this way and that to look at it in different lighting, and spotted the rest of the party. From their positions, either he, or someone nearby, was their target. The way one lived to a ripe old age, in his kind of life, was to assume he was the target. He smiled inwardly. *'And the Lady Lusommi wanted me to stay in the main market where I'd be safe!'*

Thotgol tossed the trinket back on the stall. He ignored the insistent shout of the stallkeeper that this piece was really a bargain and that he hadn't even spoken about price. He walked over to the produce stall. He took care not to completely ignore the ruffian, which would be as much a giveaway as staring him in the eye. Instead, he looked at him, and appeared to dismiss him, turning instead to the stall itself.

He picked up a melon from a stack, and tossed the vendor a silver coin. The vendor gasped in shock; even a wild barbarian knew a silver coin should buy nearly half his stock!

Thotgol whirled and threw the melon at the head of the ruffian. "Now look what you've done, you great bumbling lump of ox-dung!"

The ruffian was caught by surprise; Thotgol was doing essentially what they had planned to do to him. He raised his hand just too late to ward off the melon. By the time he had reached for the cudgel thrust through his belt, Thotgol had kicked him in the groin. As he was falling, Thotgol laid his ox-goad across the side of his head for good measure, and moved off to meet the others.

The other three were also taken by surprise. They had a little more time to react. To ready themselves to carry out their job. Thotgol moved so, rather than having to face them all at once, he could get one of them alone for at least a moment.

He feinted a thrust at the man's middle. When the man struck to ward that off, Thotol struck a backhand at the man's forehead, which dropped him where he stood.

The other two were coming at him, trying to take him from two sides. Meanwhile the market-crowd screamed and shouted and tried to move away from them. Thotgol jumped over, warded a downward blow from the cudgel of the man moving to his left, while kicking him in the shin. He then turned to the other, who was coming in with his club upraised. Thotgol thrust the point of the ox-goad in the man's throat. Then parried the weakened downward swing of the cudgel.

Whirling again, he saw the other man trying to limp away. He caught up with him in two swift steps, and hit him across the back of the head.

From the look of the man he'd stabbed, he was no longer any trouble, possibly never again any trouble. Thotgol moved off, with no one hindering him. He could probably use the Lady Lusommi's name to get him out of trouble, but he didn't like the thought of that. Having had experience dodging the City Watch in various cities over the years, he was able to make his way back to the palace.

HE WAS SUMMONED, A little later, to appear in Lusi's quarters again.

"I understand you bought an expensive melon today."

Thotgol looked up at Lusommi. Well, she was smiling, so matters couldn't be that bad. "You have spies watching me?"

"No, but a quarter of the city knows I have a guest from Batan-ji. And Batans are few in Askos, you understand. So when a Batan kills or seriously injures four men in the market-square, using a stick with a metal tip, it is a foreseen conclusion the Masters of the Market will bring it to my attention.

"No," she said, "you needn't frown so; the Watch did their own investigation, and the men were all known to the Watch. So far as the Watch Captain is concerned, you did the city a favour."

"Those were not the sort that usually haunt the Market."

It was her turn to frown. "No, they aren't. That suggests they were hired to find you and attack you. By whom?"

"Doctor Gobnash?"

She shook her head. "Not Doctor Gobnash's way. His method is a quick knife in the ribs by some harmless-looking person, or something fatal slipped into a drink. I'm afraid I know who, but I'm also afraid there's little I can do about it."

"Who?" When she looked hesitant, he demanded again, "Who? Have I no right to know my enemy's name?"

Suddenly the answer came.

"Dalthorio! Fierce flying pig guts! It's Dalthorio, isn't it?"

"It is. And without the forces he can bring to the muster, we would be in sad shape. Not merely for the lack of the forces themselves. Which would be bad enough, but there are many others who, witnessing our numbers lessened, will be less than eager to support us. They may do such things as coming late to the muster, or merely melting away on the battlefield.

"So even though I am certain who is behind it, I must pretend to have no idea. And I must ask you to join me in the pretense. I will, of course, make sure you are well-guarded."

"Wardesh keep me from being a ruler! It seems a ruler is required to be courteous to the people he'd most like to punch in the face. How did you come to choose this life?"

Frowning, she shook her head. "I didn't choose it, it chose me.

"My own family were only minor cousins to the royalty. High enough to have considerable land, but not so high as to even consider the notion of taking the rule.

"You may not have heard, but most of the Old families have protective talismans. As it has been explained to me, they are little more than powerful good luck talismans, specifically tailored against violence.

"However, even the best of luck will eventually fail. So the families suffered grievously. First of all, many sons went to battle, and in battle the effectiveness of the talismans is reduced. When the great battle against the First Narnash failed, many fell, and all the Old families were proscribed by him and his successors. Assassinations and skirmishes, illness and accidents, cut back the numbers.

"My own close family were dead, and I was living at an old hunting lodge with a few servants. One day a body of nobles rode up to tell me I was the heir to the throne of Askos.

"It had not been nearly so simple as they had made it sound. The fact was none of them would support any of the others as King, so they picked me. A mere girl, they could bend me to their will as need be."

She sighed. "Fortunately, I was not entirely untaught. I had read some histories—Vahherod the Scribe takes credit for that—and I knew some pitfalls to avoid. Mostly, I avoided immediate decisions, no matter who pressed me, saying it was a matter required some thought.

"I asked advice when I was able, found out as much as I could, of the reasons why this person might be demanding that. Then mostly made decisions that left no one entirely unhappy. I also gathered a few people whom I knew could usually give me unbiased advice, and made sure when there were biases, I knew about them. So here I am."

She paused. "So, now it's your turn. Tell me how one such as you becomes an ox-driver. It seems an odd use of your talents."

"Ah, I spent the usual childhood in Batan-ji, practicing with wooden swords, certain I was going to become a famous warrior, covering myself with glory.

"When the king—I never knew which king—called up warriors from our village, the elders declared I was too young to go. I recall what a sulky and bad-tempered brat I became!

"Twenty-one young men marched away from our village. Three returned. My elder brother came back lacking a right hand, another had a leg which no longer served him. He walked with a crutch, his left leg dragging in the dust. The third had no wounds at all, but a sickness of the chest which kept him from all but the lightest chores.

"I've learned since then such losses are not always common to every village. At the time, though, I was horrified. My brother had been stronger, more skilled than I, yet he came back with no glory. Just a crippling injury that left him an angry and bitter man at eighteen.

"I gave up practice with wooden swords, found myself a place as a helper in an ox-train, and went travelling. The next time the king called on our village for warriors, I would be far away.

"I discovered, Of course, even in the world of merchant-trains. There were reasons why a man must fight. Reasons that had nothing to do with Kings and Armies. My training with wooden swords had not been entirely wasted. Though a sword is an expensive item for an ox-driver. I eventually had the ox-goad made, to my specifications, and learned to live in the places ox-drivers frequent. By the time I could afford a sword, I no longer really needed one.

"And every so often, I do something like kicking a Zhotani in the behind, and get in trouble for it."

Lussomi measured Thotgol with her eyes, "Do you have any hopes, any plans for the future?"

"Other than surviving long enough to leave Askos, you mean? Oh, I suppose I'll keep on travelling, working for this caravan master or that. Perhaps if the Dwarves' Bones fall right and I get the money, I might set up a train of my own, hauling for this merchant or that."

And suddenly his circumstances struck him. "That's right, if I see this through, I'll be nigh unto rich, won't I? Perhaps the notion of my own train is not so far off!"

"And you'll bring goods to the Royal Lady of Askos, by special commission?"

He grinned, taking up the notion. "But of course. The finest silks from the Faraway Lands, spices from the land of the Kondellini and jewels from beyond the Zhotani lands."

"Being careful not to kick any behinds on the way through."

She was laughing, but this comment sobered him. "I'll have to watch where I go. I show up in the wrong place, and there'll be Half-faces hunting me before I can breathe twice."

"How long will they carry on that feud?"

"Zhotani? I've heard of it lasting twenty years or more."

"No way of weaseling out of it? Buying your way clear, something like that?"

"I'm not sure. Never heard of it being done," He shook his head, "That's a problem for later on, though. First I have to survive this year."

NEXT DAY THE SITUATION became more pressing. Lusi walked into the chamber just as Vahherod was explaining a particularly naughty phrase in the initial chapter of Zoltario's ride through Algasor.

"Vahherod, would you excuse us for a moment?"

"Certainly, Lady." He walked from the room with the air of one taking just enough time, but not so much as to earn him a reprimand.

When he had gone, she took a small piece of paper from her pocket. "A messenger-bird has just come from one of our agents in Wennz. Previous report was Narnash was mustering for war. This report says four days ago he and most of his army have begun to march."

"So the reading-lessons have to be rushed?"

She nodded. "He knows we have the talisman. It cannot be ruled out that rumour of your reading-lessons has reached him. If he was unable guess the meaning of that, Doctor Gobnash certainly could. He hopes to be on us before you've mastered the use of the talisman. I suppose it's too much to hope he's wrong?"

"Well, ever since my first lesson, when all I was certain of were the shapes of some letters, particularly 'a,' I unrolled the scroll just to see what I could make of it. If only to see every place where 'a' occurred.

"Last night I discovered I was able to make out every word. But by then I was becoming fascinated with the idea of reading. That someone a thousand miles away and a hundred years ago could set down their thoughts on a matter, and I could read them here, today.

"There are still some things unclear about the instruction scroll. But I could speed matters up by asking about them specifically."

"You have been wasting our time?" There was an edge of wrath to her voice.

He held up a hand, almost as if warding off a blow. "No, no, not really wasting time. There are some sentences in which, though

I know every word, the sentence makes no sense. I was trying to get round that by asking about various meanings a word might have. I thought the fewer people who know any of the exact wordings of the instructions, the better."

She still frowned, but now it was in concentration. "You're right about that. Vahherod is a very good teacher, but a little prone to self-importance. My people have already had words with with him about muttering over a cup of wine about the *'very important student'* *he's teaching. 'And by the Request of the Royal Lady, no less.'*

"If you were to ask him about some mysterious sentence, I can only guess what he'd do."

"Do you have any possible suggestions? At some time, someone is going to have to explain these sentences to me."

She drew a deep breath. "Would you object to taking lessons from me?"

He grinned. "Not at all. But won't some of your people object?"

"Some will, of course. But I'll explain the situation to the ones that matter. I doubt there's a person in the city who doesn't know you've brought something special to help in our war against Narnash. Knowing that I'm meeting with you to help plan how to use the thing will be all the explanation needed by most."

LORD DISIKOMIN WAS on the march, annoyance fueling his steps. The galloper was rattling off his message. The basic point of it being Narnash had hurried his departure, and trusted Lord Disikomin would overtake him shortly.

Nor was Lord Disikomin mollified to learn several other commanders were left in the same situation as he. Narnash had apparently not left any instructions as to the victualling of Disikomin's men. This meant he either paid out of his own funds—a physical impossibility—or he gathered his supplies in the king's name, on the king's lands.

He noted where this led in its turn. The king now had another weapon to use against him, if he decided to turn against him. Requisitioning supplies in the king's name on the king's lands could be twisted to appear as an intention to supplant the king.

The man had wound up his message. Disikomin waved a dismissive hand. "Find yourself something to drink, a bite to eat. No return message just yet."

Finding himself alone with his son, he asked, "You understand the import of this all?"

"The king has marched without his full muster. He clearly feels anxious about what the Askos might do, and hopes to forestall them by making the first move."

"Very good, so far as it goes. But he has left no orders for our provisioning. How do you read that?"

"That we are expected to gather our own supplies."

"Ah, so simple! But there is no specific order, written or verbal, to that effect. And if King Narnash decides Lord Disikomin Rudashin is getting too high and mighty, why there is proof. He went about requisitioning supplies in the king's name on the king's land, just as if he were king himself."

The boy had long ago ceased to be surprised at the notion of duplicity among rulers. "But we've given him no reason to fear, father."

Disikomin smiled grimly. "What is considered a cause by a ruler is not necessarily what you or I might think. The line of Narnash Skalsland has survived by using bloody means to cut back whatever seems a threat. And when Disikomin Rudashin appears to be growing richer, more popular among the nobles. That fact alone, without any overt sign of treachery, may mark him in Narnash's mind as a dangerous man."

There was silence then, but for the sounds of their horses' hooves, and the noise of the army marching behind. He hoped Folsidon would not ask him how one was to survive in this kind of situation where good stewardship and good fortune might be taken as tokens of possible treason. The only answer he could give was one tried to guess what was being thought in the Palace, and to prepare for any eventuality. And as far as answers went, that was no—-

"Ambush, father! Watch out!"

With the clear and horrible slowness of such events, the matter unfolded. Folsidon put himself and his horse between his father and the men standing up in the brush at the roadside. Disikomin flung himself from his saddle to haul the young man down, only to feel the impact of arrows, feel the boy go limp.

They had been wearing leather, this far inside friendly territory. The three arrows had gone through cleanly, deep into the boy's chest. Disikomin was oblivious to the shouting and chasing and screaming of horses. He watched helplessly as his son quietly stopped breathing.

"The bandits are being pursued, Lord."

He did not look up. "Bandits? Bandits who attack an armed force of soldiers?"

"Askos, then, Lord?"

He did not answer that, but pulled himself stiffly to his feet. He was old and weary, and the taste of life had suddenly become bitter. He looked up to the horizon in the supposed direction of the king's march. "Oh Narnash, Narnash, did you fear me so much? Did you think to kill me and then bend my son to your will? Or was your only thought *'The old man worries me; away with him?'*

"Always the slippery thought, is it, Narnash Skalsland? Attack someone slyly, and the others will understand the message?

"Oh, yes, Narnash, never my king again, yes, I will follow you into Askos, and may you have the joy of it when I do!"

Chapter IX
Maneuvers, Skirmishes, and Tests

T hey did not march immediately. First they interred Folsidon and set a cairn of stones on the grave. Disikomin called one of several stonecutters who had been conscripted into his army, and had him cut these words on one of the larger stones:

> *FOLSIDON RUDASHIN,*
> *DIED IN HIS FATHER'S PLACE,*
> *ON THE ROAD TO KING NARNASH'S WAR.*

There was every likelihood the king's men might commit the impiety of destroying cairn and grave. Such a deed would serve to declare to those who followed him just what sort of man the king was.

And in the meantime.... In the meantime, anger's heat having cooled a trifle, Disikomin's mind went to more effective notions than merely marching up to throw his force against Narnash's rear in in a useless display of vengeful anger.

The five picked messengers stood before him, "Commander Tugashin has given you your instructions?"

"Yes, sir," said the spokesman, "We're to make our way through Askos, as unnoticed as possible, and find as many of our folk as we can in the various parts on the king's army, tell them what has happened, and order them to slip away from the king to join with you."

"Good. On your way, then, and Wardesh guard and guide you, lads," Disikomin watched after him as the spokesman took his leave, '*Lads. Yes, each of them was the son of some father somewhere.*'

He then turned to the aide beside him. "Tugashin, have you any thoughts?"

Tugashin spoke carefully, "Lord, you know your folk will follow you without hesitation. Yet Narnash outnumbers us badly."

"And it is only in the heroic ballads that good overcomes crushing odds to defeat evil? Yes. Had Narnash's army been at the top of that hill, likely I would have cast you all away to a useless death. But I have had time to think. We will use our force to hurt Narnash as best we can, and yet not destroy ourselves in the process."

"We will offer our service to the Lady of Askos?"

"Yes, but there are other matters to be considered. If we simply ride into her camp, we can expect a long period of distrust and suspicion. Along with petty little garrison tasks well away from any main battle.

"So I have a better notion."

THE TENT-FLAP MOVED slightly in the idle breeze. Lusi did not like the thought of living in such a fancy tent when her soldiers were camping outside, with no more than a blanket to keep them warm at night. On the other hand, as her advisors insisted, she was not an ordinary soldier, and needed to act like a ruler.

Which also included making challenging decisions as the one that was before her.

"We are in a difficult situation here, Lady. Certainly, we are being joined by new troops nearly every day. But every day we hold back from battle gives our troops a little more concern for our confidence in them."

Lusommi nodded. "Yes, Aelkoriat. You're telling me things I am already aware of. And I also know Narnash is coming up fast, destroying as he comes. With those he left behind coming up to swell his ranks daily.

"Everything you tell me, I know. And I know as well we are balancing on a knife-edge. If we fight too soon, we run the risk of failure. If we wait too long, we risk loss of morale and desertions.

"I assure you, I have all these things in mind."

Aelkoriat bowed and withdrew. For a while Lusi sat, staring at the tent door. Then she rang a bell, and when a servant appeared, she said, "Find Thotgol and tell him that I request his presence."

The servant knew Thotgol was not difficult to find. One simply asked a soldier to direct one to where the biggest gambling-session was going on out among the camps of the army. At the third such one, Thotgol was present.

He gave an audible sigh on seeing the servant, recognizable by his dress. "Her Ladyship requires my presence?"

"She does."

He looked at his winnings then shrugged. "Sorry, lads, I can't stay and take any more of your money. I'll be back, though."

The servant thought it to the man's credit that he made no sly and ribald suggestions. Even more to his credit that he frowned when such a suggestion was made, loudly and crudely, from one of those gathered.

As they walked, he asked, "What does the Lady want?"

"It has not been my habit to demand reasons of the Lady," answered the servant, forbiddingly. "She will certainly let you know when you arrive."

"Of course. Sorry, I had no intention of insulting you." He suspected, though, the man knew more than he let on. The servant had not asked the Lady's reasons. But servants lived by gossip. If only to know and anticipate the requirements of their masters. Thotgol, unfortunately, was in a class outside. He was not a servant, which meant servant's gossip seldom found its way to him. And as an ox-driver set into a place of importance, he was often seen as a jumped-up menial trying to hobnob with his betters.

He was not kept waiting at the Lady's tent door, the way some of her Lords might have kept him waiting just to demonstrate his place.

Nor did she take him to task for spending time gambling. She apparently understood a man could not be reading leather scrolls every hour of every day.

But she did ask, "How soon do you think you'll be ready? On the one hand we have Narnash wasting our lands, and on the other we have our own mustered troops beginning to lose confidence."

He prevented himself from shrugging, knowing that would say the wrong thing. "Well, you've been studying with me, you know the progress I've made. I can read the whole thing, some parts of it I've even committed to memory. All we can do is make the attempt, see if I can really make it work."

"You want to test it before the battle?"

He shook his head. "I'm a little concerned about the warning Hrezorio gave. That interfering with the weather can have disastrous consequences. I'd rather use the power as little as necessary."

She nodded. "Well, we will begin marching again, to close with the enemy. You continue to read the scroll, and be ready when the time comes."

LUSOMMI CONSIDERED it necessary for Thotgol to attend the evening staff sessions. Considering the talisman was to be used as a weapon, only the most finicky of the lords could deny this was only right. On the third night out, he was asked to do more.

Many lords, did their best to show that, while Thotgol was to be allowed in the sessions, he was not allowed in as any sort of equal. Most were careful to stay just short of open insults. For the tale of his use of the ox-goad, had become widely known.

Thotgol did his best not to hear or see any of the insults; for certain, he might demand satisfaction of some young knucklehead, even finding the man some night alone if, as likely, he refused to fight on the grounds that Thotgol was no equal of his. But this would only make the others more upset, putting Lusi in a continual position of having to force them to accept his presence. Even Thotgol knew that was no way to go to war when facing a foe already superior in numbers and, likely, in training.

The first order of business, as always, was Lusommi's demand, "Our forces today?"

"Shilgrothia joined us today, bringing a hundred fifty horse, five hundred pikes, and six hundred assorted infantry. This brings our total to six hundred horse, three thousand pikemen, and fifteen hundred light troops.

"Some of our pikes, though, are of indifferent quality. Even an hour's training before and after each day's march are no likely to bring them up to the standard of Narnash's best."

"Serious disadvantages indeed, Aelkoriat. Have we any advantages?"

"We have more archers, most of them are better than any Narnash can boast. If we can site them advantageously in the battle-line, they may well make up many of our other lacks. There is also the talisman, of which we have heard only rumours, so we have no notion of how it will serve. Have there been no tests?"

Lusommi looked at Thotgol. "Would you tell us of the situation with the talisman?"

He hadn't wanted to talk in this company. They already resented his presence enough, without him actually speaking as if he were one of them. She'd told him, though, she was going to call on him.

"You'll be using it. I could explain it, but that would be just me telling it as I understand it. I think it best you tell the tale. Bad enough that you are who you are, without me seeming unwilling to dare to allow you to speak for yourself."

So he stood, well aware that for most of them, nothing he could say would make them more accepting of him.

"The talisman is known as the Talisman of the Winds. It gives the user the ability to call on the winds, from the east, west, north, and south, and also the whirlwind.

"The wizard Hrezorio, who made it, warns of the dangers of excessive tampering with the weather. It is not to be used heedlessly.

"The user must be in sight of the place where he is going to call the wind, and preferably not more than five hundred yards away. A wind may be called for an area of about one hundred yards wide. It ought not to be allowed to continue for more than three hundred heartbeats. Else it may have irremediable consequences."

Irremediable consequences' was a phrase direct from the scroll, and Thotgol couldn't help using it himself. It was so distinctive, so rhythmic. But he carried on.

"To prevent severe weather reaction, it ought to be used only once a day, and for every wind used, an opposing wind ought to be called within seven hours, of as near exact duration as possible.

"Even these precautions will not necessarily prevent after-effects, though it will at least ameliorate them.

"The whirlwind, though potentially the most powerful, should be used very sparingly, as there is no known counteraction to its effects."

"Given all this, I have decided, and the Lady concurs, testing the talisman is too dangerous. Best to use it only when the time is upon us."

This caused uproar. The main thrust of the outcry was on the line of "We must put ourselves and our land at risk, hoping in unproven magic?"

Lusi answered this. "Hrezorio knew well what he was doing. His intent was to produce a talisman that needed no particular magical ability to use. He warned us in the scroll, as Thotgol has said, tampering with the weather can have drastic results. What good would it do to win a battle and suffer seven years' drought after? Or have weather so consistently cold and wet that low-lying lands are flooded, crops and hay rot in the fields?

"Hrezorio sent his warnings and his assurances about this talisman. He warned us the effects can be ameliorated, but not necessarily prevented. Should we then do forty tests, each time risking some effect? And, at the worst, perhaps have thirty minor effects coming back to bite us? Which of you is going to be willing to look at your people's destroyed fields and say, 'Well, at least we made sure of the talisman's working'?"

That silenced them for a bit, then someone called out, "Why must it be this foreign ox-driver who wields the talisman? Why not one of us?"

Lusi's first glance was at Dalthorio, whose face was too carefully void of expression.

"Interesting that you should put the question thus. Might I ask in return if the soldiers you have brought with you are all men from your lands? None of them mercenaries from other nations, fighting for pay? And if there are mercenaries in your forces, why should it matter that the talisman is used by a Batan. So long as he uses it in our service?"

She gave no sign of the rage that roiled in her, *'Dalthorio, I went to extreme lengths to make up to you, and you pay me back by feeding this question to that young troublemaker? Is this the way life will be with you? Always having to beware of any little spiteful thing you might do because you think your pride is threatened?'*

And of course, answering the young nuisance's question with direct truth was impossible. That Thotgol knew so little of talismans that he could accidentally cause one to become attuned to him, and therefore must wield it. This was not something to give the army confidence in him.

It was no secret Thotgol was taking reading lessons. The corollary, that he had been previously totally illiterate, was so logical, she feared daily someone might hit on it. Their situation was already so shaky that this could bring it down. And was she agreeing with Thotgol's decision about tests partly from a nagging fear he might mess up the first test, destroying the army's morale before they came within sight of Narnash?

She looked around at the company, willing them not to say anything more. Whether it was the force of her personality, or whether it was something else. There was only a bit of muttering as the gathering broke up.

Aelkoriat stayed behind. Stepping close, he said quietly, "Dalthorio planted that question, of course."

"Of course. But what would you have me do? Accuse him before the company, thus admitting the point was a valid one?"

"At some time the value of Dalthorio's following could be outweighed by the trouble he causes. Say the word, and he will meet with a fatal accident."

She looked at him closely. Yes, he would do so if she wished. But they were looking at a time full of death and killing. She couldn't see taking on one more which would be directly attributable to her. Worse, however well planned and executed, it might still be traced to her. What would that do to the realm?

She shook her head. "Believe me, it means not a little that you would offer to do this for me. But no, not such a measure at such a time."

"As you wish, Lady."

THE DUSTY ARCHER IN nondescript clothing stood before the king.

"You were successful?"

"After a fashion, Highness. We were just taking aim at him when that boy of his yelled and jumped in the way. Three arrows got the boy, the old man ducked off his horse to catch his son. Got an arrow each into their horses, the last went Chaos away."

"You killed the boy, left his father alive?"

"Yes, Highness."

"And you call that success '*after a fashion?*' You know what I call it? I call it worse than a failure! Now once I've finished this job in Askos, I'll have to go back and deal with Disikomin, him and any others that might join him!

"I wanted the boy left alive, because he doesn't have the prestige his father does, and I could keep the boy in his place.

"I call this akin to wilful disobedience. You're lucky Gobnash doesn't accompany me into the field, or I'd turn you over to him! Guard! Get this lump out of my sight!"

"Yes, Highness." The guard stepped forward, took the man by the elbow, and pulled him, still stunned, from the palace.

EVERYONE KNEW NARNASH'S army was just ahead, and the two forces would likely be meeting in the morning. For the past five days there had been occasional grumbles among the nobles, though seldom in public, about the untested talisman.

Most of the common soldiers, though, seemed to have taken the attitude it was too terrible a weapon to be tested casually, which made it good for them.

There was the sound of a minor disturbance outside her tent. A servant came in to say, "Lady, the scouts have come across something their leader feels important."

"Send him in." It might be nothing at all, but it would help to pass the time in this night which seemed unlikely to ever end.

A man entered. He was a scout and it was easy to see from his small stature and the way he moved, he excelled at scouting. After bowing, he said, "Lady, we came upon a Wennz out there alone, bearing tokens of truce. When we questioned him, he claimed to have come from one Disikomin Rudashin. This Disikomin claims to wish to desert Narnash and join you."

"And where is he?"

"We have him outside, blindfolded, in case you wish to talk to him."

"Bring him in."

They brought in the man, his hands bound in front of him.

"Remove the blindfold." Disikomin's emissary stood blinking in the light.

"Tell us your message."

"Lady Lusommi, my Lord sent me to tell you that he is willing to assist you. The King set men in ambush to kill him, for fear of his prestige among the nobility. Lord Disikomin was not killed, but his son was. He therefore has a proposition to put to you. If I may continue?"

She made a sign with her hand.

"Lord Disikomin understands you have no cause nor reason to trust his word. He does not ask you immediately accept his troops and put them into your line of battle. He rather wishes you to watch. For when the battle is joined, he will strike Narnash from the flank and rear. Thus proving his willingness to join you and fight for you."

"And in return?"

"All he asks in return is that you meet with him after the battle, and discuss his situation."

"So. And are you expected to take a message back?"

"He said it was not necessary. He himself will choose the time and the place for the attack. Until he has made that attack, there is little reason to communicate further."

"I see. You will understand I must keep you under guard until the battle is done?"

He bowed. "I had expected no less."

NARNASH HAD LEARNED long ago to ignore the itch that started between his shoulder-blades as soon as he had donned his armour. Even the knowledge that every man in the army who wore armour was likely in the same predicament, made it no easier for the king to bear himself. He had discovered, once, that some of his guards would send in a junior member of their company with a trifling message just after the King had put on his armour. They would then laugh themselves to Chaos away at the outburst.

He had put a stop to that!

About the time he was beating that Destroyer-eaten itch into submission, his Aide was begging leave to speak to him regarding desertions.

He allowed the fool just time to bow before demanding, "Desertions! What is this foolishness about desertions? Of course there'll be desertions, that's for the commanders to deal with! Am I expected to run after these deserters and beg them to come back?"

One of the reasons the aide had retained his position was his ability to show proper respect. Not to be frightened out of his wits by the king's anger.

"No, Highness, it is a matter of the root of the desertions. The greater part of the desertions these past few days, have been disproportionately made up of men from the contingents sent by Lord Disikomin."

"Disikomin! Tell me, are rumours of the death of his brat going about the army?"

The aide shrugged. "That, and a half-thousand others. You know soldiers, Highness. There is another rumour, though, that has to do with the desertions. It is said the order from Lord Disikomin has been passed, that his men should desert and join him."

The king sat up straight and drew an angry breath, "Really? I had given orders for those contingents to be broken up and scattered among the army!"

"Yes, and so they were, but only so much scattering can be achieved, for various reasons. Many of the camp-messes contained several, perhaps up to a dozen, of Disikomin's men."

"So we have lost all of them?"

"No, not hardly. The word may not have reached some. Others may have had no opportunity to desert, and still others preferred not to run the risk."

"And perhaps some will choose to mutiny on the day of battle?"

"An even more difficult proposition, Highness. Seldom were more than half of any one file of the phalanx for instance, made up of Disikomin's men. Such a group, mutinying on the battlefield, would be cut down by their neighbours in the ranks, and achieve very little. Men might take serious risks for the success of a plan, but not likely for one that leads to their certain death."

Narnash frowned, "So. All this being said, why do you pester me with this news?"

"I felt it best you should know these facts, Highness in case you decide particular action should be taken."

The king sat quiet for a moment, then, "Yes, There is action that should be taken. Our scouts report continual motion of troops to our rear and most of them positively identified as groups that were late to the muster. Given Disikomin has sent orders to his troops to desert me, we must see to it we know where his force is. The bastard is almost certainly planning an attack on our rear. See to it."

"Yes, Highness. I have already given the necessary orders. And Highness?"

"Yes? What else?"

The aide produced a small wooden wand. "I carry several of these with me on campaign. I can slip it under my cuirass at the base of the neck, and relieve the itch between my shoulder-blades."

THE ARMY OF ASKOS WAS arrayed for battle. A line consisting of a series of sections of differing colours. This depended on whether they were uniformed, like the phalanx, or not, as with most of the light infantry and slingers. Iron gleamed and winked up and down the line as spearpoints caught the sun.

Aelkoriat had set them up in what seemed the best order, the phalanx in the centre, flanks guarded by light infantry. With the cavalry mostly massed on the right.

A screen of archers was well to the fore, ready to do their best to wear down Narnash's phalanx before they came to close quarters. The command group was on a knoll behind the cavalry.

Thotgol and the talisman, with a small guard of mounted archers, was on another knoll near the center of the battle line. But close to the cavalry, and across from the bright-coloured array of Narnash's cavalry.

Now that the battle was imminent, he was feeling tense and edgy, *'I'm not supposed to be the sort that gets caught up in some king's war. Or some queen's. And here I am with a leather pouch and a leather scroll, and a hundred thousand of Bloody Narnash's men are coming to chop me in pieces.'*

He idly ran his mind through the events that had led him here. He tried to decide just when he had suddenly decided to join the fight. And it wasn't just the offer of more money than he was otherwise likely to see in a lifetime, either, though that was part of it.

Funnily enough one thing that stuck in his mind strongly was Lusi punching him in the jaw. And from there his mind leaped to their sessions studying together, with him trying to keep his mind on the leather scroll and Lusi sitting so close beside him he could feel—-.

"Thotgol!"

He jerked upright. Tahheron was grinning at him. "This is no time to fall asleep, man! They're moving!"

He decided, scanning the battlefield, it was best not to tell the Captain he wasn't sleeping, he was daydreaming about the Lady Lusi. It also occurred to him, not for the first time, he was glad his guard was made up partly of the men he'd met in the mountains.

He ran his mind over the instructions he'd memorized from the scroll:

'Point with a rod, wand, or even a finger.

The winds all have particular qualities as described in the spell to call them.

'Easiest is to call a wind from right to left or left to right in front of you, sweeping the rod across as you speak.

'You merely say, "O such-and-such a wind, blow, blow, blow!"

Each repetition of the word "blow" causes the wind to strengthen.

Never repeat more than three times.'

And "never" had been underlined three times.

He reflected that it might be nice for commanders to align their armies in straight lines, either north-south or east-west.

Narnash would be the preferred target. But no, there he was in back, with the cavalry reserve, out of range, but ready to ride in and make the killing blow. Well, what about disrupting the cavalry presently advancing?

He could have used the goad, but it didn't seem right to use it for magic. And he couldn't see himself pretentiously carrying a wooden wand like some hedge-wizard intent on impressing the locals.

He pointed his finger at the front rank of the cavalry, sweeping it from left to right as he spoke. "*O North Wind from the frozen lands, blow, blow, blow!*"

He was not sure what he was expecting. A part of him expected a complete failure, or perhaps a gradual building up from a light breeze to something heavier.

What actually happened was, out of a clear sky, a blast of frigid wind. Which, striking the warm damp air, brought sudden hail on a strength of wind that sent horses staggering and men falling. And further, even horses on the edge of the effect shied and became unmanageable. The whole cavalry charge in that section dissolved into a struggling, screaming mass of horses and equally frightened men. They were slipping, sliding, and falling on ground rendered treacherous by the sudden precipitation.

Thotgol, so shocked at what he had wrought that he could only stare. He barely recalled the warning about not letting it go on too long, and managed to gasp out, "*O North Wind, cease!*"

He realized he hadn't been counting his heartbeats. He hoped he'd be able to guess at the length of time to run the opposing wind. Or worse still, had he let it go on too long?

He couldn't take his eyes off the wrecked cavalry force. He could see that some, on the edges of the spell, were able to pull their men together, and form some sort of order.

While they were attempting to sort themselves out, Aelkoriat had brought his own cavalry forward, cantering across the field. Finally breaking into a gallop at a distance that would not wear their horses out completely, and allow them some impetus when they hit.

Some of the Askos archers, who had been concentrating on pestering the phalanx, turned their attention to the already disrupted cavalry. Having done his part, Thotgol could only watch and wonder if perhaps sometime the situation might be so desperate as to require him to use the talisman twice in one battle.

DISIKOMIN AND HIS FORCE ran into a cavalry screen a little to the rear of Narnash's right wing. *'To be expected,'* Disikomin thought, *'given the desertion of my men from the king's army. But the alternative had been to simply charge in and risk having men kill their own brothers and cousins. Some of that will still happen, of course, but I've done what I could.'*

He did not pause when he saw the cavalry screen waiting for them, but ordered the charge.

He was in the front rank, and as they went forward he began to sing:

"Folsidon hey! Folsidon hey!
Folsidon comes this bloody day!
Folsidon hey, Folsidon how!
Folsidon brings his vengeance now!"

They pushed the cavalry screen in and back. But holding the cavalry from striking back at their own wings and rear robbed their charge of much of its impetus.

Disikomin, sill singing, went on forward, putting all his will into smashing the light troops. The core of his own troops were with him, now singing themselves, and it was the song as much as anything else that carried them through.

For all that, their number was few enough that when one of the local commanders realized what was happening and turned his men to face them, they were halted. They might even have been overwhelmed but for the fact the army of Askos had arrived by then. Too many of the light-armed, half-trained Wennz levies on that wing, with fighting going on in front and behind, cast aside shields and weapons to flee.

SEEING THE IMMINENT destruction of his main cavalry force, Narnash slapped his hand fiercely on the saddlebow. "Black bloody Destroyer's teeth! The Morkerr-Eaten ox-driver has the talisman working!"

Then, as he watched, he noticed something. "Once! He's only used it once, when he could have wiped out all the cavalry by using it twice or more! Either he can't, or what he's done already has petrified him! Either way, it's time to move!"

He turned to his commanders. "Follow me!"

He knew that the best he could do from this mess was to retrieve a drawn battle, withdraw what forces he could, and come back on another day.

But at least he would not be destroyed!

They went round the sides of the place of destruction. But when it came time to charge home, all they could do was to drive into the melee that was the remains of their cavalry desperately trying to hold back Aelkoriat. The impetus of the charge hardly made a difference. But the fact they were coming in fresh, not trying to rally after the center had been smashed out of their formation, told heavily.

There was no hope of bringing a victory out of such chaos. But he had managed to turn a near rout into a nasty, grinding melee. Both sides fighting themselves to exhaustion. Narnash considered it a victory Aelkoriat withdrew first. Though he had to admit to himself he was just about to order his own withdrawal.

He certainly did not consider a pursuit. Instead, he withdrew his own cavalry.

This allowed the bad news to be brought to him that his right wing had practically disintegrated, and that his phalanx, hearing rumour of destruction on the right and left, had begun to withdraw.

In many cases the light troops had gone into headlong flight. He knew what had happened. Being poorly-trained and with little or no experience, they had mistaken the command to withdraw for an admission that the battle was lost. The troops flung aside their arms to flee the faster.

Only the steadiness of the phalanx had kept the troops immediately to the right and left of them in order as they pulled back.

And even here, the superior training of Narnash's phalanx showed itself. They were able to fight, moving backward step by step. While the Askos phalanx tended to lose formation as they advanced on a retreating enemy. This caused heavier losses among them than they ought to have taken. For the strength of the phalanx is in its steady formation, always presenting a steady front of pikes to the enemy.

The Askos commanders finally withdrew their infantry as well.

The army of Askos camped there. In the morning, they found Narnash had withdrawn, leaving them in possession of the field.

They held a war council in the morning. "We have a technical victory," Aelkoriat said, "being left in possession of the field. But we are also left incapable of following up the victory, unless we depend heavily on the use of the talisman."

Chapter X
Betrayal

There was no question. The army of Askos had to pull back, at least

until they had time to do more recruiting and training. They had

been sitting on the grassy hill country next to the battlefield for over

a week. Now foraging parties were being forced to go further and

further afield.

"If you'll permit, Lady, we'll send out scouting parties of greater than usual size. At the least, they can warn us if Narnash resumes his advance. At best, they can hinder him by ambushing his foraging parties and the like."

"Yes, do that. And Aelkoriat?"

"Yes, Lady?"

"Tell me honestly, do we have a hope of winning this war?"

"Oh, yes. This last battle was a bloody murdering hell of a fight. And if we've lost heavily, bear in mind Narnash has lost even more heavily. And has to bring in his reinforcements from further away.

"Our people have had few pitched battles recently. Our commanders will have learned from this fight, and will train to avoid the mistakes we have made.

"It also occurs to me Thotgol might benefit from some tactical advice." He held up a forestalling hand. "I'm not finding fault, mind. His choice this time was well done. Another time, though, there might be more profitable choices."

Lussomi looked out over the field, "I see. I'm sure we could convince him of the need"

THE MAN ESCORTED INTO Lusi's presence by the servant was tall and slender. His dark hair was being overtaken by grey. He had a long, craggy face, and eyes that looked into a bleak future.

"Lord Disikomin Radushin," the servant announced.

"Welcome, Lord Disikomin. Very welcome indeed."

He nodded, brusquely. "You know, Lady, in ordinary circumstances I'd have cut off my hand before joining you."

"Very honestly spoken, Lord Disikomin."

His mouth quirked up in a grimly humourless smile. "I've little time for courtly manners and bowing and mouthing polite phrases to people who disgust me thoroughly. I'm sure by now you've heard from your own sources what my messenger told you?"

"Yes. I sympathize with your loss."

His eyes turned fierce. "Do you indeed? I wonder. Do you know that Folsidon was the only son of my late wife, who died in bringing him into the world? Did you know I could see her face in his more clearly every year? Did—-" He clamped his mouth shut.

It was obvious to Lusi he was hating himself for baring his grief for her to witness. She could think of nothing to say to ease him or comfort him. Her intelligence had, indeed, informed her he had doted on his son, because the boy resembled his mother. But his doting had not taken the form of ignoring errors nor being unforgiving of them, but rather of training the young man well.

The only safe thing to be said was, "You will serve in my army, then, lord Disikomin?" As she said it, she realized how brusque and selfish it sounded.

But he merely nodded. "I will serve with you, until the overthrow and death of Narnash."

"Very good. My commanders will wish to be assured that you will follow orders. That you are not likely to take your men out of the battle line in some wild quest for vengeance."

She saw him stiffen. *'I put that badly, didn't I?'*

"Lady, I could have thrown myself and my men away the other day in an attempt to charge into the rear of Narnash's cavalry reserve. I did not, because I thought I could do more damage to him by attacking in another place, where I would be alive to assist again afterward."

Lusi nodded. "Your pardon, Lord Disikomin. I ought not to have insulted you so. Might I ask that you assist Lord Aelkoriat in the training of our troops? Our phalanx, in particular, is in need of drill and training."

"A phalanx of Askos? Hmm. Well we will do what we can." There seemed to be a further, unspoken, *'But don't expect miracles'* look on his face.

It was Lusi's turn to feel insulted, but she didn't let it show.

Disikomin was ushered out of her presence. As he was led away, she considered it mattered less he maintained his Wennz prejudices against the Askos, than he was willing to help. It would probably be best if he were to give advice to Aelkoriat and his commanders.

Who could then pass it on to the drillmasters, stripped of all the expectations of inherent Askos inability.

THE ARCHER IN NONDESCRIPT clothing watched Narnash's army from the cover of a clump of brush. It ought to have been nigh impossible to escape from the guard-tent. But in the confusion surrounding the withdrawal of the army of the King '*Not my king anymore.*' he had managed it.

He'd slipped out to the battlefield under cover of night. Then he rearmed himself, dagger, short sword, bow, and a collection of arrows. Though he didn't trust these arrows as much as ones he'd fletched for himself, they would do for now. He'd also picked up a few coins, whose owners no longer needed them.

He hadn't loaded himself down; he was going to be travelling light and fast. He wasn't sure what he wanted to do. Ideal was to be looking down the shaft of a draw arrow at Narnash, but that was very unlikely. Maybe he'd find a way and a place to hurt the bugger, though.

A MESSENGER WAS SENT to Thotgol's tent requesting him to attend the Lady's tent. As they sat in the tent, the army carried on outside as sounds of various people moved about the camp and interacted with each other could be heard. Every so often a slight breeze would carry the scent of grass, trees and the occasional smell of a cookfire into the tent.

Lusi tried to hide her anxiousness, "The talisman works better than we'd hoped, then?"

"Oh, it works for true and sure. Not something I'd want to be doing every day."

"It was that bad, then?"

"Bad enough. It's not the way I'd prefer to fight."

"You won't be giving it up, though?"

"Oh, I made the bargain, I'll hold to it. But I hope you won't be asking me to use it for every little skirmish."

She shook her head. "No, definitely not. The battle, with the usual weapons of men, was bad enough. The talisman seems worse somehow."

He shook his head in agreement with her.

"It's the kind of thing," she went on, "That I'd want to keep out of the hands of Narnash and his sort. They'd use it, use it in every skirmish. Use it to punish towns, villages, or territories that had displeased them in any way. Could you imagine that?"

"Yes, I could. I wonder, sometimes, if Hrezorio thought of the danger of it falling into the wrong hands when he had the thing made?"

KING NARNASH HAD COMMANDEERED quarters in a rich merchant's brick house. The sounds of the city of Hellafriad, and the sounds of the city came faintly to him in the inner room where he listened to his advisors.

"Our cavalry is in sad shape, Highness. We have three contingents that are wiped out completely. All men either killed or wounded, most horses dead. We have five others so battered they had to be absorbed into other contingents. The morale of our horse is universally low.

"Worse, the cavalry of Askos has shown themselves to be far better than expected. And those Morkerr-eaten archers were too wicked for comfort."

"What of the phalanx?"

"They're peeved, Highness. They think they could have won the battle on their own, but for lack of support from the light troops and the cavalry. Not having suffered the effect of the talisman themselves, they have little patience with the cavalry, which they view as having let everyone down over a little wind."

"I see. Are any efforts being made to round up the light troops that broke and fled?"

"Yes, Highness. We've recovered a fair number of them so far, a few more every day."

"Good! Haul out one in a hundred of those for execution. By the Mother-goddess' belly, I'll make them more afraid of me than of the Askos!"

"There is a further difficulty, Highness. We are low on supplies, and there is little in the local area. The country we marched through was picked clean." He carefully avoided mentioning that this had been done on the King's orders.

"Sending foraging parties further afield is presenting dangers. The local people have heard you did not destroy Lusommi's army. Therefore they believe the converse, that you have been defeated. They have become sullen and unco-operative. They are hiding their grain and cattle, and even occasionally ambushing foraging parties."

"The army has to be moved, then?"

"That would seem to be the best measure, Highness. The reports we hear are that the Askos are in little better shape than we. They are in no condition to pursue us and seek another battle."

"That's fine enough, but neither can we stay in the field indefinitely. There are crops to be managed back home. Can we whip our army back into shape for another try this year?"

"We might, Highness, but I wouldn't want to be the one to promise it for certain."

THOTGOL WAS A LITTLE at loose ends. The army was busily training, drilling, foraging for food, and there was no place for him in all that. He'd talked to Aelkoriat, and the upshot was that he just didn't know what might be more important on a battlefield. Therefore, if there were a battle any time soon, an experienced officer would accompany Thotgol to give him advice and suggestions. The actual choice would still be up to him, the man who held the talisman.

Thotgol had borrowed a scroll from Lusi called A History of the Land, by a Rubellio h'Garvannad. He suspected the man was a famous person, but since he had never heard of the man, he wasn't sure. But, even reading of history, no matter fascinating, only took up so much time. Most of the troops were dispersed widely for foraging, so it was hard to find a decent game. And even then, the men who would no longer be there were just a little too present for Thotgol.

One of the long-time soldiers had told him, "Look, it happens. A soldier gets used to remembering the ones who're gone, then letting them go. You get too tangled up in the memories of who's died already, sometime you'll be a little slow on the parry and it'll be a sword in your own guts."

Which Thotgol recognized as good advice, but still, he wasn't a soldier, wasn't likely to be, and it was a difficult matter for him to get around. And on occasion his elder brother haunted him.

"Your pardon, sir?"

He turned. It was a servant, and a high-ranking one from the look of his clothing.

"Yes?"

"My master, Dalthorio h'Anavoto, wishes to speak to you."

As Thotgol immediately went wary, the man continued. "Lord Dalthorio bids me tell you he realizes that relations between the two of you have not been amicable. But since you are going to be on the same side, you ought to be friends. He would invite you to take a cup of wine and a meal with him this evening."

Thotgol might have sent the man off, but he had come to know how important Dalthorio was to Lusi's war. Best at least attempt to make an accommodation. "When does Lord Dalthorio wish to see me?"

"He invites you to come immediately. If you will accompany me? I have mounts for us over here."

The ride was not a long one. The Askos army had had to disperse for foraging. But given Dalthorio's importance to the campaign, it was no surprise to Thotgol that h'Anavoto was fairly near to the main headquarters.

Dalthorio's contingents covered several brushy hillsides, and the air was full of the scents of men, horses, crushed grass, and flowers. Dalthorio's tent was a fancy pavilion. Though he didn't hold any bad thoughts about Lusi's own tent, only a little less fine, Dalthorio's, for some perverse reason, annoyed him.

The greeting Dalthorio gave him was polite, though not effusive. Thotgol had expected little more. In fact, it seemed the Lord was forcing himself to be welcoming.

'No surprise,' Thotgol considered, *'Since I'm feeling much the same myself.'*

"Welcome, Thotgol, I'm glad you were willing to come! We are on the same side, fighting the same war, and it would be better if we could be at least civil to each other."

"I'm willing to put aside all grudges," Thotgol agreed, noticing again how short the man was. "Lus-—Lady Lusommi needs us all to work together."

"Good, good! Come into my tent and we'll have a cup of wine before we dine."

The servant held the fringed tent-flap open for them to enter. Two glasses of wine were already poured out. Thotgol was concentrating so hard on minding his manners this did not strike him as unusual. Real glass goblets on a military campaign, however, struck him as in keeping with Dalthorio's personality.

The servant picked up one glass and handed it to his master, then picked up the other glass and handed it to Thotgol.

"Shall we drink to success, then?" The little man was smiling.

"To success." Thotgol drained his glass, as Dalthorio drank down his own. He copied the lord's gesture in handing his glass back to the servant, and saw Dalthorio watching him fixedly, as if watching for something.

'Have I made a mistake, then?' He wondered. Dizziness swept over him. Thotgol made a step towards Dalthorio. He raised his hands to strangle the man, realized his hands barely moved, and his foot moved only enough to throw him off-balance. He felt himself hit the floor, then nothing more.

DISIKOMIN SPOTTED THE Askos brat for the fifth time in two days. It was the same boy, curly brown hair, impudent smile. He always lurking behind some bush or rock or tree in the hilly country where Disikomin's force was camped. It was the same boy, though some of his people professed not to be able to tell one Askos sprat from another.

The boy had never tried to steal anything and never committed any mischief. But he was too quick to slip back and away when any soldier tried to approach him. He appeared to be about eight summers old, still sure the world was a fine place and that everybody loved him.

His hanging around annoyed Disikomin, so the Wennz lord gave orders. On the sixth time the boy showed himself, Disikomin waited for a bit. Then he stepped towards the boy's lurking place. As usual, the boy vanished.

Disikomin returned to his seat in front of his tent. Shortly thereafter, three scouts came in, one of them clutching the boy by the scruff of the neck. There was a bruise on the boy's forehead.

The lord looked up at the scouts. "I ordered you to do him no harm!"

"By the Mother-goddess' toenails, we didn't! He ran when he saw us, tripped on a root, and banged his head against a tree."

Disikomin looked at the man for a moment longer, then nodded. Few of his men would lie to him. He turned his attention to the boy.

"Well, boy, a lesson to be learned about scouting: always be aware of who might be on your back-trail. Who are you?"

With eight-year old defiance, the boy said, "I'm Adelfio h'Astolkad, heir to the lordship of Asklervoy."

"A big title for a small boy. Do you know who I am?"

"Yes, of course! You're Lord Disikomin Rudashin, who has joined Lady Lusommi to fight against Bloody Narnash."

"And nobody's warned you that I eat small boys?"

"Huh! That's silly! I've seen your cook preparing chickens and pigs and sheep for your table."

"You're not at all afraid of me, then?"

"Why should I be? If you did anything to me, my Ma would fetch you such a clout!"

That caused him to smile a bit. "No, whatever else I might be, I don't make war on small boys. Why do you lurk around my camp? Surely you'd be more interested in your own peoples' army?"

"Oh, I've seen 'em. But yours is more interesting. You're different." As if the difference was the most intriguing thing in the world. And probably, for an eight-year-old, it was.

What had Folsidon been like at eight? No, not like this boy, but much more serious. The pain was still too near. He felt his grief. Disikomin noted the wary look come over the boy's face.

"Well, would you like to work in my camp? Sort of an under-page?" His intention, when he'd had the scouts bring the boy in, was to give him a scolding and let him go. This was certainly not what he had intended to say, but he realized at the same time he did mean it.

"We'd have to ask my Ma."

"What about your father?"

"He's gone away. He died in the battle," The boy's brow furrowed. Disikomin could tell, almost as if it were written there, the boy had been all through this. He didn't quite understand death, but was working at accepting the fact his father would never come home.

"I see. Could you ride on my horse in front of me on the way over to talk to your mother?"

"Of course!" The young voice was full of scorn. "I rode with my Da lots of times."

"Good, then you can be my guide." He called for his horse to be saddled, then chatted with Adelfio while he waited. "Do you intend to be a soldier when you're grown?"

"Of course! I have to, I'm the heir." It sounded like something he had been told sufficient times he believed it. Though he might not sense all the meaning of the notion.

"I see. What kinds of warriors does your territory produce?"

"Mostly mounted archers. We have a few pikemen, but Da says our phalanx is nowhere near as good as Bloody Narnash's. Or yours, I suppose."

"Interesting. Were you trying to learn how to make your phalanx better by watching my troops?"

"Oh! Yes, that's what I thought I'd do." Disikomin could tell the boy had thought nothing of the sort until just now, but he didn't call Adelfio on it. Little boys were often like that, trying to impress adults by agreeing with them about something that sounded important.

"Well, we must see what can be done. Ah, here's my horse."

He was pleased to observe the boy showed no fear of mounting the horse. Very likely, then, he had ridden with his father "lots of times."

The village itself, the chief's seat, was only three miles away, a fairly easy walk for a boy. Disikomin expected the boy's mother to be some young woman barely a third his age. He was surprised, therefore, when the boy called "Ma! Look at me!" and the woman out of the knot of women who looked over was no child, but definitely a mature woman. She might be more than half his age, and she was no beauty, though my no means a plain woman either.

She didn't have the look of one who had achieved her status through a combination of looks and conniving. But by demonstrated ability and concern.

He swung down from the saddle, and lifted the boy, down. "Now, Adelfio, introduce me to your mother."

In fairly proper fashion, Adelfio said, "Mother, this is Lord Disikomin Rudashin, who is serving Lady Lusommi. Lord Disikomin, this is my mother, Lady Junommi h'Astolkad, regent of this territory."

Lady Junommi looked Disikomin up and down. "Welcome, Lord Disikomin. We'd hoped to see you at some time. But all we've seen are your servants and aides telling us *Lord Disikomin requests so many measures of grain! So many sheep! So many hogs, and fodder for so many horses!*"

He felt a flash of anger that this woman. This Askos woman, should chide him about manners. Then he realized he really had been at fault. He had taught Folsidon better manners than this. What excuse had he?

"I apologize, Lady Junommi. I fear I have allowed the death of my son to turn me into a sour old man."

He observed the shadow come over her face, and realized he'd reminded her of the so-recent death of her husband. He was about to apologize again when she spoke.

"Yes. Well, we've all had losses, haven't we? But welcome, anyway. Will you come inside and take a cup of our new apple wine with us?"

He would have refused, but having had his bad manners chided once, however mildly, he nodded. "Yes, that would be fine."

"Very well. Delfi, you come with us. You can have a cup of cider. Hlanis, would you pour some wine?"

One of the other women bowed and went inside.

'Yes, an intelligent woman. She saw the boy come riding in on my saddlebow. She knew that, at the very least, she'd want to have him near once she's spoken with me. If only to warn him that Wennz Lords eat small boys.'

He wasn't sure what he would have to chat about with a woman until recently an enemy. Would he be forced to continue his rudeness by simply speaking about the reason for his visit?

He was grateful when she took the matter out of his hands by asking, "Have all the supplies been satisfactory, Lord Disikomin?"

This question, so far removed from what had been going through his mind, took him by surprise. "Oh, very satisfactory, thank you."

'Oh, Disikomin! Didn't you just this very morning complain the fodder for the horses was scant?'

"And tell me, how do our highland sheep compare to those of Wennz?"

Which led to a discussion of the relative merits of breeds of sheep. How sheep being bred for the warmer lowlands, though fatter, did not thrive well in the less salubrious foothills and mountains.

It was a discussion in which both knew their subject. There was scarce a lord in all Wennz-Askos who did not know intimately what his territory produced. As for sheep, he himself had turned out every year at lambing time, along with the least of the shepherds.

It was said that there were lords in other lands who did little but sit in their halls. Lord who cared only that their rents were on time. How could they know who could afford what, if they themselves knew nothing of sheep except they turned up dressed on the table from time to time?

It was even more interesting a recent widow knew her topic so well. One would have thought she would manage the house, leaving everything else to her husband, but she knew as much as he, in her way.

And the conversation might have continued longer, but for the fact she finally said, "Well, Lord Disikomin, I'm certain you did not come all this way to discuss sheep with me."

There was a little quirk of something in his mind—sadness that the visit must be cut short? But he went on with the reason for his coming.

"Lady, your boy has been hanging about my camp." Realizing at once this was beginning to sound like a complaint, he held up a forestalling hand. "I remember about small boys. Too often, if you tell them not to do something, they'll find it that much more interesting. *Folsidon rarely did.*' I wish to keep him out of trouble. If he continues to hide around my camp, he may get hurt by accident. If he comes openly, by my invitation, he will be safer.

"If you agree, I propose to employ him in a number of tasks, running errands, that sort of thing. In return, he gets to come in, watch what we're doing, ask all kinds of questions, and keep out of most mischief."

She frowned. "It seems a bit much for a boy of only eight summers."

The boy was about to object, but Disikomin responded quickly. "Lady, the boy need stay no longer than he wishes. He will sleep here nights, and if he wearies of the whole affair, he need only come and tell me so."

"And if battle comes?"

"Battle is no place for a boy." Adelfio snorted. "If we go to battle, he goes home."

"And perhaps I will have to lock him up securely until the battle is done? Well, my Lord, it seems not unreasonable. When would he begin?"

"Well, today is near over. He can come to us tomorrow after sunup. I'll see to it that the guards are expecting him." He turned to Adelfio.

"Come down the trail openly tomorrow, no sneaking through the brush. You are reporting for duty, not scouting an enemy."

He was pleased as the boy straightened and became serious. "Yes, Lord."

He was willing to wager, though, that this seriousness would not last.

THOTGOL WOKE UP, GROGGILY. The surface on which he was lying, along with the heaving, jouncing ride, told him he was in an ox-cart. Why? He seldom rode in an oxcart, save if he were ill, and the train-master was a generous fellow. But who was he working for?

Then he took into account that his hands were bound behind him. There was a gag in his mouth, and then other thoughts returned to him. Dalthorio! The little lord was having his vengeance.

He'd have thought Dalthorio would just make away with him immediately, and tip him into a hole somewhere. Was he hauling him off somewhere, in order to kill him slowly somewhere?

He felt the talisman against his chest. Well, the little horror hadn't taken that! Of course, even if he had, it'd be of little use to him. And he'd have to explain to Lusi how the thing had come into his care, and Thotgol had disappeared.

He'd just have to wait and be ready. Given there was any chance to fight, he might force them to kill him quickly. If that was the only choice he had.

Opportunities were scant. The first time they brought him out of the cart, they said, "You can relieve yourself here. We'll loose your hands, but don't touch the gag. I reckon one of us can lay a spearshaft across the back of your head before you come close to undoing it."

When he was done, they bound him up again, then the spokesman said, "We're going to take out the gag and let you drink a bit of broth. Don't try to say anything. You try to speak a word, spell or no, one of us will get you in the gut with a spear-butt. Won't kill you, just make you wish it had for a while."

This left him wondering. *'You didn't feed someone, however sparsely, if you were planning on taking him off and killing him.'*

After the third day of travelling, it occurred to Thotgol that Dalthorio might be turning him over to Narnash. The battle had been a near thing. A very near thing despite the talisman. He could see the little lord leaving Lusi for the man who had the bigger armies. And to make sure of his welcome with Bloody Narnash, he would bring along the talisman and its wielder as well.

This was all speculation, of course. He was bound and gagged in the bottom of a covered ox-cart that smelled of all the cargoes it had carried in its lifetime. He had no way of telling what direction they were travelling.

So he was not at all surprised, on the fifth evening, to hear the Common Language spoken with the harsh accents of the Wennz.

The guards who had watched over him on the trip were there to haul him out of the cart. "You belong to King Narnash now. His guards know all about you. The King'll want you alive, but a spear-butt won't kill you, just remember that. Enjoy your stay with the king."

With raucous laughter at this joke, they left him in the company of some guards who looked less friendly than Dalthorio's men had.

Their commander said, "Well, he's told you everything important. King Narnash wants an audience with you immediately. You willing to walk in on your own legs, or do we bash you and dump you in front of him like a bag of turnips? Nod if you'll walk without making trouble."

There didn't seem to be much alternative, yet. He nodded.

The guards marched him into the presence of the King, a small room, and somewhat crowded. Even on a campaign trail, there were those who made sure of their presence in the King's audience hall. If only so the King could witness that they were agreeing with his every whim.

The audience chamber was filled. There were those who had serious business, such as aides reporting on the status of the scattered army. Then there were messengers with word from the capital about decisions that had to be taken. There were also decisions which it was thought best to leave to the King himself.

Thotgol was aware, as he walked into the king's presence, that Dalthorio was standing near the king. But Dalthorio was carrying no weapons. So the King didn't quite trust him, did he?

"Well. You are the ox-driver who bid fair to destroy my army? No, I don't expect you to speak. I don't want you to speak, until I can bring in Doctor Gobnash to see to it your talisman can't harm us.

"Now, Lord Dalthorio assures me you are the one he claims you to be. But he would, wouldn't he? It would hardly do to bring in some person or other and make a claim which it could not be substantiated. It would mean trouble for him.

"And you don't look like some half-wit duped into playing a part. Nod if you are the one."

He considered shaking his head in hopes of making trouble for Dalthorio, but it didn't seem feasible. They'd keep him around for

Doctor Gobnash anyway, who would likely be able to tell the truth. All Thotgol was likely to get out of it was someone taking it out of his hide afterward.

He nodded.

"Aha!" said the king triumphantly. "So this most deadly talisman doesn't protect you against everything? Good, good. Guards, stash him away and keep him safe for Doctor Gobnash!"

Chapter XI.
Retrieval

L usi was becoming a little annoyed with Thotgol. He seemed to
have disappeared, and no one had seen him recently. Surely he
hadn't gotten into some game that lasted this long?

He'd missed three meetings, none of which were terribly
important. But missing them hinted at discourtesy to those who had
attended.

She wondered, idly, if her annoyance with Thotgol had anything
to do with having to be very careful about chiding Dalthorio. Who
had also missed the last two meetings. She could scold Thotgol,
who would grin at her and ask if she was done now, because he was
missing a great game. But he'd probably try not to miss a meeting
after.

Dalthorio, on the other hand, would take umbrage at the least
suggestion that he really ought to attend meetings. Then go sulk in
his tent. He'd probably even dream up some scheme of petty revenge.

A servant came in, keeping the sort of straight face servants
kept when on the brink of delivering bad news to their masters or
mistresses.

"Well?" It came out more brusque than she intended.

"Lady, he hasn't been seen for five days. None of the gamblers can
recall seeing him more recently than that. He may have deserted us."

"What?" She sat up straighter.

"You recall, Lady, he was greatly disturbed at the result of using the talisman. Perhaps he felt he could not do so again."

"And he left without a word? Without even leaving a message to be given after he'd gone? That seems unlike him."

"All I know, Lady, is that he has not been seen anywhere in the presence of the army for five days."

"I see. Well, continue your inquiries. See if anyone has noticed him leaving."

"Yes, Lady."

THE NEXT SHOCK CAME a few hours later. A servant entered and said, "Lady?"

"Yes?"

"The messenger who was sent to Lord Dalthorio is back, and he says he has important news."

"Send him in." The man had been sent with an ordinary message, asking Dalthorio's attendance at the next meeting. The same message had been sent to all the other leaders; what response could be so important?

The messenger followed the servant in. He was dusty and sweaty, and stiff from a long ride, but he bowed. "Lady, Lord Dalthorio's forces are gone."

"Gone where? Gone home?" Lusi interrogated the messenger, '*And why didn't he inform me, or at least Aelkoriat?*'

"Lady, I don't know. I asked at the local village and was told, three days ago, the lot of them had marched Chaos Away to the north-east. Rather than follow a three-day-old trail, I thought it best to come back and inform you."

"Well done. Go wash and rest, but hold yourself ready to to repeat this to Lord Aelkoriat, if need be."

When he and the servant had gone, she sat staring at the tent-flap and thinking. Why north-east? If he had left for better foraging, that was not the direction to go. Between her army and that of Bloody Narnash, the territory had been picked clean.

Was he going out to do battle against some part of Narnash's army? She shook her head. If he knew for certain in a place nearby, he could find a force he outnumbered badly enough, just perhaps. But her own scouts would have been bringing back the same information that Dalthorio would be getting, and there had been no such reports.

Was he deserting to Narnash? Unlikely. He was a major figure in the Askos alliance, and Narnash would not forget that. Particularly since he had nothing important to offer in the way of strategic information. None of the meetings so far had had any result beyond the reiteration of the fact the army of Askos were still recovering from the battle. There were altogether too many strategic possibilities, most of them dependent upon the nature of Narnash's first move. And pretty much all of those possibilities would have already occurred to Narnash.

She shook her head. Ridiculous. Dalthorio was many things, but he was not a traitor.

THOTGOL LOOKED UP AS the guards entered his cell. They came round twice a day, with a bowl of soup. It was a bit better than what Dalthorio's men had served. For it usually contained a withered vegetable or two, and a couple of times a shred of mutton. They would unfasten his gag, hold the bowl up so he could drink out of it, and replace the gag. They were always prepared to prevent him speaking.

He wouldn't have thought it feasible, anyway, to call a wind in such an enclosed space, where he would likely suffer as bad as the guards. But they took no chances. One time, after drinking the soup, he had a belch come up just as they put the gag in. Even as the first noise escaped his lips one of the guards put a spear-butt in his stomach. As he bent over, the other slapped the gag in his mouth, and tied it in place. Mainly by force he kept the soup down, but it was a narrow thing.

The one who had wielded the spear shook his head. "Shouldn't've tried it. Didn't think we'd still be watching out, did you?"

They never, ever, unfastened his hands, which were cuffed behind him.

Today, there were no mishaps, no difficulties, and they went out. Which left him to his daily chore of feeling around the walls. He was filthy and he stank, and his confidence was beginning to ebb. But still he searched, from as high as he could reach to as low as he could bend. He looked for any slight roughness or projection that might allow him to abrade away the gag knotted at the back of his head.

He'd have to manage it between feedings. Because if they noticed the gag was worn away at all, they'd replace it, and possibly move him to another cell.

NARNASH TOOK THE MESSAGE that had been tied to the bird's leg, then casually wrung its neck. He'd had experiences in receiving messages by Doctor Gobnash's "trained birds." The things, if left alive, would dash themselves against walls, windows, or cage bars until they fell unconscious. If they recovered from that, they would do so again, and again, until at last they did not recover.

He was willing to use cruelty against any human being if it would suit his needs. But Narnash saw no reason to be needlessly cruel to animals. The message was brief. "Light two fires, each ten paces long, in a cross-shape this evening at sunset, and I will come to you immediately."

Well, the man had his ways and his means. He handed the message to a servant. "See to this."

"At once, Highness."

The king sat in silence for a time. He would dearly love to have someone stick a dagger into this Dalthorio h'Anovoto, but that was not a good idea. It would make anyone think a second time about joining him, if all the reward they could expect was a dagger in the ribs.

But he'd keep an eye on the man, never allow him near a battlefield. Nor anywhere he might do serious damage if he had a change of heart. And of course, he must make it known on the other side that Dalthorio had joined him.

THOTGOL HAD FOUND A small, slightly jagged edge on one of the stones making up his cell. It was not overly sharp and protruded just enough to be felt. From what he could feel of the stone's consistency, it would be a race as to which wore away first, the gag or the stone. Well, it was the best of a bad lot.

Patiently, he began to rub the knot of the gag against the stone. He had to restrain himself from feeling for the stone from time to time to check if it was still sharp.

In the course of his rubbing of the knot, he also had to rub his back against the wall. Most of that was fairly smooth stone, but even so, it was less than comfortable.

His back eventually became so scraped and bruised he had to force himself to continue to deal with the gag. One thing that kept him going was what he knew of the reputation of Doctor Gobnash.

How long would it take for the magician to arrive? A message might go one way in what? Four days? And the magician would be a week or more returning. And how long had he been here? With little light or sound from outside, it was difficult to tell. Had he spent four days feeling every inch of the wall, hands continually chained behind him? Or had tit been five?

A thought occurred to him Gobnash might have other, quicker, means of travelling. No, don't think about that, just keep scraping.

THE FIRES WERE LIT and burning, according to Doctor Gobnash's specifications. Narnash tapped a forefinger against his thigh. He was not about to say out loud he hoped this was not all a lot of foolishness.

It would be just like that little sand-coloured horror to wait until Narnash had expressed his doubt anything was going to happen, then flash himself over. But Narnash determined he would wait until the fire had burned to ash before he said anything at all.

He continued to tap his forefinger on his thigh.

THOTGOL COULD FEEL the knot parting. It was a double-knot, though, so he wasn't sure just how much he had yet to go. Did the binding feel a bit looser? Should he convince himself not, so as to have a heartening surprise later, or should he convince himself so, at the risk of growing discouragement?

He pushed his tongue against the gag. He was certain it was a bit looser. But, the pressure of his tongue wasn't likely to be able to break the knot, not until it was worn to a shred.

He continued to scrape the gag.

DOCTOR GOBNASH APPEARED near the fires, between the north-pointing and west-pointing arms of the cross. Most of the gathered crowd gasped. Narnash merely growled, "About time."

Narnarsh noted the Doctor was a little unsteady on his feet at first. But he seemed to recover as he stepped forward.

"Good evening, Highness."

"And a good evening to you. I'll have a servant show you to your quarters."

But the magician was looking up and around, sniffing the air. "No time. Send a message, quickly, to the jailers to open up the ox-driver's cell and see to it he is secure!"

Narnash didn't waste time asking foolish questions. How did Gobnash know? Well, the fellow was a magician. Even as these thoughts went through his minds, he pointed at a servant.

"You! Get up to the prison, tell the jailers to check on the ox-driver's security!" It occurred to him he'd pretty much repeated Gobnash's directions, like an over-servant to an under-servant. He grimaced.

"Run, Morkerr eat you!"

THE GAG FELL LOOSE. Thotgol wet his dry lips and gasped '*Karda-ezusht lovagolni!*'

He heard noise and shouting outside. Then the jailer, clearly a little panicked, clattered the key into the lock. Fierce flying pig guts! How long would it take for Shapak-ailesh to get here? If they moved him to another cell, would the little man find him? The door swung open.

Shapak-ailesh appeared beside him, mule and all, as the guards rushed in, spears ready. The merchant grasped his arm and pulled. Thotgol flew from his feet and suddenly he, the mule, and the little merchant were standing on the rim of a volcano looking down into the white-hot rock in the crater.

"One more step, please." Thotgol might have tried to get up and take that step. But Shapak-ailesh, still holding his arm, stepped forward.

They were in a dark wood.

"WHAT HAPPENED? HE WAS safe in jail, gagged, with his hands chained behind him!"

Doctor Gobnash peered around the cell in the flickering orange torchlight. Then he picked something up. "Here is the answer, Highness. He was gagged, but managed to rub away the gag. He then called... Someone. Hmm. If he has such friends, I may have to reassess my attitude toward this ox-driver."

"Such friends? What does that mean?"

Doctor Gobnash turned his gaze on the king. "Highness, I would explain, if it were worth the time. Suffice it to say this is aimed more at flouting me than you. The forces against which I find myself fighting do not care much about you, one way or another."

Narnash took a deep breath. This was an insult! He didn't matter, did he? But Gobnash spoke again.

"Highness, my apologies. This means of travelling is not merely wearying, but wearing. Please be assured I meant no insult. This is a war of power, and though you direct my powers to some degree, it is at me that the attack is aimed."

Narnash managed to control himself by taking up another subject. "This method of travel, that brings you here instantaneously, I wish you had told me of it sooner. There are ways and times when it could have been of use to me."

"I regret, Highness, an ordinary man, after the trip I had made, would be unable to function for a day or more. Perhaps never. It is only because I have done years of specialized training, preparing body, mind, and spirit, that I am able to manage. And even so, I must have a long rest tonight.

The king growled wordlessly. "A hint, I suppose? Well, there seems to be nothing more to be done here."

THE ARCHER HAD WATCHED for three days, then chosen his target. The fellow was not the headman of the hamlet, who would have too many armed followers around him. But rather a man of some respect among the ordinary people.

Late at night he slipped down into the town, managing to get all the way to the man's house without alerting any dogs. He was glad of that. He liked dogs, but he would kill one if he had to. Much better not to have to.

All the windows were shuttered, of course, but he knew ways to deal with this. He was inside very shortly, and shortly after that he touched the tip of his dagger to the man's throat, which woke him.

"Keep quiet. Don't want to kill you, but I will if I have to. Understand?"

"Who is it? Who are you?"

"Doesn't matter who I am. Keep quiet. Now, see that? You've woken your wife. Keep her quiet, or I'll have to kill the both of you."

There were a few minutes of whispered questions and explanations between man and wife. Then the man said, "What d'you want? We've no gold here."

"Don't want your gold. Listen. I have a message here, written on a chip of wood, which has to be sent to the Lady of Askos.

"I can't go myself, so I need you to either go, or have someone else sent. The message is important. I've been watching this town for a while, and none of you has seen me. I'll probably be watching for a bit longer, and if people come out hunting me, I'll come back some night to visit you. Understand?"

"Yes, I understand."

The archer slipped back out. He hoped he wouldn't have to come back. Not that he wouldn't carry out his threats, if necessary, he just didn't like the trouble and bother.

SHAPAK-AILESH STEPPED behind Thotgol and clicked something against his manacles, which fell away. Then he moved to face Thotgol again and said, "I myself am used to suffering any number of hardships and discomforts. My mule, on the other hand, is a creature of delicate constitution, and is easily upset by certain rank scents.

"The spring next to us is warm water. To spare my mule's delicate feelings, would you mind going and washing? And unless you have a particular sentimental attachment to these garments, may I dispose of them? I have at least one outfit in my packs which would fit you. I will give it to you, and perhaps on another day we can speak of payment."

Thotgol, was scraped and battered. Despite this he found freedom had brought him from the depths of despair to a lightness of mood which he had never expected to experience again. It felt good to grin.

"You know, there are certain things a man can't do with his hands chained behind him."

"Come now, did I intimate that the fault was yours? Though if you continue to delay, I shall begin to wonder."

The water was warm, as Shapak-ailesh had promised. Thotgol left his garments on the edge of the pool and sat, soaking, savouring the comforting sensation of the water against his battered skin.

Shapak-ailesh picked up his old garments and dropped them onto the fire that he had built a little way away from the spring.

"I dislike to disturb a man in such comfort," he said when he returned, "But I have a bit of food ready, if you'd care to come and eat."

"It isn't soup, is it?"

"No, not today. Only a bit of cured pork, warmed to sizzling and some bread to go with it. You have a preference for soup?"

"Wardesh guard and guide, no! I'm afraid my late experience has brought about in me a detestation of soup. And now listen to me! I'm beginning to talk like you!"

The little man looked aggrieved. "Is there something strange or improper about my manner of speech? Beware, gratuitous insults may cause the price of your new clothing to increase."

"Wardesh love you, no, there is nothing wrong with your manner of speech. In fact, I'm so happy to hear you I'm near to coming round the fire to kiss you."

"Are you indeed? As much as I appreciate the compliment..."

"Ah my fair ox-driver, I know when my fine personality and good looks have been rejected. But tell me, is not Narnash likely to feel rejected as well? And will he not take it less well than I? For instance, to the point of having his army out beating the bushes for miles around?"

The little man smiled. "Ah, well he might wish to. But I fear even the most powerful King Narnash would have some difficulty beating *these* bushes. The disagreeable Doctor Gobnash, now, he might possibly manage. But not immediately, and not without warning."

Thotgol frowned. "You make it sound as though we were of the far edge of the world from them."

"Well, actually, it's as though we were on the far side of a sheet of silk. One who knows how might pass through the sheet. However,

Doctor Gobnash's methods are often direct and forceful, making pinholes in the silk and slipping through. But even making these tiny holes causes such reverberation all across both sides of the silk that anyone sensitive to such things will be able to feel them."

"And you, you do not make holes in the silk?"

Shapak-ailesh grinned. "No, in my case I merely ooze through the weave like a drop of water. My comings and goings may still be noticed, but they are not so blatant.

"All these, of course, are analogies, and do not completely describe the facts of the situation. They only give a means for a very general explanation."

But Thotgol had gone off on another topic. "You sounded as though you've set yourself up in opposition to Doctor Gobnash."

Shapak-ailesh shook his head. "It's more as though I've been set into opposition to him. I've been asked, by one I'd not turn down lightly, to do a few things to hinder him. I believe the intention is to eventually destroy him, though I doubt that my own part will extend so far."

"Interesting, for true and sure. You speak as though you're some special servant of the Gods."

Shapak-ailesh shrugged. "There are gods enough, and various beings of power, and not all of them agree with all the others. There are several, though, to whom the works of Doctor Gobnash are worse than detestable. You see some of the things he has done, and call them evil. Yet these things are only a part of the sort of things he does. And it is his less-publicized deeds that have made him powerful enemies.

"And now, however interesting this conversation has become, I think it time for us to rest. There is a good deal more travelling to be done tomorrow."

IT WAS CERTAIN NOW; Dalthorio had gone over to the King.

Lusi read a report to Aelkoriat in private, a report that had been sent out at great risk by her spies in Narnash's train.

"'The lord Dalthorio has appeared in the King's camp, asking forgiveness for his recent transgression. As a gift to purchase this clemency. he has brought along with him as a prisoner, the ox-driver who wields the Talisman of the Winds.'"

She looked up at Aelkoriat. "I've checked the decoding twice. There is no mistake. Dalthorio has gone over taking Thotgol with him as a prisoner."

Aelkoriat was not a man to be panicked. "You think Narnash might be able to force Thotgol to use the talisman in his service?"

"Not immediately, at any rate. I would prefer to say never, but who knows what any man might do if the torture is too strong? Not to mention the works of Doctor Gobnash, of whom we have heard numerous stories.

"But leaving the talisman aside, Dalthorio's defection robs us of a significant port of our forces. I have no idea *how* to deal with that."

He shrugged. "A problem, for certain. One possibility might be an immediate attack on Narnash. Just before the end of the campaigning season. Depending on the surprise to give us some advantage."

"Would that advantage be enough?"

"Nothing is ever certain in war and battle, Lady. It is probably the best alternative. Waiting until next year will only make Narnash the stronger, and us, likely the weaker."

"And the only other alternative is for me to negotiate a surrender with Narnash. Seeking for the best conditions we can obtain."

"You do have that alternative, Lady. But when one considers Narnash's intent to *'turn Askos into a howling wilderness,'* one must think carefully about what surrender might purchase.

"He might indeed agree to various conditions for the surrender. But when your army is dispersed, whether or not he keeps to those conditions depends entirely on the mercy of Narnash. And we all know what Bloody Narnash's mercy entails."

"And if I fight another battle, the greatest likelihood is that I will achieve nothing but the slaughter of more men on top of whatever revenge Narnash wishes to exact when the army is defeated."

He bowed. "As I said, nothing is ever certain in war and battle. Whatever your decision, I will support you."

"So, then. Call a meeting for tomorrow, at which time I will announce my decision."

She was left with her thoughts. Well, surrender would mean her own death; Narnash wouldn't leave her alive for further resistance to coalesce around. Indeed, all her most powerful nobles would forfeit their lives.

She wondered if she might have the strength of will to take her own life, depriving Narnash of that one victory.

And what of Aelkoriat's suggestion that they try a surprise attack? What Aelkoriat had said was true, when she was gone, Narnash would revenge himself upon her land. Was there a possibility of preventing that by risking another battle?

She continued to sit, going over and over the facts and likelihoods.

THE PHALANX MOVED TOWARD Disikomin and Delfi across the sunlit grass, pikes presented, a bristling hedge of pointed metal.

"So, what do you see, Delfi?"

The boy frowned. "No one can get at them, with all those spear-points out there."

Disikomin grinned, "Exactly! They needn't do anything but stand still, and no enemy can get past the pike-points to hurt them. And if they advance, they can push anything back. Because their pikes will prevent anyone from getting close.

"But what if they came up against another phalanx?"

Delfi thought about that. "They'd both be stopped, wouldn't they?"

"Yes, they'd both be stopped. They can't get past each other's pikes. And whatever thrusting they did with the pikes would mostly be stopped by the small shields they carry."

"But my Da says—-said that no matter how good you are, someone else might be better. Or luckier. What happens if someone is lucky enough to get one of the front rank men? When he falls, won't that make a hole in the line?"

"Very good, Delfi! That is the reason why the phalanx drills so much and so thoroughly. They need to be the steadiest and surest, and they need to know what do for themselves. Watch, now."

Disikomin blew a three-note call on a silver whistle he carried. A moment later there were shouts from the drillmaster on the field, and here and there a man would fall. No sooner had he fallen than the man behind him stepped into his place, and the hedge of pikepoints was unbroken.

Delfi looked on in wide-eyed amazement, "How do they do that?"

"They keep practicing and practicing until they do it without thinking."

"No, I mean, how do they know who's supposed to fall?"

"Oh, each man has a number according to which rank and which file he's in. The drillmaster calls out numbers, and that man pretends to die."

"What's a rank and a file?"

Disikomin pointed to the phalanx, "See how they're all in lines, right to left? Well, each of those lines is called a rank. And from the front, they're all in rows one behind the other. Those rows are called files."

"So everybody knows which rank they belong in, and which file?"

"Exactly."

"But what if somebody's real sick one day, and can't come out to drill?"

"Oh, they fix that first thing. Everyone lines up in their proper ranks and files. Then the drillmaster gives a command to fill blank files forward, and everyone behind a hole steps forward."

"But what if—" Delfi insisted.

"Just a moment, boy." Disikomin smiled. "A man spends months in the phalanx learning to do all these things. You can't expect to master them all in three mornings.

"Now, you were given a task to do. Have you done it?"

"Yes, Sir. But don't you have leather-workers and such to fix up the men's boots?"

"Yes, when we're all settled in camp, we do. But every man must know how to fix his boots in case the need arises in the field."

Delfi's eyes narrowed in slight disbelief, "Even you?"

"Oh, I believe I could still manage it. But my job is making sure that my soldiers are ready, that they have all their food and equipment. So it's best that I have a servant or two to look out for my kit. When I was a boy your age, I did learn all these things. If only so I knew what my troops had to do, and thus knew how much could be expected of them.

"Now, let's go look at how well you did."

"SO. THE TALISMAN OF the Winds is loose again. And you say that this action is aimed more at yourself than me. I ask, then, what do you plan to do about it?"

"I?"

"Well, it seems that if they. This strange and nameless "they" did this as an attack on you, it seems that you owe me one Talisman of the Winds."

"I regret, that is not possible, Highness, at least if I understand you correctly. The Talisman of the Winds is one of a certain class of talismans. Only one of which may be operating in any one of the quarters of the world at one time.

"Since Hrezorio was first to produce the talisman here, no other talisman may be made to call winds. At least, I could make such a talisman. But until the talisman of Askos was destroyed, mine would be but inert scraps of leather, feathers, and such."

The King frowned. "I believe I understand you. however, this still leaves the question, *'What will you do?'*"

Chapter XII.
Winter Quarters

They took a step into the Hidden Ways, into a place where winds swept across a bare and sandy plain. Just to their right lay the skeleton of a fish, dry and white in the pale sun. The skull of the fish was huge. It was so large Thotgol estimated it to be twice his height from the bottom of the jaw to the top of the skull.

They stepped once more, and now they were in as territory that was vaguely familiar. "Ah, here we are."

"Where are we, then?"

"Ah, my doubtful ox-driver, look to your left, on the ground."

There, tossed aside into the grass, was his ox-goad. "You brought me here for this?"

"Yes, indeed. It's not a thing you need desperately, but it seemed right we should recover it for you. Now pick it up; we have other places to be."

Thotgol picked up the ox-goad, realizing his sense of familiarity was right. This had been the place where Dalthorio's forces had been camped. But the absence of the soldiers, tents and all had prevented him from recognizing it immediately.

Shapak-ailesh spoke again. "We won't bother with the Hidden Ways from here. That would be akin to damming a creek to make a lake so as to dip out a cup of water."

A SWEATY AND URGENT scout was ushered into Lusi's presence. *'What now? Narnash is advancing with four times the force we expected?'*

"Lady, there's two people coming up the road. One is a short little one, knee-high to a grasshopper, the other is the ox-driver, Thotgol!"

"Thotgol? But he's a prisoner of Narnash!"

"He says the little fellow got him loose yesterday. But of course, he's making that up. It'd take a week or so to travel from Narnash's camp to here."

"How far out are they?"

"They'll be in by evening. Duty officer's rousted out a small patrol to escort them in."

"Well done." She pulled out a couple of coppers. "Here, take these, with my gratitude."

Early that evening, Thotgol and the little man were escorted into Lusi's tent. "Welcome back, Thotgol. We were afraid you were lost to us."

"Indeed I was, Lady, but my friend here, Shapak-ailesh, freed me."

She looked at the little man. "Well, my thanks to you, too, Shapak-ailesh. What is your trade?"

"I, Lady? A mere merchant, a peddler, a traveller with gewgaws of this sort and that in my packs." It almost seemed for a moment he was going to begin a spiel and offer her a great bargain. But instead he went on, "I met Thotgol at another time and another place. And there was that about him that required me to give him assistance, when the such was needed. I therefore came to his aid and brought him from the prison of Narnash, away from the clutches of Doctor Gobnash."

She looked at him a moment longer, then said, "The two of you have made my quandary more difficult. Dalthorio has taken a substantial portion of my army with him. Lacking both the troops and the talisman, my choices were between a last desperate attack on Narnash, and surrender.

"Now, however, we must assess whether the recovery of the talisman can make up for the lack of troops."

Thotgol bowed. "Lady, having experienced the hospitality of Narnash, I can say that I will not surrender to him.

"You may do what you feel you must for you and yours, but I will not be put in his hands again."

"And if the battle is hopeless?"

"Then I will die. Or perhaps I will flee far and fast. But I will not be Narnash's prisoner again."

"So. It seems it would do me no good to surrender, then. Narnash's first demand is sure to be that I hand you over to him."

"You seriously considered surrender?"

"If it might save my people the least part of his revenge, yes."

"And you'd trust any promises he made?"

"What choice would I have? Another bloody battle with more men dead? and at the end of it the great likelihood that Narnash would be free to do as he wished?"

Thotgol opened his mouth to speak, then stopped, frowning. Finally he said, "The crown is a heavy burden. I, I can afford to consider only my own welfare. The queen must think of so much else."

"Yes. And I must think of matters such as getting the farmers back to their lands, as well. Aelkoriat has convinced me that we must keep the bulk of our army together until Narnash has gone into winter quarters. The numbers are such that he might choose to make his own unexpected attack.

"But all this is stuff for meetings. We will be meeting this evening, Thotgol, and I would appreciate your presence."

THE MEETING IN LUSI'S tent that evening was a vigorous one. There was the "surrender now and hope for mercy" group. There was the "attack immediately, catch Narnash unawares, and destroy him with the talisman" group. Finally in the middle, there was a "let us see to our lands and herds and farms, and come back freshly prepared next year" group.

There was much heated talk and few minds were changed. But those of standing who spoke up were heard.

Lusi finally held up a hand for silence, and looked around. "One person we haven't yet heard from, one person who has a great stake here. Thotgol, what have you to say?"

Thotgol stood and looked around. There were people present, who would have protested his presence, let alone his right to speak. But that attitude was tied too closely to Dalthorio, and no one wished to put himself in that camp. It was one thing to advocate surrender, it was another to negotiate a private surrender, leaving erstwhile companions in the lurch.

"My contribution to this discussion will be brief. I doubt there is one here who does not know I was, just recently, a prisoner of Narnash for some days. I tell you, for what it may be worth, I have no intention of falling into his hands again.

"And further, if the decision from this body is to fight, then fight I shall. If your decision is to surrender and hope for mercy, I know the kind of mercy available at Narnash's court.

"I will not surrender."

Which set several spokesmen, from each of the groups, to shouting at once.

This went on for a short time, then Lusi rose and began rapping on the table with a dagger-pommel. It took a little time, but even the most vocal of those present realized the Lady was standing.

"I thank you all for your contribution to the discussion. There are things to be said for and against each possible decision, but in taking these all into account, I find one of them to be best.

"We will begin to send home those who are needed at farm and homestead and herd, beginning with those who must travel the furthest.

"Our scouts will keep track of Narnash, and see to it that we are apprised of every movement he makes. Narnash was badly battered in the recent battle, but to assume he will not take the field again this year is to take a serious risk.

"Next season, we shall march once more. And having learned from the events of this year, we will do the better.

"Think also of this: throughout the year, men will be going back to Wennz, telling tales of the battle and the dread talisman, so that next year the new men, and many of the old, will be half-beaten before they take the field.

"That is all."

DISIKOMIN HAD HIS MEN called together. "Soldiers, you have followed me well and faithfully into a situation you had not imagined at the time when we left our home. There are many of you who have left families back in Wennz, families, farms and lands which need your care. To those of you in such case I say report your status to your commanders, and I shall see to it your are sent home, without prejudice or hindrance. Only beware when you have gone home. For, if it becomes known that you followed me here and fought behind me, Narnash and his bootlickers may not forgive you.

"For those of you without family ties on you, I ask you stay with me in our new place. When matters here are properly settled, I will see to it that you are rewarded."

As he stepped down, leaving his commanders to dismiss their men. Tugashin said quietly, "You'll find more than a few making claims of family affairs just to be able to go home."

"If so, don't you think we'll do better without them?"

"At what point, then, will we cease to be an effective fighting force, and become merely an expanded honour guard for you?"

Disikomin smiled his small grim smile. "You speak bluntly, don't you? Well, I have already had a thought or two in that direction. When the commanders have the lists of men wishing to go home, have them pick some dozen or so steady and reliable men from those. Have them brought to me before they leave."

HE HAD EXPECTED DELFI, in the manner of most boys, would lose interest in the game eventually. But still, every morning, the boy came trotting up the trail, eager to learn something new.

There were, of course, parts of the soldiering trade that interested him less than others. The necessity of latrine trenches, for instance, was not something that caught his imagination. Disikomin suspected the reason for that was he didn't have the build or stature to handle a man-sized shovel. Making his attempts at digging less than satisfying.

Troop maneuvers, however, and all the reasons for any evolution of troops, on parade-ground or battlefield, continued to fascinate him.

The men took to him, and referred to him as "The Little Commander," with no mockery intended.

And once in a while he could come bearing something special "from my Ma;" a fresh loaf of bread, a half-dozen eggs, a fresh cheese, or the like.

The boy, of course, handed these over as though they were nothing special. Disikomin wondered if she was sending them as some sort of payment. Though he'd never spoken of payment. Moreover, he hadn't thought of it as a matter for payment.

He'd tried to think, on occasion, of a way to politely let her know these gifts were not needed. But recalling his interview with her, he always held back. How did he refuse without seeming discourteous.

Which reminded him he had to go visit her for supper sometime. He passed the word through Delfi he would be happy to come dine with them whenever it might be convenient. He added a note that, while he appreciated the gifts she sent, he regretted he had nothing worthwhile to send to her in return.

The boy came back the next day with a suggested date. Two days later, and a little note at the end assuring him that keeping her son occupied and out of trouble was gift enough.

He could practically see her smiling as she wrote that.

AELKORIAT LOOKED AT the chip of wood Lusommi had handed him, and read the phrases of the Common Language. Written by someone from Wennz, with idiosyncratic spelling.

"'Narnash gooes hoome'" he read. "'Hes foorce is baadly baatered, and not fit tou fite agein thiss yeear. Hes caavallry in partiklular, is sorly strikken. I will watsh, aand sennd you ferther werd.'

"And no signature."

"None." She looked up at him, while all around were the noises of an army preparing to march. "This message was sent by a villager who claimed it was given to him late at night by someone he didn't see, who made threats against himself and his family if it wasn't brought to me.

"The message doesn't tell much beyond what spies and scouts have already reported. I am loth to dismiss it. But it could merely be a plan to make me believe the things he says, until a day when he can send a message to seriously mislead me."

Aelkoriat shook his head. "Unlikely. Narnash knows you have scouts and spies, and have to assess the various reports they make. If one report varies so much from the others, most likely we would discount it completely.

"What concerns me is he asks no money. A person doesn't hang around taking the risk of spying on Narnash, all for nothing but a good feeling."

"That had occurred to me as well. Perhaps he sends us this for free. And, after he has sent another two or three, when we have some faith in his reports, he will send a request for a small bag of silver.

"Well, we will watch what he sends us, and if it continues to support what we know from other sources, we will use it."

THE LADY JUNOMMI H'ASTOLKAD had wine poured for herself and Lusi. The two of them sat in Junommi's kitchen, chatting about various things.

Then Lusi got down to business. "Lord Disikomin and his army, they haven't been a great deal of trouble to you?"

"No, not much. Occasionally, one of his younger men gets too full of wine and notions of Wennz superiority, and makes himself a nuisance. Lord Disikomin takes care of that, issuing punishments and apologies and, if the case is serious, paying a fine.

"And to be honest, on occasion one of our own young hotheads, who hear "Wennz" and think "enemy" will cause trouble. Usually beating some half-drunk soldier. In which case I see to it punishments and apologies are made. And occasionally, a fine.

"I must admit, though, my lands cannot continue to support them indefinitely. We have fertile and productive lands, but not infinitely so."

"You wish to be rid of him?"

"Oh, not immediately. There will come a time, though, when supporting our own people along with a small army will be too much."

Lusi frowned thoughtfully. "I see. I had hoped to leave him here until such time as I can find lands to reward him with.

"I wouldn't burden you excessively, though. Suppose I make contributions toward his upkeep until that time?"

Lady Junommi fiddled with her winecup. "Lady, that would be most helpful. Might I ask, though, the contributions be in kind rather than coin? With the armies that have been in these territories, the land is so picked over that even gold is unlikely to buy an extra sheep."

"WELL, SHAPAK-AILESH will you be on your way soon?"

"What sort of treatment is this? Shapak-ailesh, come rescue me, clean me up, deliver me home, and now please be gone and don't hang around! You fear your status as ox-driver will suffer from having a mere merchant in your vicinity?"

Thotgol grinned at him. "Now, if I thought you really felt yourself to be aggrieved, I would apologize. But as you very well know, you were on your way from somewhere to somewhere else when I called you. I didn't want you to miss your appointment."

"Ah, but I am not one to be sent here and sent there, carrying my goods only to certain markets. I am a free merchant, free to go where I will, and if I make a few coppers more here or less there, so be it. And if I have a mind to go to the Old City of Askos, why, there I will go. And if I choose not to breathe the dust and other fascinating scents at the tail of the army, then I have other ways to travel which are less crowded."

Thotgol chuckled. "And I'm afraid the Lady Lusi will not let me out of her sight again, so I must travel with the army. Not at the tail, mind you, but with the army."

The little man raised his brows. "She will not let you out of her sight? Is this a romance I smell a-brewing?"

Thotgol snorted with laughter. "An ox-driver and the Queen of Askos? Not hardly! It's only she has great concern for the weapon which may help win her freedom from Bloody Narnash."

Shapak-ailesh put on a mournful face. "Ah, no romance, then? So sad. I'm something of a scholar of tales of romance, you see, and it would be fascinating to be there at the beginning. To watch the development of the tale. Ah, well."

"How many subjects are you a student of? Philosophy, ancient epics, and now romance!"

Shapak-ailesh grinned. "I'm sure you would be surprised to know the subjects of which I am a student.

"I'm sure we shall see each other from time to time around the Old City. And we shall have time and opportunity to discuss philosophy once more."

Chapter XIII
Plans, Preparations, and Stratagems

"**S**o, what is it now, Doctor Gobnash? You've developed a Talisman of Earthshaking that will allow me to flatten the mountains of Askos around the Lady Lusommi's ears?"

"Nothing quite so eye-catching, Highness. It is only I thought that, given Disikomin's defection, I ought to pay special attention to the lands that were his. Watching for people who might have come back from his forces."

The king went alert, his position straightening slightly. "Ah, messengers! And I would guess your presence here means you found something?"

"It was not entirely straightforward. Most who had come home were simple louts, knowing only that they had to come back to see to their little plots. The most intensive questioning revealed nothing. One, however, let slip he had heard that certain ones had been called to Rudashin specially. Though he knew no more than that. He knew no names for certain, could only guess at some of them.

"Having further direction to focus my questions, I was able to fashion a list of likely candidates. Of these, most had taken their families and disappeared. I was able to find and seize two, and one of them finally admitted he had carried a message to a certain Lord Komsallit.

Though the man did not know what was in the message, he guessed Disikomin had written to tell what had happened to his own son. And probably to invite Komsallit to join him."

"And now?"

"Now, Highness, it is a matter for you. The ordinary people I can deal with, but when it comes to Lords, I can only gather evidence. Once I have done this, the matter is in your hands."

"Well, continue to gather evidence. I scarcely think that a great number of my Lords will desert me for Askos. But even a few of them being dilatory coming to my service could be something of a hindrance. I shall have to consider how to approach Komsallit."

'Archers from ambush? That worked so well for Disikomin, didn't it? Perhaps something more subtle?'

THE ARCHER MADE HIS way to the edge of the field, then stepped into the open. He didn't call out. His intention was not to startle the woman. He definitely didn't want to alarm her. She called to the ox, and turned the plough at the far end of the field, and even then, she didn't notice him immediately.

A few paces later, she saw him, and her hand went to the dagger at her waist. She took in his appearance, clothing and all, and said bluntly, "What do you want?"

He warned himself to go carefully. This was a a woman who had just recently lost a husband, and was trying her best to keep herself and three children alive.

"I want to make an agreement with you. Will you listen?"

She sneered. She'd had sufficient time alone with her bitter thoughts to be able to put sincere feeling into that expression. "O man of Wennz, whose countrymen slew my husband in battle, what sort of agreement might we two make?"

This alarmed him. He'd expected caution, even dislike for his race, but not that she would near blame him, as a Wennzman, for her husband's death at the hands of other Wennzmen. But he had learned long ago to be careful just what feelings he let show on his own face. "I propose a bargain to suit us both. I need food and a roof over my head until Bloody Narnash (he used the nickname consciously) begins to move again next year. You need help in running this farm so you and your children should not go hungry. I will supply that help if you supply me with the food and shelter."

Her face remained grim. "And, of course, sharing my bed is a part of the bargain?"

"No, your bed is your own. If you wish, I will swear whatever oath you like that I will let you be."

She relaxed, but only a little. "And no man has ever broken an oath before, of course."

He spread his hands. He had immediately dropped the notion of telling her he could have taken her unawares, disposed of the children, and taken over the farm. That would only make her more wary. "You must believe what you must believe, but I promise you the only agreement I wish is the one I stated."

She was still not completely easy in her mind, but he could see her turning the matter over and looking at it from all sides.

"All right," she finally said grudgingly. "But you mind your manners, Wennzman."

DELFI HELPED WILLINGLY, fetching and carrying while Disikomin's men built huts for themselves. They could well have stayed the season in tents. But morale was already something of a problem for this relatively small group of men. As they sat in the midst of people still getting used to not thinking of them as *'enemy foreigners.'*

The camp, like any group of soldiers, was full of rumours. Most were laughable, but the occasional one required serious intervention. Such as this morning.

"Men," he had told his gathered army, "I don't know, nor do I wish to know, the source of the story that Doctor Gobnash has laid a curse on us all. And, if you use your heads for purposes other than a handy place to put your helmet, you will realize this is foolishness. If he had the ability to lay a curse on us, don't you think there would be more likely targets?

"We are but a minor nuisance to Narnash. His real concern is the Lady Lusommi and her aides. A curse on us would accomplish little. A curse on her would probably put an end to his problems for good. And since she is still alive and working, what do we need to fear?"

He stood looking at them for a bit. "Now, I know forbidding you to pass rumours is a bit like forbidding water to flow downhill. However, rumours which have a deleterious effect on our ability to be an effective fighting force are not allowed. I am giving orders for your commanders to take the names of anyone heard repeating rumours. And if find myself out here again having to repeat this lecture, the punishment may well go beyond extra drill and fatigues."

DELFI'S EYES WERE WIDE. "Those silly stories the men tell, are they that dangerous?"

"It would hardly seem so, would it? But think, stories like this touch a little fear in everyone. Suppose, for one or two, the fear is too much and they desert? Every desertion makes others more fearful because we are so few. And how many rumours will it take until we are down to so few men that we cannot fight effectively?"

"I see. There're lots of things to think about if your want to lead an army, aren't there?"

"There certainly are."

"Oh. And Ma says I'm to invite you to come for supper tomorrow."

"Tomorrow? Hm. Perhaps. Tell her that I may not be able to come tomorrow, but would the next day do?"

Actually, there was no real problem with coming tomorrow. It was only that he did not want to appear to be leaping to her orders.

THOTGOL HAD HAD A FAIR bit of luck with the Dwarves' bones, and as Lusi was looking after his food and quarters, his expenses were not high. He therefore took one of the histories Lusi had lent him to have a copy of his own made. Since his memories of the scribe who had first taught him reading were still negative, he took the scroll to a different scribe. A certain Hostragl of Garras. Hostragl was a tall, slender man, with snow-white hair and trimmed beard, and a very prominent nose. If his name had not proclaimed him a foreigner, his features would have done so.

Thotgol held up the scroll he had borrowed and asked, "How much would it cost me to have a copy of this made?"

"Let me see it." Hostragl held out a long, slender hand. Thotgol handed over the scroll, and watched with fascination as the scribe set it on the reading stand. then rapidly rolled it from beginning to end, and back again. He clearly couldn't have read a word of it, but he said, "Forty silver."

"But you didn't read it!"

The scribe frowned at him. "Young man," he said crisply, "I wouldn't presume to tell you your business. Please do me the courtesy of believing that I know what I'm doing."

Then he softened slightly. "You see, by merely glancing through the scroll, I can see how long it is, what margins are left, and the size of the letters. From that I can make an estimate of the amount of paper, ink, and time that would be required.

"And of course, with such a relatively well-known work as this, I already know most of these things. So the price is forty silver."

Thotgol had, before coming, asked Lusi what a reasonable cost would be, and this price was within the acceptable range. However, not to bargain would be strange, even somewhat discourteous.

"Thirty."

The price finally agreed on was thirty-eight silver. Having handed it over, Thotgol continued to look around the shop. Small sheets of paper were hung here and there about the shop, samples of books written in various styles. The first one he looked at appeared to be from a horse-doctor's manual. The next was incomprehensible. Though it was written in the characters of the Common Language, the words were not the Common Language at all.

"What is this?"

"That? That is an interesting one. It is one of the Ancient Writings of the Kondellini. In the Old language of Kwandel, but transliterated into the Common Alphabet."

"Oh, really? And are there many works in the Old Tongues that have been, uh, transliterated?"

"No, not really. You know how various languages have sounds which some of us find it difficult to get our tongues around? To transliterate, one either has to ignore such sounds, or insert letter-combinations to represent them. This one is mostly a curio. One who is throughly versed in the Ancient Writings of the Kondellini would be able to make it out. One who did not know the language would get a very mistaken notion about it from reading the scroll from which that bit was copied."

"I see."

But Hostragl was off on his favourite topic. "Here is something perhaps a little more interesting." He pointed to another page, written in what looked to Thotgol like rows of shapes and squiggles, some of them done in red ink.

"This is the Priest-writing of Gon-Wakb. It's called that because the Priests first used it to record holy documents. Later on, of course, it became more generally used. This is a bit of the history of one of their kings.

"And before you ask, I can't read it. Not properly, anyway. There are about six hundred or so signs in the alphabet; a scribe in that land would find failing memory a disaster." He smiled at his own humour.

So Thotgol left the scribe's shop with many new thoughts. All the way from alphabets with six hundred letters, to men he'd known who would scratch their names on walls or cart-wheels or anything handy, just to make themselves known.

AFTER A WEEK IN WINTER quarters, Thotgol was bored. After two weeks he was extremely bored.

He went out to a wineshop one evening, and got into a bit of a game. His heart wasn't really in it, though, and after losing a couple of pieces of silver, he pulled back. A hulking labourer sneered at him. "Can't take it, eh, boy? Better run along home and let men do the gaming."

Most times, Thotgol would let such jibes go by without comment. But he had just enough wine in him, added to the general boredom, to say, "Must be comforting to have no mind. Saves time having to think, like the rest of us."

The hulking labourer was so drunk that he had to think it over before he understood he'd been insulted. Then he roared something unintelligible and swung at Thotgol, who had been standing, smiling, and waiting for him to act.

In a fight like this, Thotgol was happy to use his fists, unless someone else went for a weapon. Of course, the wineshop was a bit crowded. There was also more than one fellow present who objected to having either an ox-driver or a labourer bouncing off them. So they were willing to do some pushing and hitting of themselves.

The wineshop owner with his truncheon was unequal to the task of restoring order. But the City Watch eventually came in. For the task at hand, they used spear-butts. Though, if anyone gave them too much trouble, they wouldn't hesitate to use spearpoints.

Because of his status, Thotgol was not merely knocked on the head and dropped into prison to await the magistrates' displeasure. He was, instead, knocked on the head—he was too drunk and too wild to listen to reason—and held for the Lady Lusommi to deal with.

She was not happy.

"You make matters awkward, Thotgol. Look at you! I suppose I am to be grateful you've never found it necessary to cheat at gambling, or things might be worse. I don't suppose you know what the fight was about, do you?"

He didn't lose his smile. "It seemed like the right thing to do at the time."

"It seemed like the right thing to do at the time! Oh, Wardesh guard and guide! What next? Will it seem like the right thing to go and trim the beards of Wardesh's priests?"

"Now, that's an idea!"

She found herself half an instant from grabbing something, anything, and throwing it at him. Drawing a deep breath, she calmed herself.

"Can't you find something useful to do?"

He sighed. "That's just it, I suppose. Every called up farmer or potter or stablehand has his farm or his trade or his occupation to go back to. But what of the ox-driver with the talisman? He's left at loose ends until the next campaigning season starts."

"Well, you'd better find yourself something to do. Write a history of Batan-ji or something. As it is, I'm going to fine you fifty silver. That is, thirty for the damage to the White Dove's Rest, and ten silver for the innkeeper, plus ten for the city."And the next time, I will be very hard on you."

He grinned. *Yes, he would!* "So, I must either find something worthwhile to do, or continue to have good luck with the Dwarves' Bones?"

She managed to hold her face in a serious and grim expression until he was ushered out.

HE CAME ON SHAPAK-AILESH a little later, while wandering around the market. The merchant was selling little toys. There were spinning tops and dancing figures. There were also toy flutes which, when one blew into them, produced the sounds of a whole band, including strings and drums. Many children had been fascinated, first by the mere sight of the small merchant, and then by his marvellous wares.

"Ah, Thotgol!" he cried. "Here you are, out and free. There were those willing to wager you'd be hung by the heels in the dungeon!"

Thotgol grinned, a little ruefully. "I think it was only the fact I can use the talisman which saved me from decorating the front gate with my head."

"Ah, the course of young love," said Shapak-Ailesh, almost as if quoting someone.

"Only in silly ballads do folk like me come to wed princesses. And then only after it's discovered they're long-lost princes themselves."

He picked up one of the figures and, turning it over, discovered on the bottom of each foot a set of small marks. "What are these, some kind of writing?"

"Yes indeed. They say, if I remember correctly, Tharak-haval, which is the name of the owner of the workshop in which they were made. Please don't tell anyone; most people think of them as parts of the magic that makes them move. It adds to the exotic appeal."

He looked up at Thotgol. "Still interested in reading and writing, are you? Perhaps you should do a history of your own peoples."

"Ah, yes. *'Glories of Old Batan-ji,'* by Thotgol the Ox-driver! No, my writing is likely to be more in the lines of the scribble I saw on the prison wall. *'Here stood the Misfortunate Manorio,'* including some such non-word as Misfortunate.'

"I did wonder a bit whether Manorio was hung for some terrible crime. Most likely he was given ten lashes for public drunkenness and rioting."

"Ah, how true. The human mind can always find a way and a means to call up the most interesting happening from the most mundane evidence. Now, please hand me that dancer, lest people get the feeling that the magic wears out so soon that they only do one small dance."

Thotgol stood watching while the little man wound up his little figures and sent them spinning and dancing again. A sly grin crossed his face, "Next time I get bored, I'd better get you to take me through the Hidden Ways to the town of Hellafriad. Then I can take the garrison commander by surprise and truss him up in his underwear, and take the town for Lusi."

Shapak-Ailesh gave him a discerning look. "You'd best be joking about that."

"Hmm. I don't suppose you could take me and a hundred others into Hellafriad? They're going to be storming some of the garrison towns to start off the campaigning season. Mostly to relieve the supply problems a bit. A small party might be able to do the thing with a lot less losses than a storming-party. I hadn't really been serious, until just this moment when I got wondering *'why not?'*"

"The first reason is I could take thirty, perhaps forty, through the Hidden Ways. Unless we all hold together physically, there's too much chance that someone, maybe more will be lost along the way."

Thotgol sighed. "It was too easy a notion for it to be possible. Ah, well."

He had been leaning against the wall. Now he was scraping with his thumbnail at a small fault in the mud-brick, turning it into the letter Th. *'Misfortunate Thotgol!'*

Suddenly the sight of the letter brought an idea to his mind. "What if, one morning, the residents of Hellafriad woke up to find something like, *'The Winds of Askos blow bitter,'* written on various walls, in all parts of the town. Including walls behind locked doors?"

"Remember, few people can read."

"But if these things are widespread enough, people will see them who can at least puzzle out a few letters. Some will be able to read fairly well. Market rumour will see to the rest."

Shapak-ailesh shrugged. "A nine-days' wonder. Perhaps a little more if the garrison commander decides to turn the town upside down in search of rebels and seditionists."

"For true and sure." But Thotgol was caught by the notion. "But what if one came back in oh, four days, a week, and repeated the effort. Always being careful to put the phrase in some locked places, such as garrison stores or the like?"

"And returning for how many times? And to what eventual purpose?"

"As often as necessary. I hadn't thought that out altogether. And the eventual purpose would be so when the Army comes to summon them to surrender *'lest the Winds of Askos blow'*, the garrison will be one-quarter beaten before they start.

Shapak-ailesh grinned. "You have a wicked, deceitful mind! Yes, I will help, though there may be some limitations on our work. What preparations will you need to make?"

"Preparations?"

"Yes. You hadn't thought to do all this with your thumbnail, had you? Even tough thumbnails as yours are not up to such hard usage."

"Ah. paint of some sort. And brushes. I'll have to do some shopping."

"Before you go off to do this shopping, what do you intend to tell the Lady Lusi of the Fair Locks?"

"'Fair Locks?' Wardesh guard and guide, you know she has dark and curly hair!"

"Oh, you'd noticed? But a fair-haired lover always seems to do better in the Romances." He waved a hand to quiet Thotgol's immediate protest, and went on. "Lover or not, what will she say of this plan?"

This made Thotgol stop and think. "You're right. I can't tell her; she wouldn't have me locked up, just have bodyguards with me night and day. Suppose I tell her we two are going off for a little, visiting other marketplaces. No lie there—and we'll be back soon."

"And the Lady Lusi has spies in every town, particularly the ones garrisoned by Narnash. So you just happen to buy some paint and brushes, and come back just about the time she's learning about mysterious writing appearing on walls?"

Thotgol shrugged. "She'll probably scold me. And maybe set nursemaids to watching me. When that comes about, I'll have to see what I can do."

"No, but perhaps we might put off the day of reckoning a bit. It would be nothing particularly strange if a merchant were to go about looking for paint and brushes. The timing of our going and returning, and the timing of the mysterious writings on the walls, will almost certainly make her suspicious. though perhaps we can allay that a bit."

"Ah, good. When do we leave?"

"Such a rush! Give me at least two days, possibly three, to gather the supplies. And don't get into any mischief in the meantime!"

"Mischief? Me?"

"IT HAS COME TO MY ATTENTION the vile traitor, Disikomin Rudashin has sent communications to various of my loyal lords, summoning them to join him in treason. It would be well received if all lords were to report any such communications to me."

The king looked at the scribe. "And put on the usual titles and so on, then leave them for my signing. Address one copy to each of the persons on the list you were given."

"Yes, Highness."

The scribe, being seated for the dictation, could not bow properly. But he did bob his head down toward his writing-table and back up again.

DOCTOR GOBNASH APPEARED in the king's audience chamber. The king smiled at him. "So, you have bad news for me again, Doctor Gobnash?"

"Unfortunately, yes. It appears a sizeable number of young men with no family ties have been slipping across the border to Askos.

"We have managed to catch a few of them. It seems they were leaving, not because they were summoned, but because the notion of serving Rudashin appealed to them. They were all young and foolish, the sort who might dare a lot for some whim. Many of them would be poor soldiers once the excitement wears off. but even a few additions to Rudashin's numbers are a matter for some concern."

"Concern? Yes indeed! I'll have men patrolling the frontiers, with orders that any such should be taken for punishment."

"Good enough, so far as it goes, Highness. But I have a further notion. Suppose among the newcomers to Rudashin were a few fellows with specific orders?"

The king smiled. "Ah, yes! An assassination would be very useful. Even a failed assassination would force Rudashin to look carefully at all volunteers who come to him."

"I have a further plan, one which will cause difficulties, at least, to the Lady Lusommi. I will keep you informed as the plan matures."

"Still no Talisman of Earthshaking, eh?" The king was near jovial.

"Regretfully, no, Highness. But I have something only a little less effective."

Chapter XIV
The Garrison Town of Hellafriad

S hapak-ailesh had brought them to a place near to Hellafriad.

A place where casual patrols from the town were not likely

to find them. They camped there until evening, when they prepared

to go in. Shapak-ailesh began to pack up the mule.

"You don't want to take her along, do you? Best leave her until we get back."

"No, that's not possible. She's such a delicate creature, you know. She'll become terribly disconsolate if she's left alone."

"But—-"

"Young Thotgol, do you have all the knowledge in the world?"

"Of course not, but—-" He was reminded of his dealings with the scribe Hostragl.

"Then consider you have learned another small trifle. She will come with us."

Thotgol wondered if it might be the mule which travelled the Hidden Ways, and just brought Shapak-ailesh along. But that sounded too silly.

Shortly, after a little philosophical discussion with the mule regarding packs, they stepped into a dark place. There a huge moon, much larger than natural, hung in the sky. Far off in the distance was the sound of roaring water.

Another step brought them into the town, in the poorer quarter. Here the houses were shoddily built of whatever scraps of wood were handy. Shapak-ailesh brought out a pot of paint and a brush. "Where will you write first?" Thotgol asked.

"Ah, no, this is your plan. It's for you to do at least the first one."

Thotgol looked around. One of the buildings had a wall which looked fairly solid. On it he wrote in great bold letters, *'Bitter blow the winds of Askos.'*

After a bit of thought, he had decided on this phrase as having the better rhythm.

He stepped back, looked at it, and nodded his satisfaction.

They moved through the Hidden Ways into various parts of the city, leaving the phrase on various walls and doorways. However, while they were in the main Market, Thotgol had just begun writing when they heard the tramp of feet. "Soldiers!"

And these wouldn't be any "foreigners-hired-to-keep- the-peace-and-a-few-coin-in-my-hand-will-make-me-forget-   this-whole-business" soldiers. These were men of Bloody Narnash. They were quite willing to stick a spear through someone who was supposedly doing something wrong.

Thotgol hurried through the phrase as much as he could. He was just putting in the last letters when he heard the tramping stop. There was a shout from across the market square, something on the lines of "You there! What're you up to?"

He turned to see the soldiers rushing toward them with levelled spears. As the soldiers approached, Shapak-ailesh swept them away to a starlit grassy plain.

"Have you risked my hide sufficiently for the night?" asked the little man.

"Could you get us into their weapon-stores?"

"Meaning you want to try once more for a spear in the brisket? All right, come along."

They were inside a building, that much Thotgol could tell by the wooden floor. But there were no windows nor open doors, so there was no light at all. "I should have brought a torch!"

"Wait a moment, I believe I have something useful in my packs."

There was a sound of rummaging and muttering. Next, a faint glow began, and grew in strength. As it grew, it revealed itself as coming from some device in the little man's hand. "Now, go to work."

The walls were inaccessible, save for places behind stacked crates and kegs. He decided it would be best to have the message visible to whoever opened the door first. He painted the phrase across a row of stacked crates and turned to Shapak-ailesh. "Done."

"So let us be gone."

One step took them through to a place where large and slender people warred with each other, casting balls of flame as a man might throw a stone. One more step, and they were at their camping place.

"I HAVE A NOTION TO make this plan of ours more effective," Thotgol said, stretching his legs out toward the small fire.

"'This plan of ours?' I seem to recall it was you that made the plan. And convinced a certain merchant to accompany you, providing transportation and the like."

"And I seem to recall comments on my *wicked, deceitful mind.* Did you want to argue as to where the blame should be placed? Or, did you want to hear my notion?" An impish grin spread across Thotgol's face.

"What now? We slip into Doctor Gobnash's workroom and paint *'Doctor Gobnash is kind to spiders and vipers,'* in the Ancient tongue of Kwandel?"

"Now, that's an even better notion than mine. Providing you know the Ancient Tongue of Kwandel."

"Certain things are feasible, and certain things are obvious jests. Obvious, at least, to anyone but a Batan ox-driver.

"There are places I wouldn't want to attempt by the Hidden Ways. And Doctor Gobnash's workroom, while not chief on the list, is definitely on the list."

"Ah, well, back the the mere Batan ox-driver notion. Suppose we go to one of the other garrison towns tonight, or tomorrow, and do as we have done in Hellafriad. And perhaps visit another town next day, and another the day after that. Would it not appear more serious than a mere nuisance restricted to one town?"

"It seems we will be extremely busy. Will we be allowing ourselves a little time for unimportant matters such as sleeping and eating?"

"You want to be responsible for me going to jail?"

Shapak-ailesh's brow furrowed. "Now, how does that follow?"

"Simple. If I'm not kept busy, I'm likely to get into trouble. If I get into trouble, the Lady Lusi will lock me up."

"Ah, but you've already stated your possession of the talisman renders you immune from imprisonment."

"Not for the kind of trouble *I* can manage."

"Singing drunken songs at night in high praise of Lusi of the Fair Locks?"

"I hadn't thought of that one!"

"Well, give me some time to rest, and we'll see what can be done."

"THE COMMANDER OF THE Hellafriad garrison sent a message. Seditious graffiti has been appearing in the town, and he is concerned."

"Concerned? What kind of fool is he? Have him pick out ten of the leading citizens, and give them five lashes. If the graffiti continue, give them ten. If they still continue, hang them."

The aide hesitated, jittering nervously. "Well, what is it? Clearly there is more to it from the way you're dancing about!"

"Yes, Highness. The graffiti has also been occurring behind locked and guarded doors. Such as garrison food stores, the Commander's antechamber, and the like. It seems unlikely any of the locals would have been responsible. The guards have been questioned closely, with no result. The only evidence is that, on the first night, a city patrol spotted a man, a boy, and a donkey across the Market Square. They disappeared before the patrol could get there. But one of the graffiti was freshly written on the wall where they had been.

"Despite cordoning off the area, they could find no tracks that led anywhere."

"I see." The king partially turned his head. "Servant, summon Doctor Gobnash." He turned back to the aide. "If there is magic involved, then Doctor Gobnash will sort it out. If it's merely some kind of devious trickery, Gobnash is also the most devious and tricky person I know."

But Doctor Gobnash was not available. He left word that he was to leave, on the king's business, but would return in three days time, at the outside.

A certain servant, whose task it had been to ensure the king was informed of Doctor Gobnash's departure, was given ten lashes and reassigned from palace duty to mucking out the stables.

LUSI FINISHED DECODING the message which had arrived by bird. She looked at it once more to be sure what it said and rang a small bell.

A servant entered. "Yes, Lady?"

"Find Thotgol and request his presence before me as soon as may be."

She spent a moment being proud of herself for maintaining a calm "business-as-usual" expression and tone of voice until the servant was gone. Once the servant was out of earshot, she slapped the message down on the desk and glared at it. *'What kind of fool does he think I am, anyway?'*

He hadn't appeared to try to make himself scarce, either. Momentarily the servant returned. "Thotgol awaits you, Lady."

She slipped the message into a pocket, went to the audience chamber, seated herself, and waited for Thotgol to come in.

"Well?" She demanded. "What have you to say for yourself?"

"I suppose it won't do to thank you for pulling me away from a game where the Dwarves' Bones were seriously nipping my fingers?"

'Why do I always have an urge to throw things at him?'

"I have received a message from an agent in the garrison town of Tropolloi. Someone has slipped in and painted *'Bitter Blow the Winds of Askos'* on various walls. Including the wall of the Commander's outer chamber.

"Do you take me for a fool? Did you think I wouldn't remember your small friend's rescuing you from a locked dungeon? What did you hope to achieve?"

His smile grew a little broader. "Why, to sow a little doubt and concern in the minds of Narnash's soldiers. Perhaps at the end make them a little more ready to listen to reason when we call them to surrender."

"I see. And did it occur to you to think what might happen if you ran afoul of a patrol while you were sowing?

"Taking the garrison towns is a thing of importance, for certain. But it is only a prelude to the war, which will involve at least one full-scale battle. And if we don't have you and the talisman available for that one battle, all our hopes are well-nigh doomed. Did you think of that?"

He grinned again. "And perhaps I might trip on a doorsill and break my neck. Or choke on a chicken-bone. Or go off to trim the beards of the priests of Wardesh."

"Everything for you is a matter of lightheartedness and carefree dancing through life, isn't it? Some of us can't join you in the dance, though. So we must hope your wild dance doesn't jostle us while we walk, or worse still, send us sprawling on the cobbles."

"Lady, that was very poetic!"

"Do you hope to flatter me enough to make me forget what I've called you for? There's no hope of that, my friend! I'm assigning you a bodyguard. Tahheron and his men will watch over you."

"Ah, Lovely Lady Lusi of the Fair Locks! You have such solicitude for a poor ox-driver."

"Fair Locks? What d'you mean by *that*?"

"Oh, Shapak-ailesh assures me a fair-haired lover is always more popular in the Romantic ballads. I'll have to go study my ancestry; perhaps I might be some long-lost prince of Batan-ji."

"You are the most arrogant, ridiculous man I've ever met! Go on, get out of here, and don't make trouble. I'll give Tahheron special orders to knock you on the head if you start another fight!"

But she could barely prevent herself from laughing long enough for him to be removed.

THE LAME MAN READJUSTED his grip on his crutches and swung himself in to the group entering the gate of the Old City of Askos. The man in brown-—His mind shied away from that thought. *He* had instructed him to do so, when he had transported the two of them to a place two days' walk from here.

He wouldn't disobey those instructions. No, even if his mind refused to think of them, tied as they were to so many other memories. He couldn't face what might happen if he disobeyed. What *would* happen.

He no longer had the strength of will to curse the torturers of-—Who had it been? They had left him lame, but the brown man-—No, keep that thought away. Stay with these people most of them so happy and cheerful. Had he ever been cheerful? It seemed so, once, long ago. Before—-.

The guards at the gate counted the people who came through in this lot. Though they, like guards all over, were so hurried that a miscount, too many or too few by only one, was put down to a mistake in counting. The party was pushed on through to make room for the next.

The lame man stayed with them for a little while, then moved quietly off by himself. His instructions were to find a quiet place to sleep. To sleep. Perhaps he would sleep deeply enough to avoid the Dreams. Perhaps.

TAHHERON GRINNED AT Thotgol. "Now, you know my loyalty is to the Lady Lusommi. Don't bother trying to convince me or bribe me to disobey her orders, and we'll all get along just fine."

Thotgol smiled in return. "And you have orders to spoil all my fun?"

"Only if it appears the fun is becoming too destructive or dangerous."

"You'll knock me on the head if I start a fight in a drinking-room?"

"Worse. We'll draw swords and form a circle around you, announcing that this man is under the protection of the Lady Lusommi."

"And mark me forever as the fellow who starts trouble, then hides behind the Lady's skirts? You'd do that?"

"Well, if nobody does anything too foolish, we won't have to find out, will we?"

So, when Thotgol visited Shapak-ailesh in the Market, Moxtarum was with him. "Shapak-ailesh, this is Moxtarum, one of Lady Lusommi's men. Moxtarum, this is Shapak-ailesh, a good friend of mine. Apparently, I'm to have guards with me, whether I like it or not. And I can only hope they won't insist on sleeping in the same bed as me. None of them would like it either; I tend to kick like a mule."

Moxtarum grinned. "Does he get as grumpy as this with everyone who tries to keep him alive?"

"I'm sure he does. I have yet to divine whether it is a fault of the man himself, or a standard attitude of all Batans. Don't let him discourage you. And don't let him gamble with you."

"No fear of that! He has quite a reputation with the Dwarves' Bones."

AFTER A SCRUPULOUSLY few cups of wine, Thotgol made an early evening of it, back in his own bed by twilight.

Shortly thereafter, Shapak-ailesh and the mule passed through. The little man grabbed Thotgol's arm on the way. One moment they appeared to be on a small sandy isle barely large enough to hold the three of them. Then they were in the camping-place outside Hellafriad.

"I wasn't sure you'd be coming."

"Oh? After you'd as much as said to me *'Come by with the mule when everyone's asleep, and pull me out?'*"

"You can't say that. My hint was very subtle."

"Subtle as a hammer blow. I was surprised your chamber wasn't lined with guards, spears levelled to catch me as I came in."

"But they weren't!" declared Thotgol triumphantly. "Which shows that I was subtle enough!"

"Hah! Well, shall we stand here arguing all night, or shall we get on with the job?"

There were no untoward incidents tonight. Nor were there any near-encounters with patrols. Soon Thotgol was back in his quarters in time to sleep a bit before morning.

"AND WHERE HAVE YOU been, Doctor Gobnash? We have a problem that could use your talents."

"I was delivering a little gift to the Old City of Askos, Highness."

"Only four days, there and back?"

"You know, Highness, I have other means of travel."

"The king's brows lifted. "You had someone there light beacon fires for you?"

"No, Highness. I picked a landmark nearby, and travelled there. A good part of the time was spent in pulling my passenger out of the worst effects of the journey."

"Passenger? You told me that—-"

"Exactly, Highness. My passenger very nearly did not survive. And I had to expend a good deal of my power to keep him alive long enough to do his task. To do the same thing with an army, or even a small troop, would be well-nigh impossible."

But Narnash was on a new tack now. "His task? To assassinate the Lady Lusommi?"

"Not directly, Highness. But it will certainly discommode her. I shall keep you informed on the progress of the matter. Now, there was another problem that required my attention?"

"THESE NEW MEN, TUGASHIN. What d'you make of them?"

"Mostly youngsters, Lord. Out for a lark, thinking to be heroes. I've put them into a separate section, drilling them and training them apart from our own men. The ones who stay through the training will then be put into our main force. A lot of them have taken to the training well, partly because they know they don't dare go back. A few have left us altogether, and I fear they may become bandits in the locality."

"Not a good thing, Tugashin. We are still barely welcome here."

"I know that, Lord. I've taken it upon myself to send messages to the Lady Junommi, warning her of the possibility and apologizing. But Lord?"

"Yes?"

"One further thing. Have you thought Narnash might slip one or two of his own men in, with orders to kill you?"

Disikomin scowled. "Yes, I'd thought of it. I'll be as careful as I can."

"I've also had a word with your own personal guards, Lord. Just to make sure they're aware of the situation."

"YOU KNOW, YOUNG THOTGOL, eventually the word of this is going to come to Doctor Gobnash, who will quite certainly begin laying traps for us."

Thotgol's head came up. "I ought to have thought of that myself! D'you have any notions as to what we might do in that case?"

"Be ready to turn and run very quickly."

Thotgol grimaced. "This is the best you can think of?"

"Better than not having thought of it at all!" retorted Shapak-ailesh. "And for most things, I think it will work better than any complex scheme I might come up with. I might, indeed, work out a series of possibilities of traps and the like. Then work out a series of possible counters to each, but I think running is the better notion."

This conversation made Thotgol a little nervous. But after they'd paid their visits to the three garrison towns, he began to relax. They had one sighting of a town patrol, but far enough distant to be of no real concern. The most interesting occurrence, in fact, came at the tail end of the night. They came into a better-off quarter of the town, when they had put their slogan once before.

Most of the walls here were neat, well-kept, and solid, an ideal surface for writing on.

"Look at that!"

Their earlier depredation had been scraped off and painted over. However, on top of that someone had written, fairly recently, '*Biter blow the winz of Askoz.*'

"And don't be telling me that they left it there from last time, either. I never made errors like that, not even in a rush."

"And this means somewhat important, does it?"

"It means—-" Thotgol calmed his voice. "It means, as you very well know, you little rascal. That someone, at least, is joining us in our endeavour, which will be more than a little assistance to our cause. It would be even better if they could spell correctly."

"Ah, and now Thotgol, having lately learned to tell one letter from another, has taken on the task of criticism of all writing?"

"Perhaps not. But Thotgol has a feeling we have been standing around here nattering far too long."

"THOTGOL, MESSAGES CONTINUE to come in to say that this graffiti-writing is still going on. And also that much of it appears to be in the same hand. Though my agents have not been able to view more than a few samples without drawing suspicion.

"Furthermore, a thing *has* become conspicuous. That you are going to bed early, and rising very late, often still tired.

"Since we know your small friend could slip you out of your quarters with no-one the wiser, I must consider other measures."

"What will you do? Have Tahheron chain me to my bedpost every night?"

"No, that might be a bit excessive. Perhaps only have the guard inside your room rather than outside."

"And might I ask a question, O Lady Lusi of the Fair Locks?"

She glowered at him. "What question is that?"

"Do your agents mention any effects these graffiti might be having?"

"The soldiers are a little nervous, but not to the point of surrendering to anyone who comes against them."

"All the more reason not to stop now. See, they know the people don't like them. A little scribbling on the walls just reminds them of that.

"But when the slogan turns up in locked rooms which the local people couldn't get into, it makes them sure things other than local unrest are at work here. And further, it reminds them of the stories they've likely heard, of that battle last year and the use of the talisman.

"If we begin the season by summoning them to surrender *'lest the winds of Askos blow.'* Don't you think that would at least hinder their will to fight?"

"I hate to dampen your eagerness. But I've already told you if some soldier gets lucky and puts a spear through you while you're painting the walls, we could lose you and the use of the talisman. And if we lose that, we might well have lost the war."

"Lady, any number of things might happen to me to lose you the use of that talisman. Is protecting me like a toddling child really going to have the proper effect?"

She looked at him. Then her eyes widened suddenly, as though she were seeing him for the first time.

"Anything I do to try to keep you safe merely pushes you the harder to take risks, doesn't it?"

"Not at all!" He protested automatically. Then he stopped. "You know," he said slowly, "there's a lot of truth in that."

"I see. So even if I put a guard inside your room, you'll find some way to evade him, won't you?"

He grinned. "Does a mere ox-driver dare to disagree with Lady Lusi, Fair Queen of all Askos?"

"If that ox-driver is a Batan named Thotgol, he will dare pretty much whatever he wishes! And he'll even make some silly joke and grin as the headsman takes his head!"

"This would not be, of course, until after I've won your battles for you. Ah, the Misfortunate Thotgol!"

"There! Just like that. And Wardesh guard and guide, what kind of a word is '*Misfortunate?*'"

"Oh, back when I was in jail, awaiting your displeasure. I saw someone had scratched on the wall, '*Here stood the Misfortunate Manorio.*' The word caught my fancy. Perhaps because it doesn't exist."

"Now we're drifting away from the matter at hand. The more carefully I try to protect you, the more determined you are to evade the protection. And you will take greater and greater risks as you do so. Perhaps we could come to an accommodation?"

"What sort of accommodation?"

"You speak as warily as if I were Bloody Narnash himself, offering you a *'special cup of wine.'* My offer is simply this: Go do as you will do, and try not to risk yourself too unduly. And take at least one of Tahheron's men with you."

You really think one extra man is going to make much difference?"

"Probably not, but it will ease my mind a little."

"Just take him along? No stipulation about taking his advice?"

"Would it do any good? I only ask—not demand, mind you—that you not reject any advice out of hand."

"For my own part, I would agree. I will have to consult my partner, though."

"ANOTHER MAN? WOULD you also like to take along some jugglers and a musical troupe?"

"You said you could take thirty. This is only three. Plus the mule."

"And the four of us will fit so well in those crannies behind the locked doors where you insist on going."

Thotgol sighed. "We must make allowances. I'd prefer not to upset the Lady Lusi. And don't give me any snickering about young love and such nonsense. I'd just as soon not come up to the campaigning season with her treating me as some sort of necessary evil. We still have to fight against Narnash."

"So." The little man shrugged. I suppose the only thing to say is, *'Bring in the guard so we can show him what the Hidden Ways are like.'"*

Chapter XVI
Opening Moves

"You're mad, Thotgol!"

"Does that mean '*no?*'"

Shapak-ailesh took a deep breath. "As to the exact question, yes, it is quite possible for me to detect a trap such as the last one. Unlike certain people, however, I do not lay claim to all the knowledge in the world. It is possible someone might have developed a trap I don't know."

"You won't help, then?"

"Why are you so set on doing this?"

"Well, thanks to you, the plague was not as serious as it might have been. Still, we've taken losses from it. Anything I can do to make up for those losses would be to the good. Even if all I do is to make a few Wennzmen a little less eager to fight."

"Have you talked to Lusi yet?"

Thotgol shook his head. "She's got enough to deal with. She gave me instructions a while ago, and they haven't been rescinded."

"And it's not because she thought you'd have the sense to refrain from going?"

Thotgol smiled, spreading his hands. "Can I read anyone's mind?"

"And you're not going to bring it up to her, are you?" Shapak-ailesh said, disgustedly. "And her last orders required you to take a guard. Who had you thought to take?"

"Moxa was practically ready yesterday." They were both silent for a moment. Moxtarum had come down with the plague toward the end of the outbreak. For a time he did not respond to the "plague-drink," as the concoction was called. At last, however, he had come out of the illness and begun to mend.

But all Shapak-ailesh's efforts had not saved everyone, nor could he bring anyone back from the dead. There were dead, all too many dead, throughout the Old City.

MOXTARUM SHOOK HIS head. "I'm not in the best of shape. If we had to run from one of those Gigglers, I doubt I'd make it."

"We're hoping not to have to run from anything. And I'd prefer not to have to take the time to train someone new."

"If I go along, and we all get killed because I'm not well enough to fight, Captain Tahheron will skin me alive and use my hide for a saddle-cloth."

"But if we get killed, he won't be able to get at you."

"This is supposed to cheer me?" said Moxtarum sourly. "All right, let me do a little moving around, a couple of sword-drills, and we'll see how I'm doing by evening."

By evening, all three were waiting in their camping-place near to Hellafriad. Shortly after nightfall they went into the town.

For all his cheery optimism, Thotgol was wary, almost nervous, and he noted Moxa was in much the same mood. He couldn't be sure about Shapak-ailesh. However, for the little man held his face expressionless. He had, however, expressed his feelings earlier. Thotgol was sure they were going to hit on a patrol coming around some corner at any moment. Or worse, a sending from Doctor Gobnash.

But nothing happened. They finished their work in the open town. Then began making their decision as to which locked premise they should invade.

"Weapon stores?" suggested Thotgol.

Shapak-ailesh thought a moment. "I've got a bad feeling about that. Nothing definite, just a feeling."

After the previous experience, Thotgol was not about to press him to go against a feeling. "Commander's antechamber?"

"Nothing magic in the antechamber, just the same couple of talismans that've been there every other time."

"All right, let's go there."

Despite Shapak-ailesh's assurances, Thotgol had a hand on his ox-goad as they went in. Everything was quiet. His hands shook just a little as he wrote *Bitter blow the winds of Askos!* on the wall. He stepped back to look at the final result. In that instant, a key grated and clicked in the lock then the door was flung open. Four armed soldiers stood in the doorway.

The Wennzmen were caught by surprise, their spearbutts still resting on the floor. Regular inspection of stores had become one of the duties they had to do on their rounds. But none of them expected anything to ever come of it.

Thotgol recovered first. He whipped his ox-goad from his belt. Then jumped towards the soldiers. They tried to move back to have room to use their spears. But Thotgol was already too close, slashing and stabbing with his weapon.

Moxtarum, took advantage of Thotgol's attack which had taken the soldiers' attention. followed up by stepping in and thrusting with his own spear. One of the guards was already down. So Moxtarum was able to take another in the side as he sought to come to grips with Thotgol. The odds were even, and immediately swung the other way as another went down. Then the last one, trading spear-thrusts with Moxa, realized his situation and turned to flee.

Which was fatal for him.

"MESSAGES HAVE JUST come in by bird from Hellafriad, Doctor Gobnash. The Askos graffiti-writers made their way into the Commander's Antechamber two nights past."

"Is the Commander certain it's the same people?"

"Tolerably certain. On the first evening, a patrol spotted a man, a boy, and a mule across the market-square. And when they got to the square, the three had disappeared. But a message was written on the wall. Survivors of the patrol that surprised them in the Commander's Antechamber the other evening, insisted there had been two men, a boy, and a mule in the room."

"A second message said indeed, traces of mule hoofprints were found there."

Doctor Gobnash said nothing for a moment, and Narnash experienced a moment of triumph. A definite sense that, for all the doctor's smooth brow. Behind that mask was a bafflement that would have twisted the ordinary face into wrinkled mass.

"A boy and a mule?" Did he detect the slightest puzzlement in the voice?

"Yes. A boy and a mule. None of this speaks to you, does it?"

Doctor Gobnash bowed slightly and then said, "Not at all, Highness. Let me return to my workroom and see what I might discover."

"Go on, good doctor. I hope to see results soon," Narnash dismissed the doctor.

As he leaned back into in chair a very slight smirk crossed his lips. *'Got you, you, little bugger! Baffled to the core!'*

Narnash watched as the doctor made his usual calm departure. Then he became aware some of his less-experienced servants were casting glances at him, as if wondering what madness had stricken him.

"Orribash, if you cannot provide me with servants who don't jump around and twitch all the time, perhaps I should put someone else in your place!" He was gratified to watch the lot of them stiffen, knowing they were in trouble.

"Who's to see me next? Not the local merchants again, I hope?"

LUSI DIDN'T SEEM ANGRY today, just upset, and perhaps tired. "Thotgol, Captain Tahheron has reported to me the result of last night's foray. He has also reported to me what happened in the previous foray. Before the plague interfered with everything. Don't you think it's becoming a bit dangerous, even for you?"

He smiled and spread his hands. "Yes, I'm afraid even I must admit we've pushed our luck there as far as we dare. On the other hand, though, we are gathering our troops for the campaign. Might I propose a flying column to Hellafriad? We could demand they surrender *'lest the Winds of Askos blow,'* and if they refuse, I could give them a sample of the wind."

"And if they still refuse to surrender?"

"Then I blow down the main gate. But I doubt if it'll come to that."

"The notion has much to commend it, and not merely for the small prestige such a victory would bring. We would also have command of supplies from the surrounding area. Which would make things a little more difficult for Narnash.

"But I still dislike the risk to you yourself, if some archer on the wall makes a lucky shot."

"We've discussed that before. I'll be as careful as I know how to be."

"And I won't say yes or no immediately. I'll want to talk to Aelkoriat before I decide."

"I'll wait for that, then."

"What?" she said, her humour a bit forced. "Thotgol agreeing to wait for my decision? You're not going to get a band together and ride off tonight, just to show me?"

He grinned and spread his hands again, "Regrettably, Lady, your captains are entirely too loyal. I could take myself, perhaps Shapak-ailesh. And maybe find a dozen others willing for a romp, but even I have to admit this venture needs more than that."

THE ARCHER LOOKED UP across the fire at the woman. "I'll be going tomorrow."

Her face was the blank mask he'd seen before, whenever she felt emotion she didn't want to show. "Tomorrow?"

"Yes. Bloody Narnash will be on the march soon, and I have to be out there to watch his host."

"Will you come back?"

"I'm going into a risky situation, and I'd be a fool to say for certain I'm going to live through it."

"But if you live…?" Her voice trailed off.

"Do you want me to come back?" Two weeks back she'd invited him into her bed. But it was only two people, alone, sharing something to keep back the loneliness.

"If you want me to come back," he said into the silence, knowing she was trying to conquer her pride to ask him, "I'll come back."

"There'll be a place for you."

And he suddenly realized coming back might indeed be a good thing.

"I HEAR YOU'RE SENDING ten men to help train Lady Lusommi's phalanx," Delfi, like most children, always seemed to be able to ask the most apt questions.

"Where did you hear that, Delfi?" Disikomin raised his eyebrow and forced himself not to smile.

"Well, they talked about it some last year. And now the men are saying the orders will come any time. And making bets on who will be sent."

"Have you told anyone?"

"No, Sir. Only my Ma."

"Be careful, Delfi. What you hear in camp ought not to be repeated outside. Sending men to help train Lady Lusommi's phalanx is something that would be expected. So it matters little who hears that. But if you make a habit of not talking, you won't say anything where it might be heard. And eventually repeated, in the ears of one of the spies of Bloody Narnash."

The boy's eyes grew round and serious. "Not even my Ma?"

Disikomin found himself smiling. "No, it's safe to tell your mother. But be careful who's around when you tell her."

"Yes, Sir!"

THE AIDE APPROACHED Narnash's throne and bowed deeply. "Highness, Lord Komsallit is marching, with all his folk, toward the Askos border!"

"Bloody Black Destroyer's Teeth! I should have had him done away with last year. Send orders that he be headed off and stopped!"

"Yes, Highness. But given the time of this message, any intercepting force would be unlikely to arrive in time."

"Tell them to force their march! If he's taking his people, he'll be slowed. If they can't head him off, they can at least pursue him and bring him to battle. Go on, get out of here, and send the orders!"

Narnash looked around. "Someone go fetch Doctor Gobnash!"

Doctor Gobnash was his usual calm self.

"Well, Komsallit is off for Askos, Doctor Gobnash. I'm sending a force to catch him and, I hope, to destroy him. But I have a feeling this is only the beginning. I think we'll see a few more lords being dilatory at the least. Some of them even managing to send their contingents until too late. I doubt if it'll leave us outnumbered, but it will certainly cut back our advantage.

"And this means we must have something to counter that talisman. Have you any ideas?"

"I've been working on a few notions. I expect that before you march, I'll have something for you."

"I'd feel a good deal better about it, Doctor, if you'd deign to take the field with us." It was the sort of speech that would have anyone else in his kingdom swearing they'd had no intention of doing anything else.

Doctor Gobnash merely said, "Ah. If you wish, Highness, I will come."

THOTGOL RODE IN VERY familiar company of Tahheron and a detachment of guards. They moved with a clatter of arms and armour. The total force was under the command of one Neltrahhio, reputed to be some sort of cousin to Aelkoriat. He was also reputed to have gotten this task for more reasons than his high connection.

They were all mounted, for speed, and they carried little in the way of supplies. What supplies they did have were not in oxcarts, but on led packhorses. This severely limited the amount and type of supplies they could take.

Thotgol looked back over his shoulder. "We're not really hoping to take Hellafriad by surprise, are we? With the cloud of dust we're raising?"

Tahheron grinned. "Well, there are degrees and degrees of surprise. Best would be so suddenly show up at the gates, totally unexpected. We can't manage that. But what we hope to do is to appear sometime between the time they send a galloper out to the nearest garrison town, and the time that reinforcements can arrive."

"Well, so long as they don't arrive just as we're trying to convince Hellafriad to surrender without fighting."

"Don't start getting nerves now, Thotgol. Everyone knows this was your idea."

HELLAFRIAD HAD NOT been a large town. But it had been chosen, because of its location. Hellafriad was to serve as a local government center, to keep a garrison of Wennz troops, and to serve as a supplying point when necessary. Its status as a seat of local government drew some population, mostly from Wennz, to fill the necessary posts. This in turn drew people to provide services for the soldiers and the general population. From a very small place, it had grown into a town of respectable size.

Its walls, under the rules of various Wennz kings since the initial defeat of Askos, had been carefully maintained and strengthened.

"It might be possible to take this place by storm. But we're not enough to do the job," Neltrahhio had features similar to Aelkoriat. But he lacked the axe-carved planes of chin and cheekbone and brow. One could predict, though, that a few more years would remedy that.

He looked at Thotgol. "You're sure they'll surrender?"

Thotgol had been wondering why he'd been called to the command session. Mostly he'd been treated as a weapon, albeit a weapon one had to be polite to. He shrugged. "The groundwork's been laid, and I'm fairly sure it's had its effect. Am I sure they'll surrender? No. I think, though, a demonstration or two will change a lot of minds in there."

"Could you blow down a wall?"

He glanced at the walls, suddenly realizing his whole experience with the talisman consisted of that one battle last year. Could he blow down a wall?

"I don't know. Perhaps, but don't bet on it. It might be possible to take out a gate."

"I see. You're singularly ill-informed for the man who's going to use that thing."

"I'm afraid so." He wasn't going to go through the whole story about accidentally attuning the thing to himself and everything which had come of that bit of mischance.

Neltrahhio looked at him. almost a glare, and suddenly the features of Aelkoriat were more clear in his face. "The Lady Lusommi won't be happy if we've come all this way to no purpose," he said. "But more importantly for you I won't be happy."

'At least he's not a short one!'

"If it makes you any happier, Commander, this was my idea. And if it doesn't work out, I'll be annoyed at the instigator myself."

It clearly didn't make the Commander any happier. He glared at Thotgol for a moment longer than said, "Well, let's get to it. You'll go up with the party, along with the herald. The herald will summon them to surrender, and if it's necessary, you'll use the talisman."

He looked for a moment as though he wanted to make some further statement or threat, then he turned away.

Thotgol understood the purpose of the guards with him, of course. It wasn't likely to come down to protecting him against a sally from inside the town. But they would be expected to interpose their shields, or even their bodies, between him and any arrow, slung stone, or even a javelin from the walls.

He remembered Moxtarum's statement about people who weren't afraid, and congratulated himself on being sensible. It was against all custom and tradition to attack heralds, or parties coming to parley. But that would be little comfort if he ended up dead.

They were within calling distance of the walls now. The herald cupped his hands at his mouth and shouted, "Hello, you on the walls, do you hear me? I wish to speak to your commander!"

One of the men on the walls shouted down, "Just a moment, I'll send for him!"

Which was intended as a ploy, as if a hostile force appearing outside the walls would not have drawn the Commander to the walls long ago. On their part, the party with the herald did their best to seem unworried and casual, as though none of them considered the possibility that a sudden sally might, against all expectation, be made from the town.

But finally a new voice spoke. "I am Maltash Howaldin, Commander of the forces of King Narnash in this town! What do you want?"

At which the herald answered, in the agreed words, "Lord Neltrahhio h'Alikor summons you in the name of the Lady Lusommi h'Askevoto to surrender, lest the Winds of Askos blow!"

The answering shout came back in a moment, "The Walls of Hellafriad are safe against a little wind!"

The herald looked at Thotgol who nodded. He hadn't really expected them to surrender without a demonstration. He pointed his finger and swept it along the wall. *"O wild storm wind from the Eastern sea, blow, blow!"*

The wind that struck against the wall bore a tang of salt which drifted as far as the Askos parley group. It smashed a sudden driven rain against the wall, and the men on the wall disappeared. Whether blown away by the wind or simply ducking behind the parapet it was impossible to say.

With his memory of the first experience of the talisman, Thotgol was able to judge more carefully the amount of time that went by before he called, *"O Western Winds, stop!"*

And the wind that had raged the length of the town faded as suddenly as it had come.

After a moment the herald called again, "Will you surrender now?"

It was a short while later before a voice answered tersely, "No!"

The herald looked at Thotgol. "What now?"

"One of you go back and tell Commander Neltrahhio I'm going to make a try at the gates."

One of the guards went off at a gallop. Thotgol considered the matter, and decided not to wait too long. *"O wild dancing whirlwind, come against the gates before us!"*

The little whirlwind which began dancing in the grass in front of them was disappointingly small. Despite its size, it caused the horses to shy. By the time they had controlled their horses, the whirlwind was rushing against the town. It was gaining speed and strength as it went. By the time it reached the gates, it was a massive dark funnel. It was pulling up bushes and carrying dust, small rocks, and other debris.

When the wind finally struck the gates, it ripped them from their hinges, broke them up, and flung them aside.

"O wild-dancing whirlwind, stop!" The whirlwind was gone as though it had never been, leaving complete silence. Thotgol considered what that might do to massed troops. Then he thought perhaps it was best the strictures against using this wind were so strong.

Neltrahhio was quick to seize his advantage. A sudden sound of hooves announced the first assault on the broken gates. Someone inside had recovered their wits quickly enough, though. For one of the riders went down just before they reached the gates. Those in the rear ranks spread out to launch arrows to keep the heads of the Wennz archers down.

Neltrahhio had not sent his whole force in. Thotgol, although he was no soldier, could understand the reasoning behind that. Getting everyone jammed up in one narrow gateway would be worse than useless. Sounds of battle came from inside. Someone had recovered from the smashing of the gate.

Moxatarum murmured, "Now, we will see."

"What will we see?"

"Well, for one thing, if our lot can make a start at clearing the walls over the gate, we'll have an easier time of it getting our men in."

The first detachment of Askos horsemen was now out of sight inside, and the second was coming in. There was a danger of coming in small groups, too. If the Wennzmen inside could rally sufficiently, they might be able to defeat the smaller detachments. While leaving the city still in the hands of the Wennzmen, and Neltrahhio outside with too few people to make a difference.

On their side, the Askos had the advantage of morale. Both their troops and many of the Wennzmen had seen the first demonstration of the wind. They also witnessed the whirlwind that had smashed the gate. The Wennzmen could not know there were problems with overuse of the talisman. Indeed, few of the Askos understood that. Thotgol himself was not sure what he might say if asked to use the talisman against a particular force of Wennzmen who were intent on making a stand.

It was frustrating sitting here outside, knowing only that there were sounds of fighting still inside.

Then a banner flew over the gates, a pennon showing Neltrahhio's Boar's Head. The men of Askos cheered, and the last of them rode toward the gate, as the sounds of battle diminished.

"Let's go!" said Moxatarum.

They urged their horses into motion, and pulled in behind the last of the main force as they went through the gates. The sounds of battle continued. But they were farther away, as the attackers pressed inward and encountered troops rushing from other places to the point of greatest danger.

"Stay with us, Thotgol," Moxa said. If someone slips past Neltrahhio's men, we don't want them getting you."

A MESSENGER FROM NELTRAHHIO requested Thotgol's presence at the Commander's Quarters, so Thotgol went on over and waited. He listened as messengers made their reports. "It was the gate did it," one of them said. "Men running from the battle met up with men marching toward it, told them the tale, and kept running. Often as not, parties met up with our troops after a quarter or so of their numbers had disappeared into alleys along the way. And of course the tale kept being told and retold, so that many times we'd meet men ready to surrender at the first demand."

That report, with minor differences, was a reflection of most of the others. One of the later messengers reported, "About five hundred or so, most still armed, marched out the east gate. Commander Menorio thought it best not to pursue without your order, sir."

"Tell him 'well done.' Our main purpose here is to take the town for Lady Lusommi, and we might well have to hold against an attack before any relief reaches us."

When this messenger had gone, Neltrahhio turned to Thotgol. "So. It worked out in the end, did it?"

"It did."

"Why didn't you just use the whirlwind as your first demonstration?"

"There are warnings against the overuse of the talisman in general, and in particular against the use of the whirlwind. It's likely the land will pay for today's whirlwind with unseasonable weather later on."

"Hmp." Neltrahhio did not seem convinced. "You could smash the whole of Narnash's army with that."

"And if, later on, the cost were found to be too high?"

Neltrahhio scowled, but Thotgol felt the scowl was not so much at him, personally, as it was at a situation where Neltrahhio didn't have enough information to argue for a point he'd like to make.

"Well, I'd best send the first bird to let the Lady know we've taken the place, with reasonable casualties. I wish we had a few more men; it'd be nice to be able to present her with another garrison town or two. Ah, well, if wishes were fleece, the world would wear wool."

Chapter XVII
Campaign

The word reached Narnash on the march. Worse yet. The word had to come by bird to the capital and thence by galloper to Narnash. Which meant it was old news by the time it got to him. Anyone who could not avoid being in his presence, such as his servants, noted his mood and walked carefully around him. The hangers-on who wished for favours from him, at least those of them who were more experienced, made themselves scarce. Many a man had turned the king against him by some chance word or deed during those times of anger. Such a stain was well-nigh impossible to erase later.

Everyone was glad his anger seemed to fall heaviest on Doctor Gobnash.

"Hellafriad has fallen, Doctor Gobnash! A small force of Askos came up! They blew the gate away with a whirlwind, and drove out that lot of fools and cravens who called themselves my garrison! What have you to say to that?"

"Unfortunate, Highness."

"Unfortunate?! Dark Destroyer's Teeth! *'Unfortunate'* says my most wise and highly favoured master of things magical! The man has known for more than a year of this talisman! Still. When the talisman is used to take the initiative of this campaign out of my hands, all he can tell me is that it's bloody *'unfortunate!'*"

He paused a moment after this long speech. "Tell me, then, what have I paid you so handsomely for all these years?"

Doctor Gobnash showed no sign of anger or fear. "What is it you want of me?"

This was not the sort of statement to quiet the King's mood. "What do I want of you? I want Hellafriad back, and the supplies it is to provide for me. And I want you to do something about that Morrkerr-eaten wind-talisman!"

"Ah. I see. Well, I assume we are marching for Hellafriad. I can help you there. And if the talisman is there, I can deal with it at the same time."

"You say all this so calmly! I wonder, then, why you couldn't have used your magic to see what was to happen, and prevent it?"

"Magic has its ways and means and usages. Predicting futures is notoriously unreliable. If I had spent all my time scrying for the talisman to see what it was doing each day, I would scarce have had the time to develop a means to combat it."

Temporarily robbed of arguments, the king scowled at the Doctor, then he waved a hand. "Go away, then. Yes, we move to Hellafriad, but only because we need it for any extended campaign.

And every day required to reduce it is a day taken away from the main point of this campaign, the reduction of Askos!"

SEATED AT THE LIGHT folding table in her tent, Lusi looked down at the chip of wood, which bore a single sentence. *'Narnaash mooves on Hellaafriyaad.'*

"It seems to be that mysterious fellow from last year."

She looked up at Aelkoriat. "It does. Of course, Narnash would naturally move on Hellafriad. It's near to a necessity, if Narnash plans any extended campaign in our territory. It's good to have it confirmed."

"Well, our schedule appears to be holding. Even Thotgol has returned."

"You thought he might not?"

"Well, Lady, he is a bit impetuous. I could well imagine him going off Chaos away with some plan of his own in mind."

"Too true. I'm told he did try to convince Neltrahhio to let him stay to help hold Hellafriad. Neltrahhio was able to resist his notions."

"And he is an engaging rascal, as well. Should you not perhaps change his guards to prevent them from getting too familiar with him, and perhaps falling in with some plan of his against your orders and wishes?"

She shook her head. "I think not. Tahheron is one of my steadiest, and he's managed to pass that attitude on to his men. I doubt they'll be talked into anything wild."

THE CAMPFIRE CRACKED and snapped, tossing a flickering orange glow over the gathered crowd, winking yellowish gleams on polished metal. "Yes, Lady," Disikomin said, "the Raven Flying is the badge of Komsallit." He didn't bother stating the obvious. Just because someone wore a badge, it didn't mean he wore the badge legitimately.

"Well, we'd heard word that Komsallit was coming to join us, bringing all his people. We've also heard that Narnash has had men pursuing Komsallit. I'd appreciate it if you'd stay here while I question these three messengers. And possibly ask them a question or two yourself."

'A trick question to unmask false messengers?' posed Disikomin to himself silently, "Certainly, Lady. If you think I can help."

The three messengers were the type to be sent on such a mission. Travelling through hostile territory into territory only slightly less hostile. Two were youngsters, at the stage of needing a shave once a week. Full of dreams of heroism, but with a good deal of native wit and some training. The third was a grizzled man, the sort who has a fair and unbiased notion of his own capabilities. The sort who will undertake a mission for his lord, and carry it through without taking undue risks.

It would have been simpler, Disikomin reflected, if he'd been able to recognize any of the three. But that would be expecting too much good luck.

Lusommi looked at the older man. "Please tell us again your story, how you come to be here."

"Lady, I am Baradong, and these are Entoshi and Molnash. We are all Komsallit's men. Last year, the Lord Disikomin" he glanced at Disikomin, "sent messages to our lord and others. The messages suggested they reconsider how much loyalty they owed to King Narnash.

"Word of these messages came to the king. Who of course sent messages of his own, requesting any lords who had received such messages to inform him.

"Our Lord determined to leave Wennz this year, with all his people. Knowing how often a suspicion in the king's mind becomes certain knowledge of wrongdoing. Having all our people with us, we were caught up a little this side of the border by a force sent from the king. Lord Komsallit has been continuing to march, fighting a rearguard action all the way. Having nowhere near enough men to stand and fight, he asked us to come find you and ask whether you could give any aid."

Lusommi pursed her lips doubtfully. "I should risk sending out a force of my own into territory Narnash still holds? And have him pounce and destroy them?"

Baradong bowed. "Lady, you will do as you see fit, and I can only say what I know. Our people are in desperate straits. Our Lord himself would be here before you, save that he is directing the defence of our people."

Disikomin spoke up. "Baradong, you know who I am?"

Disikomin admonished himself, *'Silliness! Of course he knows, you saw the look he gave you. But the question had to be asked.'*

Baradong looked at him, without a trace of irony. "Yes, Lord, you are the Lord Disikomin Rudashin."

Disikomin remained stoic, *'And what Wennzman does not know about the Wennz lord serving the Lady Lusommi?'*

"So. Do you know the tale of my wager with your lord, how I lost two silver pieces betting on my red mare?"

The man's lips twitched. Disikomin could see as clear as if Baradong had spoken out loud, that he knew he was being tested.

"Lord, as I heard it my lord lost ten silver betting against your red mare."

Disikomin nodded, *'And how many people from one end of Wennz to the other have heard the story?'*

"So you say. But back to the beginning of things. Why should your lord be so concerned for Narnash's supposed distrust?"

"I beg your pardon, Lord, but all Wennz knows what was done to you last year, and for less cause."

The loss of Folsidon was suddenly fresh again.

Disikomin nodded. "Yes, indeed." He stepped back into his place.

Lusommi spoke. "Thank you, Baradong. We will discuss the matter, and let you know our decision."

When the three had been ushered out, she turned to Disikomin. "Well, Lord, have you anything to say, for good or ill?"

"Lady, I can say nothing for certain. My feeling, though, is they are nothing more nor less than what they claim."

"I see. And would you be willing to risk a thousand men on that feeling?"

His lips twitched upward slightly. "Lady, I will never make idle boasts in your presence, lest you hold me to them! At the risk of sounding like a housewife bargaining for melons in the marketplace, might I suggest that five thousand would be more reasonable?"

This brought a smile to her own face. "Those melons are too dear, Lord Disikomin. Whatever force you take leaves us that much less to face Narnash's main body. Can you achieve it with three thousand?"

He couldn't help but smile. "At this point I ought to demand no less than three thousand five hundred. But no, with good fortune it can be done with three thousand. So long as the three thousand are not the dregs of your army."

"STORM'S GOING TO HIT us before the end of the day," Thotgol commented, sticking out his chin toward the clouds moving rapidly up from the horizon.

"Very nice," muttered Moxatarum. "So we get to march through mud most of the day."

But the storm which came on them so suddenly was not rain. It was snow! A sudden driving, blinding storm, so one could hardly see the man or horse in front of one.

Very shortly, word passed down the line to set up camp, and try to find shelter from the storm. Tents were wrestled into place to provide some shelter from the wind. Then fires built of whatever fuel could be found.

Thotgol said nothing to anyone. Secretly, he wondered if this unseasonable storm might be the result of the use of the whirlwind. At the beginning, it was thought to be the kind of storm which might last for days. But it had blown itself out by midnight, leaving a clear sky full of stars.

Day dawned, still clear and cool, but the unhindered sun warmed things rapidly. The march began through two feet of wet snow, and as the snow continued to melt, the roads turned to mud. The feet of men and horses churned the surface into a thick grey-brown soup, that clogged boots and wearied legs.

The oxcarts, being near the end, were badly slowed, for the heavy-laden vehicles sunk to the axles. This required several methods of solution. First logs, sticks, stones and the like were tossed into the thick mud, to give something solid to travel over. Then, a team or two of the oxen behind were unhitched. Finally, the teams were hitched to the carts in front to drag them out of the mud which had near swallowed them.

Some of the carts to the rear were hauled up, not on the road, but on the slightly more solid ground beside the road. But all this was wet as well, so that eventually the cart wheels began to cut into that too.

Three miles ahead of where they had camped the previous night, the effects of the storm began to peter out. There the ground was less soft. Ten miles ahead, the ground was dry.

But the storm had delayed their march by a day and a half, perhaps two days.

"I WONDER," LUSI SAID in camp that evening, "if this is the kind of effect that Hrezorio warned us about,"

Thotgol started, then relaxed. Lusi was not reading his thoughts. She just thinking the kind of thing which would occur to anyone who had some knowledge of the talisman.

She noted his startlement. "You'd thought about it too?"

"Yes. There's little to go on, but I'd wondered a bit if the talisman might attract the bad weather it creates. After all, we had a snowstorm dropped right across our path."

"You don't plan to use the whirlwind immediately to see if you're right?"

He grinned. "I can control my curiosity."

"HIGHNESS, MY SCRYING shows the army of Askos has been held up by a sudden snowstorm."

"A snowstorm? Good work, Doctor."

"I will not take credit where none is due, Highness. The snowstorm was none of my doing. It seems there are strictures on the use of the Talisman of the Winds. One of which is the possibility of causing bad weather."

"Ah! So it's not the totally fearful destructive weapon we've been led to believe?"

"Oh, it is destructive, Highness, make no mistake about that. However, the controlled destruction is balanced by a certain amount on uncontrolled destruction. This uncontrolled destruction can be mitigated. But the process is not exact, and some uncontrolled destruction may occur.

"It could, indeed, be used to destroy an army. But the balancing destruction might well be prohibitive."

"I believe I understand. But if I possessed the thing, I could use it to destroy the army of Askos thoroughly. Then withdraw and let this uncontrolled destruction destroy the land, could I not? Then when the destruction had run its course, I could return and repopulate the land with my own people?"

"Possibly so, Highness, but doubtful, Wind and weather do not stop for borders."

"So then I can at least be assured the amount of destruction they can wreak on my army will be limited by their own fear of what may happen afterward?"

"That is true, Highness. And I hope to be able to interfere with their use of it at all."

"COLUMN UP AHEAD, LORD Disikomin," the scout said. "Looks to be mostly women and children, with a few warriors as guards."

"Badges?"

"Flying Raven, sir. It's Komsallit's people, all right."

"Right. They'll probably be worried and jumpy. have someone go in with truce-signs, explain who we are and that we've come to help."

"Sir!"

Lord Disikomin and his men drew nearer. It was soon apparent to them the warriors guarding the column were either old men still capable of holding a weapon, or young boys, frightened into seriousness at the responsibility laid on them.

None of these warriors relaxed. Even when they were assured this was truly Lord Disikomin, and not some trick of Narnash. It was clear they had lived in a constant state of vigilance for so long, they had begun to believe relaxation would be impossible.

The straggling line, consisted of women carrying burdens and babies, children and old folk, and a few wagons now pressed into service to carry those least able to walk. All of them slowly came to a jerky halt. A greybeard on a horse came forward to greet Disikomin. He was still upright, for all his years. He wore a very old-fashioned helmet which, might have looked ridiculous on another, lent him an air of archaic dignity.

"Lord Disikomin? I am Hadatison Arlashin. I am in charge of this group."

"Well met, Hadatison. Where is Lord Komsallit?"

The old man jerked his head back in the direction of the column behind him. "Back at the rear, leading the defence."

"Then I'll find him. Is there anything we can do for your people here?"

"Best thing you can do, lord, is get those Morkerr-eaten buggers off our necks."

"We'll do what we can. Any idea of their numbers?"

"Lord Komsallit'll be better able to tell you. From what I've heard, somewhere between five and eight thousand."

LORD KOMSALLIT HAD been a stout man with a chubby face. The man Disikomin saw, seated on a fallen log with his legs outstretched toward a near-dying fire, was a pared-down man. His clothing and armour hung loosely on him, whose face was now weathered, wrinkled and hard. It was clear the man was holding off exhaustion by little more than force of will. His dull eyes stared at Disikomin as they strained to focus.

"Seems fitting, you coming to rescue me, Diska. It was your letter started it all."

It was said without particular rancour. Perhaps because Komsallit was too weary for rancour. But his words struck all the more painfully for that. Sending those letters last year, all he he'd intended to do was cause some disaffection in Wennz. Clearer thought would have shown turmoil and conflict would be the result of it. Worse still, he'd known the probable results, but had ignored them in his determination.

He tried to stir himself out of self-condemnation. "How many back there?"

"Dark Destroyer's teeth, Diska, seems like a million! I'd guess about six thousand. They've been whittling away at us and we've been whittling away at them."

"Have your men got one more fight in them?"

It wasn't meant to be derogatory, but Komsallit came to his feet. "Chaos away with you, Disikomin Rudashin! My men and I have enough fights in us to get us where we need to go!"

"Easy, easy, Komsa, I didn't mean it that way! I think Bloody Narnash's men have been having it all their way too long. Suppose we give them a bit of something to think about."

THOTGOL WAS STILL A weapon. But now he was a weapon worthy of some degree of respect. This meant he was close by when the galloper came in seeking Lady Lusommi. "Lady, Commander Neltrahhio sends me to tell you that scouting parties from Bloody Narnash's army have come to Hellafriad! He says he is not likely to be able to hold three days without help."

Lusi turned to Aelkoriat. "Do we have even five hundred who might arrive there in time, and fit to fight?"

His face showed his doubts. "We might send five hundred mounted archers. But even with hard riding, they'd be likely arriving in time to find the place well-invested. And they wouldn't be able to break through the lines."

"Send them. Warn them that if they can't get in before the town is surrounded, they're to avoid throwing themselves away. They are to annoy Narnash if they can, and perhaps we'll be able to arrive in time."

KOMSALLIT AND HIS FORCE had taken up battle order on a hillside. It would be seen as a last desperate stand, a sacrifice in the hopes that most of the families would still escape. They had all had a little rest, some even an hour or two sleep, and stood in their determined ranks. Disikomin's men had shared some of their arrows with Komsallit's archers. They were as ready as they'd ever be. Short of having another week's sleep and a few good meals.

Narnash's commander took in the situation, and had his men take up their positions. They were all tired of this fight. Exhausted from pushing forward, clearing ambushes. Day after day of skirmish and sally and march. They would be glad of the chance to end it by sweeping this forlorn little army off the slope.

On command, they surged forward.

Grim and silent in the face of the war-cries of the charging enemy, Komsallit's men stood to their weapons. Archers began to loose their deadly shafts.

Amid their racket, none noticed the song coming faintly from beyond the hill. Nor did they notice, until it was too late altogether, the horsemen coming round the shoulder of the hill.

Narnash's commander faltered for a moment. The standard of Disikomin stood next to standards of Askos. He was under attack by the whole of the army of Askos. He sent messengers to pull his attack back, but it was too late. The messengers had barely covered a few yards when the enemy struck the flank of his main body.

He could hear the song, now, a song being sung by even the men of Askos:

"Folsidon hey! Folsidon hey!
Folsidon comes this bloody day!
Folsidon hey! Folsidon how!
Folsidon brings his vengeance now!"

They began to roll up the flank of the Wennzmen,

And if that weren't enough, a force of some two hundred mounted archers came riding hell-for-leather around the hill. They headed straight for the small group standing around the commander. The archers were hardly enough to overwhelm that force. But they were enough to harass them, and make calm assessment of the situation difficult.

Disikomin did not have enough men to utterly destroy the Wennzmen. Even adding Komsallit's force to his numbers. But given the advantage of surprise, he had enough to give them a fierce check, and make them wary.

IT WAS A BATTERED AND fearful troop, no more than thirty men, haggard and haunted, who sought Lady Lusommi's tent. They had no real leader, just one man who was willing to speak for all.

"Ghosts, lady! Spectres and fearful things! Against men we might have fought, but not these!"

"Where is your commander?"

"Commander Neltrahhio fell in the fighting, Lady."

"So there was fighting, then?"

"Oh, Lady, there was fighting! Narnash's advance party were no more than five thousand. And they came no nearer than two bowshot of the town walls at first. They set up what appeared to be a pole with a bundle of rags on the top, and waited. At nightfall, people began reporting seeing things. Horrible things, like dark headless figures carrying bloody swords. There were also ghastly old women weeping, and things which flew close overhead shrieking.

"I was on the wall, Lady, and I saw, near midnight, the approach of rank on rank of glowing green soldiers. I saw myself, Lady, three of my arrows went right through one of them without slowing him.

"It was clear there was no holding the town, Lady, so I got my horse and fled. It was not until morning that the spectres ceased to haunt us."

The man was putting the best face on his own behaviour. But there was no denying he had been through a terrifying experience.

"We sent a force to support the town. Did they arrive?"

"Lady, I know nothing of that."

"I see. Find a place to the rear, get yourselves some food and come with us."

A flicker of fear ran over the faces of the men. But Lusommi's calm determination in the clear daylight helped overcome the remembered fear of frightful things at night.

When they had gone, she turned to Aelkoriat. "So Hellafriad has fallen again. Do we assault it in our turn?"

"I'd suggest not, Lady. If Narnash's army is there, they'll block our way, and if they're not, they'd probably love to catch us surrounding the town."

New scouting parties were sent out, with fresh instructions. They ringed far forward and on all sides. They brought back constant reassurance Narnash's army seemed to be gathering at Hellafriad. But had come no further forward than that.

Another Askos horseman met with Lusommi on the road, just as her advance parties were reaching Hellafriad. He was one of the party that had been sent to try to reinforce Neltrahhio.

"Lady," he said, "we arrived too late. We had camped well off the road, and in the night we heard strange noises from the direction of the town. Our Commander thought it best not to go riding forward in the darkness. Into whatever might be happening.

"We heard men on horses flying down the road from the town, but they didn't stop. In the morning, we advanced with caution. We found some two dozen men scattered along it, clearly killed in flight. The town was held by Narnash's men, with more arriving all the time.

"There was no point in drawing attention to ourselves. So we pulled back and camped, sending out scouts to assess his forces.

"This fellow, dressed like one of Bloody Narnash's archers. He came up to our camp and handed over this chip of wood with writing on it, said it was for you.

"Since he'd come under truce, we couldn't hold him, and he went off. We moved our camp, and I was sent to bring you this, with a warning as to who brought it." He handed over the chip.

"'Narnaash haz a thowzaand horss, five thowzaand pikez, and twoo thowzaand lite infaantree. Doktur Gobnaash is witth himm. Sum Lorrds havv nott joynd himm.'" Lusi looked up. "Destroyer's teeth Aelkoriat! It's our friend!"

"It would seem to be. But what's his game? Why would he think we'd trust one of Narnash's archers?"

Lusi looked at the messenger. "Can you say anything about this?"

"Unfortunately, very little, Lady. When I left we were fairly sure that Narnash had over eight hundred horse. Near enough five thousand pikes, and over fifteen hundred light troops. But there were more coming in, and this may be a more accurate count."

"And what's the point?" demanded Aelkoriat. "Narnash would prefer to have us underestimating his force, so we come to fight. He doesn't want to frighten us off so he has to follow us far into our own territory. This," he indicated the chip with an outflung hand, "comes near to our own assessments of his forces, from various sources. And it's the number we've allowed for when gathering our own forces, so why should one of Narnash's archers tell us?"

Her horse, wanting either to be going, or to go nibble grass at the edge of the road, stirred under her. Lusi tightened her hold on the reins and gave the mare a little pat on the neck.

"I'd say we accept this for what it is, but stay watchful. Lord Disikomin found reason to leave Narnash and join us; who's to say this archer might not have done the same?"

"THEY'RE STILL HANGING back there, Komsa. But now they're in hostile territory, and foraging won't get any easier for them. They won't be moving so quickly any more."

"You sound like you're planning on taking your men and heading off Chaos away, Diska."

"Thinking about it. Near as I can guess, the real fight is going to happen up north, around Hellafriad. Lady Lusi is going to need every armed man she can get.

"I wouldn't take all my men, either. I'd leave you about half, just to keep those fellows from trying anything."

Komsallit frowned. "Not saying I'm not grateful, Diska, but I don't want to take my women and children onto a battlefield."

Disikomin waved a hand. "Wouldn't ask you to. Think about it this way. You're keeping that lot back there from joining Narnash on the battlefield. That in itself is a help to the Lady Jun-—Lusommi."

As he walked back to his own tent, he wondered "Where did that come from? Confusing Junommi with the Lady Lusommi." He shook his head. "Mind's starting to go, old fool!"

Chapter XVIII
Magic and Battle

In the dimness of morning, king Narnash watched his armies taking their formation. Each unit tramped away in columns. They jingled and rattled as they went, and formed themselves into the line they would hold. All the fine colours of his nobles did not show up so well at this hour. But then, neither did the niggling little faults among their men. The spearmen, swordsmen, and others, had only recently marched away from their farms. Twilight did not so easily betray their small ineptitudes as they would in the light of day.

But now the waiting was done, and the judgment of the battlefield would be seen. And, if Doctor Gobnash could provide what he claimed to be able to provide. They would be fighting man against man, not against that Morkerr-eaten ox-driver and his talisman.

He turned to the Doctor.

"Your various trickeries are ready, Doctor Gobnash?"

"Yes, Highness. I think they will serve our purpose. Even if my workings don't draw them to waste the power of that talisman, I have something special which will deal with it."

"Ha! Good!" The king wheeled his horse and set off for his chosen position, trailing his aides, assistants, and hangers-on behind him.

THE ARCHER SLIPPED onto the field. He had no intention of being caught up in the maneuvering of troops. Nor of being discovered by some underofficer or other. But he did want to be close enough to be able to maneuver himself into the right position, if the time ever came.

And Bloody Narnash's Army was marching itself to positions now. So there'd be little chance of him being seen here, behind the Wennzish lines. And maybe, just maybe, a clear shot at Bloody Narnash's broad back...

DAY DAWNED. THE ARMY of Narnash was a dark blur in the dimness, but the army gradually marched into view. And then-—"Fierce flying pig guts!" Thotgol muttered.

"Dark Destroyer's teeth!" echoed Aelkoriat. "How could we be so far off in assessing their numbers?"

"Even our most exaggerated estimates would barely allow for such numbers. Something's strange here!" Lusi stared at the troops in front, as if trying to make out something about them.

Aelkoriat twisted in his saddle. "You're not suggesting Doctor Gobnash has magicked this lot up out of nothing?"

"I'd say he had a lot to do with it. Send some mounted archers down there to shoot at that phalanx right in front of us. Tell them not to take any chances, but just see what happens."

He looked at her silently for a moment and nodded. Word was given, and a messenger trotted out to the Askos lines. Shortly thereafter, a band of horsemen headed out toward the phalanx.

As they approached, the phalanx opened ranks to allow a force of light slingers through. The slingers whirled their slings and let fly their shot, which appeared to have no effect on the horsemen. Arrows were flying, now, and suddenly the slingers disappeared. A moment after that, the phalanx disappeared as well.

The horsemen, after a moment's confusion, ordered their ranks and rode at the phalanx unit to their right. Arrows flew again, and again the phalanx disappeared. Then the whole front line, some two to ten men deep, shimmered and vanished.

The command group could hear shouting from the nearest Askos troops. "They don't altogether like this, Lady," Aelkoriat said. "They see an illusion banished, and wonder what other crafty tricks Doctor Gobnash might have in his pocket."

Down below, the horsemen attacked the second line of the phalanx. Once more slingers came forth to hold them off. This time, when the slingers cast their shot, men and horses went down. The remainder of the horsemen withdrew quickly, but in order.

Aelkoriat said, "Captain Tahheron, will you escort Thotgol over to that knoll on our right. Thotgol, let Tahheron advise you on where and when to use the talisman."

"Certainly." He had no intention of being a simple weapon to be set out and aimed by some other. He'd promised to let Tahheron advise him, but he hadn't promised to follow that advice, if he had a better idea.

If he'd thought his quiet acquiescence had deceived Tahheron, he was shown differently almost immediately. "I know you're going to do what you're going to do, Thotgol. Just think before you do it, and ask if perhaps you're only doing it because I've suggested you do something else."

"Am I so easy to read, then?"

Tahheron smiled grimly. "Not always, and not by anyone who doesn't know you."

NARNASH SCOWLED. "OUR Doctor Gobnash is very ineffective with his trickeries today."

His aide said, "Well, Highness, at least he'll have them wondering what else he might have in his pack."

"Or perhaps he'll have them wondering why they need to worry, if this is the best he can do?"

He turned his grim face back toward the field. "Order the advance!"

"Yes, Highness."

DOCTOR GOBNASH WAS not in the habit of frowning, though his forehead did wrinkle slightly as he saw the illusion dissipated. He shook his head slightly, a gesture which indicated that he had expected better, but no matter.

The small guard who were to protect his person while he worked his magic kept their eyes trained in other directions. Fear was a useful tool, though none of them was likely to be capable of spying on his work to any profit.

He took an object from the bag at his side. The object resembled a child's top, and he held it as such, in thumb and forefinger.

He uttered a few syllables and gave the top a flick. Like an ordinary top, it began to spin, but unlike an ordinary top, it spun in midair.

As it spun, it began to grow and glow.

Shortly, all that could be seen was a tall spinning light, about man-height, which barely disturbed the grass as it spun.

Doctor Gobnash spoke another imperative syllable. Then the glowing mass leaped away, zig-zagging forward, travelling in a series of straight-line rushes. He watched it go with a brief nod of satisfaction.

THOTGOL SURVEYED WHAT he could see of the field. Narnash seemed intent on overwhelming them, without any special maneuvers. He was, however, holding back a sizeable force of cavalry. Something Thotgol had become familiar with in listening to soldiers talk. The cavalry reserve could have several uses. Among them to strike at some weak point in the enemy's formation, or to reinforce a part of their own line which was hard-pressed.

His eye was caught by something, a glowing shape rushing across the field. It came in series of zig-zags, pausing momentarily before it changed direction. The glowing shape dashed first through Narnash's lines. Then it went through the Askos lines, disordering each momentarily, and kept on coming.

Thotgol heard Tahheron speaking, but the words were vague and far away. All his attention was caught by the spinning thing.

Suddenly, a hand caught his arm, and he was whipped away out of the world into a place where a forest was burning. They were at the edge of a stream. All around flames roared and snapped, sharp woodsmoke assaulted their nostrils. A mule snorted and stamped nearby.

Next they were back on the battlefield again, on a hillside looking out over the rear of an army. "How does a merchant make a living," grumbled Shapak-ailesh, "when he must spend half his time rescuing Batan ox-drivers?"

"I suppose my gratitude isn't welcome?"

"First things first. That *shoivompok* which Doctor Gobnash sent after you will be back on your track in a moment or two. Best use the talisman now, before it starts to enthrall you again."

Thotgol suddenly realized he was in the rear of Narnash's army. It was unfortunate Tahheron wasn't here to advise him in these new circumstance. But he should be able to do enough damage on his own. He considered aiming for Narnash first. But that wouldn't likely have the immediate effect he wanted. He pointed at the center of the phalanx. *"O wild storm wind from the Eastern sea, blow, blow, blow!"*

He was more prepared for the results this time, the wind flinging rain at the troops, even bowling some of them over. A whole section of the line was flung into chaos and disordered. He had to halt the wind very shortly, since the two armies were about to come together. But the wind would make no distinction between friend and foe. The Wennz phalanx demonstrated its training, and had nearly pulled itself together when the Askos pikes hit.

Struck first by the fierce wind, then by the enemy pikes, the center of the phalanx began to give way.

Thotgol saw force of cavalry on their way over to reinforce that potential gap. He was on the point of sending a wind against them when a glow caught his eye. The *shoivompok* was coming again. Suddenly all the sounds of battle were far away, and all his attention was on that glowing thing.

Shapak-ailesh's hand was on his arm, pulling him away. They were in the burning forest again. Wood burnt, popping and crackling around them. They stood near a rock that was radiating intense heat.

Then once again they were standing on the battlefield, still behind Narnash's lines. Thotgol turned to Shapak-ailesh. "How do we stop that thing?"

"Getting rid of Doctor Gobnash should do it. He's over there." He pointed to a group of men about fifty yards away.

Thotgol pointed, "*O Hot wind from the Southern Wastes, blow, blow, blow!*"

The wind struck, shriveling grass around the wizard's party. The guards assigned to protect Doctor Gobnash staggered. Suddenly sweltering in their armour, they began to fall. The slender figure of Doctor Gobnash turned toward them, and he, too, was blown flat. Thotgol halted the wind; the *shoivompok* wavered in his direction, then disappeared.

Thotgol looked around. The battle was joined. The phalanx he had hit first was still holding. But only because the cavalry had managed to stiffen them.

He realized he himself could not do much more damage to Narnash's force. Anything he did against the battle line would effect Askos troops as much as Wennz. Thotgol wondered about striking at Narnash himself, or some of his reserves. He muttered, "Now that I need Tahheron's advice, I can't get to him."

"Do you really want to?"

"I don't know. If I were there, I'd be out of range of most-—Watch out!"

The party of horsemen, no more than two dozen, had come up over the reverse slope of the knoll. Whether some cavalry commander had sent them on an errand. Or whether Narnash himself had spotted Thotgol and Shapak-ailesh and had sent them specially, Thotgol never knew. Their initial approach had been hidden in the sounds of battle, and now they were almost on top of the two.

Almost without conscious thought, Thotgol shouted *"O wild whirlwind, go against these riders!"*

Then he dropped to the ground as arrows whipped overhead. Then he dropped to the ground as arrows whipped overhead. Once more the tiny, inconsequential whirlwind started in the grass before him. Once more it grew in strength as it raced toward the enemy, to fling horses and men aside.

He turned. Shapak-ailesh was lying on the grass, an arrow sticking straight up from his shoulder.

The little man was unconscious; the arrow had gone through his shoulder right by the joint. Thotgol broke the point off, and pulled the shaft back through. "Just as well you're not awake for this. It's not something you'd want to feel."

He searched in the mule's packs, and found some cloth, which he tore into strips for bandages. "I hope this isn't some rare and expensive magical fabric."

He'd finished wrapping the shoulder when he heard a foot whisper in the grass behind him. He was on his feet in an instant, whipping the ox-goad from his belt. Four men, battered and dazed and more than half-mad, were coming at him with swords. The remnants, he realized, of the troop he had destroyed with the whirlwind. These few, driven beyond fear, gathered themselves for one more effort to find revenge. Or perhaps, to strike back.

Well, they were too close to use the talisman; he'd just have to see how good a fighter he was.

NARNASH LOOKED OUT over the battlefield. The accursed winds had done their work altogether too well for his comfort. He'd had to use some of the cavalry reserve to shore up the phalanx. Whatever trickeries Doctor Gobnash had been hatching were finished. Had he survived? A part of the king's mind said that death was only the expected price for his failure. Another said that the Doctor would be needed even more badly after this day.

So, where was the best place to send in his remaining forces?

There was a stirring behind him, and faint and far away a song was being sung by many men.

He looked over at his aide. "What's that?"

"Highness, we're being attacked from behind!"

"What?" Without awaiting an answer, he pulled his horse around and pushed through the ranks to see.

"Dark Destroyer's teeth!" A line of troops, including horse, phalanx, and light troops was coming up. In the midst were the banners of Disikomin and Komsallit, along with some from Askos.

They weren't enough to destroy him, just enough to force him to use up his reserve. If he were lucky, he'd be able to pull some sort of draw out of this. And what was that bloody song they were singing, anyway?

FINE YELLOW DUST ROSE up over the line of battle, so anything beyond it was seen, if at all, as dim shapes.

"Can't see for all this muck, but Narnash's reserve still seems to be in the same position. I'm going to take out cavalry and see if I can draw him off.

Lusommi turned to Aelkoriat and said, "Go ahead." She was queen, and in theory, had the ultimate say, but she knew her limitations in military matters. Besides, Aelkoriat's notion was sound.

She continued to watch the battle. Even at this distance, it was impossible to ignore the fact that down there men were fighting, killing, and dying. She had managed, some time ago, to deal with her share of the responsibility for it. Surely the rule of Bloody Narnash justified extreme measures to remove his heavy hand from their necks?

But that barely made the results of battle any less awful, the widowed, the fatherless children, the crippled.

Lusommi had some idea of how the battle was going. Narnash's phalanx had not completely recovered from the wind. They had only been saved from complete destruction by the cavalry reinforcements.

They were holding the Askos phalanx, fighting desperately, a mass of men on horse and afoot. They no longer fought with the cohesion of the properly-formed phalanx. On Lusommi's side, the Askos phalanx was firm and steady. Was that the result of Disikomin's cadres, or simply the result of another year's training and experience? Lusommi reflected that, according to the public, where she placed credit would depend on who she was talking to.

"Lady! Lady! News, Lady!"

A horseman on a panting horse came galloping up. A mixture of dust and sweat streaked both man and beast, and the rider pulled the horse to a stamping halt by her side. The man's expression was triumphant. "Lady, Commander Neforio sends to tell you that the standard of Lord Disikomin has been sighted in Narnash's rear! They appeared about to engage Narnash himself!"

"Well done. What's your name?"

"Hanorio h'Solkat, Lady."

"Get yourself some water and rest, Hanorio. You've earned it."

"Thank you, Lady!"

She was trying desperately to remember which of her commanders was Neforio. She knew the name, knew it quite well, but was unable to put a face to it. And as Queen, she dared not admit to anyone around her that her memory was at fault. She slapped a gloved hand on the saddlebow. She had to still her horse, at which point she realized everyone was wondering who or what had offended her. The ridiculousness of it all made her smile. Men were dying down there, and up here, people were wondering what had offended her.

There was abrupt movement on the right. The lines of battle were moving. The Wennzmen were being pushed back. Suddenly, between one instant and the next, the whole wing was breaking up and fleeing!

The people around her began to cheer. No, the battle was not completely done. But it was now a matter of whether she would have a victory, or an overwhelming victory.

THE SCRAP OF BRUSH was little cover. But the archer had occasionally bragged, "Give me a flat field and a single dandelion growing in the middle, and I'll hide myself."

Faintly behind him he heard the sound of singing. What mad bugger was singing on a battlefield?

There was a mighty stir among the horsemen up on the field. Leaving Bloody Narnash himself, staring out at the singing, as if it were bad news.

The King pushed his helmet back to get a better view. The archer went into action, a series of well-drilled movements. The arrow drew back. His body adjusted automatically for the uphill shot and the wind. Then he loosed the arrow.

He dropped himself into the fold in the ground next to the bush's root, just as some wildly singing horsemen went riding around him. He wondered if they'd even seen him, or if they'd been so fixed on Narnash they'd missed his small movements.

Chapter XIX
Aftermath

Amessenger was escorted into Lusi's tent. "Lady, Thotgol has been found!"

"Is he alive?"

"Oh, yes. I've a feeling that one would take some killing. It's said he was found on the field, behind Narnash's lines, with a half-dozen or so enemy dead around him. That little merchant was with him, also wounded, and the pair of them are in the Healers' tents."

"Thank you. Now, would you please find Captain Tahheron and give him the word?"

Tahheron had been chagrined at having Thotgol whipped away from his guard. Though patently there had been little he could do about it. And he had said he had a feeling Shapak-ailesh had been rescuing him from something. *'He was standing staring at that glowing thing, Lady, and he didn't hear a word I said.'*

But it didn't change the fact the ox-driver had been under Tahheron's care, and had disappeared somewhere. That Thotgol was alive would be small comfort to Tahheron; he ought not to have been wounded at all.

"I'm going over to the Healers' tents," she told her entourage. It wasn't that she was particularly concerned about Thotgol, she told herself. But she had a duty to at least show herself to the men who had been wounded in her service.

She looked around. It still felt strange not to have Aelkoriat's quiet presence with her. He'd led the attack, and she understood he'd been killed in the first shock, but the cavalry had carried on to do their job. Her entourage now included some who, with fervent apologies for missing the battle, swore they were eternally loyal to her.

She was on the edge of telling them all that Morrkerr Deathlord would eat her before she favoured any of them. But years of training held her tongue. She'd need them, so she acted as though she were pleased with them, quietly noting them all. She'd make use of them, and be sure for every little favour she did them, they'd give some real service!

THOTGOL WAS CONSCIOUS, though very pale. He smiled at the sight of her. "Ah, Lovely Lady Lusi of the Fair Locks! You have come to comfort the last hours of the lost Prince of Batan-ji!"

She heard some of the shocked voices behind her. How did a Batan ox-driver, Talisman or no, dare be so familiar! She ignored those noises, and snorted at Thotgol's foolishness. "Last hours! I'm told that, barring wound fever, none of your hurts are likely to be mortal. And you probably wouldn't have been hurt at all if you hadn't gone gallivanting off without your guards."

"Ah, the Misfortunate Thotgol! Always misunderstood! I was taken away by main force from the battle, where a certain small merchant fancied me to be endangered by some sort of spinning light."

"Fancied you endangered!" No one had noticed Shapak-ailesh until then. But there he was, just inside the door, sitting up, and looking much better than Thotgol, despite his bandaged shoulder.

"Who was standing there like a stunned rabbit when I took him away?"

"And who managed to stand in the way of an arrow so he couldn't get us out of real danger?"

Lusi allowed herself a smile. "If the two of your are well enough to bicker like this, I'll just go visit some people who were actually hurt. But to be serious, I thank you for what you've done."

She had been careful not to rush to see Thotgol first, nor to leave him to the last. Though she was fairly certain rumours would be passing. As she was walking to the next tent, a small party of horsemen approached. There were three of her own cavalry, with another horse bearing a body thrown over the saddle.

"Lady?" said one of the three riders. "We've been seeking you."

"What is it?"

"We've found something on the battlefield that we think you might want to see."

The horseman swung himself down from his horse. He pulled the corpse off, staggering a bit with the weight, and laid it down on the ground. She suspected if she'd been a man, he'd just have heaved it off and let it fall before her.

The body was that of an older man. His clothing and armour fitting to a person of rank. He bore the Crowned Bear of Narnash of Wennz. A broken-off arrow-shaft stuck out of his right eye.

"It's Bloody Narnash himself, Lady. He took an arrow in the eye, and a Wennzish arrow at that. One of his archers had bad aim, it seems."

One of the man's companions spoke up. "Not necessarily, Lady. Disikomin attacked Narnash's cavalry reserve."

"Destroyer's teeth!" said the first spokesman. "Lady, you're likely to be seeing every man who has ever thought of drawing a bow coming to you for a reward!"

"Your name, soldier?"

"Gevassio h'Noktor, Lady."

"Gevassio, you and your companions present yourselves to me tomorrow. You deserve a reward for this. In the meantime, bury the body."

They hesitated a moment. "No," she said, I'm not going to say I didn't hate him, nor that his death saddens me. But he's dead, and dishonoring his body is a petty thing to do. And Gevassio? Make sure a good number of our people see the body. I want it well-known he is dead. I want no big men making trouble by claiming to be the real Narnash Skalsland."

"Yes, Lady."

SHE LOOKED AROUND THE well lit tent at the men gathered to give her advice. They would all discuss matters, and in the end, she would make up her mind what to do. It was always best if she could end up with most of them agreeing her decision was the most favourable. But that was not strictly a necessary condition.

"Well, the battle is won, and we must now make a decision on our next action. We can be sure of some sort of peace with Wennz for the next few years, while the various lords decide who should replace him. But do we wait for that?"

There was quiet for a bit, then a young man, Kwadahheron h'Nevis, spoke up. "And they recruit and rearm and attack again! I say we crush them now!"

'Wardesh love you, Kwadahheron, you couldn't have done better if I'd planted you to say that!'

"That is a possibility, for certain. We could press forward and conquer Wennz while they're disordered. Then establish a new kingdom of Wennz-Askos. It is possibly even the most desirable action.

"Are there any other suggestions?"

"Do we want to push the war further?" Shanorio h'Aelofat was an older man. The scars on his arms and face testified to the fact he had fought, in his time, "If we press on, they will almost certainly give over deciding who is to replace Narnash until they have fought us again. Continuing the war is going to cost us, both in gold and blood."

Kwadahheron was quick to reply, "And we'll pay the cost with Wennzish gold!"

Someone else called, "And what will be the value of Wennzish gold if it's bought with too much Askos blood?"

The argument was well away then. It ranged over the comparative populations. Wennz with its expansive empire and Askos, which was diminutive in size. They argued about how difficult—or easy—it would be for Askos to impose its will on Wennz.

That was the trouble with councils, Lusi reflected. They required everyone who had an opinion be allowed to voice it. Even when some opinions were close to absurdity.

Nor was it a simple matter of allowing them to speak. Then making up her own mind and making a decision which ran counter to most opinions present. Her decision must be expressed in such a way it appeared to be based on most of the opinions present. And Destroyer's teeth, how she missed Aelkoriat!

Finally, she raised her hand. The men who had been leaning forward to add force to their arguments straightened again, and waited for her to speak.

"War is not something to be undertaken lightly. However, knowing Wennz attitudes as we do, we can predict that, in five years' time, whoever rules Wennz will be looking in our direction again.

"It would be sensible, then, for us to choose our time to fight, rather than wait for them to recover and recruit.

"Further, there is a great deal to be said for advancing now, when we have the spoils presently taken to make the financial burden easier." She paused.

"We will advance on Wennz as soon as may be. We should be on the road by the day after tomorrow. Make the necessary preparations."

"One thing more, lords." Lusommi waited, making sure she had their attention. "We will advance on Wennz, we will fight Wennzish armies, and we will defeat them. But we will not terrorize the people. Yes, there will be Wennzmen who find it difficult to live under an Askos Queen. If necessary, they will be punished. But there will be no casual killings or extortions from Wennzmen simply because they are Wennzmen. Justice for Askos will be justice for Wennz as well.

"I will not be known as Bloody Lusommi."

THE CAPITAL OF WENNZ was alive with rumours. One true fact was Doctor Gobnash had been seen in the city. Most took this as a sign Narnash was dead and his army beaten. Some suggested it meant Narnash had been so victorious as to no longer need the wizard in the field with him. But few believed that.

Halnash Naslund was chosen for his lack of imagination to serve as viceroy during the absence of the king. He steadfastly refused to accept rumours, waiting for some undeniable word. He had a private interview with Doctor Gobnash, rather unsatisfying to both parties.

"Well, Doctor Gobnash, what are the facts of the matter?"

"The army was well on the way to being beaten when I left. the King is certainly dead."

"Have you proof of his death?" (He did not quite have the nerve to ask why the Doctor had deserted his master.)

"Proof? The fellow who uses the talisman has more luck than is natural. The army was in desperate straits when I came away. I have scried for Narnash since I arrived back, and saw him lying with an arrow in his eye. I think you had best assume you are the ruler of Wennz."

'And why did you leave the army, Doctor Gobnash?' He could not bring himself to ask that. Nor to voice a further concern. It had been known for the wizard to stir people into unwise actions, at which time they would be reported to the King and dealt with. And because all his suggestions were so oblique, the Doctor was able to escape any blame.

True, this suggestion was not an oblique one. But Halnash was not about to make some declaration, only to have Bloody Narnash come marching back from the dead and deal with him in the usual manner.

He shook his head. "I had best wait for certain news."

"You wish me to show you what I have seen in my scrying bowl?"

"No, I think not." Which was as close as he cared to come to telling the Doctor he wouldn't trust any magical vision Gobnash might show him. "I will wait for some sure word."

THE ARMY OF ASKOS WAS on the march. The long columns of men and horses were strung out along the roads, throwing up a plume of fine dust. Scouts were out to the front and all sides. Everyone knew the Army of Wennz was beaten and withdrawing. But everyone preferred not to take chances.

When they camped that evening, a fine, mizzling rain was beginning to fall. Furthermore, when they reached the site for the night's camp, Shapak-ailesh and Thotgol were waiting for them. Lusommi rode up to them.

"Ought you not to be back there resting?" she demanded.

He grinned. "O, the Misfortunate Thotgol! He makes a supreme effort to accompany Lusi of the Fair Locks, only to have her object to his presence!"

"You were left behind so that you could recover, fool! What good will you be to anyone if you wear yourself out marching?"

"Ah, but if you'll forgive my absence from your retinue for a day or so, I will not wear myself out with marching. Pining for Fair Lusi, perhaps, but not marching."

"You realize you're scandalizing all my nobles, don't you? Sometime, one of them is likely to try to give you the whipping they think you deserve and I have already lost too many Lords." She turned to those with her.

"All of you, hear this, and pass the word to those who might not be here. If the time comes for Thotgol to be punished for anything, I will give definite orders. Anyone who attempts to do harm to Thotgol without my direct orders should think carefully as to whether or not he has served me half so well and faithfully as has Thotgol."

She turned back to Thotgol, who was frowning.

"I really don't need to hide behind you, Lady Lusi."

"And I really don't need to lose either you or some misguided follower of mine, perhaps both. Wennz is not likely to kneel and beg our mercy as the result of one fight, is it?"

THE RAIN CONTINUED overnight and the next day. Neither strengthening nor weakening but continuing a cool and steady drizzle. By the end of the day, tempers were frayed. Commanders at all levels were busy heading off quarrels before they became fights.

No dry wood was to be had for making fires. But some of the more powerful talismans of fire-lighting could start even damp wood with some effort. So those with such talismans were kept busy.

Between that and carrying torches sheltered in jugs from one camp to another, nearly everyone had a fire of some sort. Though even the best of them were smoky and stubborn, requiring constant tending.

When Thotgol spoke with Lusi that evening, he asked for a word with her in private. She dismissed her aides, followers, and hangers on. They expressed shock and horror, but departed in face of her determination.

"I wasn't able to call the counterbalancing winds on the day of the battle," he said, "and I used the whirlwind again. This weather may be my fault."

"Fault? You were wounded and unconscious for most of the day. How is it your fault?" Lusi looked at him gently.

He shook his head. "I know. Circumstances didn't permit it, and I couldn't control the circumstances. But still, we may be suffering as a result of what I've done. And the fact I couldn't help it is only small comfort."

"Well, don't work yourself into a stew over it." She smiled, "Can't you see the stone over your grave? *Here is the Misfortunate Thotgol, who could not be done in by all the trickeries of Doctor Gobnash or Bloody Narnash. But finally managed to worry himself to death.*"

Which brought a smile from him.

"Now, before all my noble followers are too thoroughly scandalized, I'd better rejoin them. Do you think I should disarrange my clothing a bit before I go, just to give some of them fits?" She shook her head. "No, that would be too cruel."

THE MIZZLING RAIN STAYED with them for two more days. By which time they were marching on roads already churned up by the Wennzish troops withdrawing in front of them. The sticky mud pulled at feet and legs, wearing and wearying men and horses alike.

A horseman from one of the scouting parties came in to report. Mud and water glistened grey on his horse, himself, and his hooded rain-cape. "The enemy are still withdrawing, Lady. They've left a scattering of rear-guards and patrols to make sure we can't come up on them without warning.

"People in the local villages say only about one in three of them still carry arms. I wouldn't take that as Wardesh's own truth, Lady. But we do know a lot of them did leave their weapons on the battlefield to flee the faster."

"Thank you. Find a fire and rest yourself and your horse for the night before you go out again."

When the man had gone, she turned to Shanorio. "How hard can we press them?"

He shook his head. "In this weather, Lady, not much at all."

"The rain is falling on Wennzmen too."

"And they are ahead of us, leaving the trail in hideous condition for a march, much less a forced march."

She frowned. She frowned. Unfortunately, he was correct. And if not completely correct, than so close to it that it hardly mattered. "So. We will continue to march, and though we will not try to force the march, we will not slack off either. It would be preferable to press them to the extent that they have scant time to rearm. Even if they do reach one of their magazines."

ON THE FOURTH EVENING, the rain petered out, and the next morning shone bright and fair. That bode well for the march, but by evening it was sweltering. The strain of marching through boggy roads carrying armour and packs under a steady heat wore on the men. Even the knowledge that the Wennzmen were marching through similar conditions was of little comfort.

The day after that, Thotgol joined them for most of the march, and it remained sweltering hot.

One of Lusi's coterie, a bull-necked broad-faced fellow named Banorio mentioned that evening in Thotgol's presence, "I've heard men grumbling about your talisman. They're wondering why you don't use it to call a little cooler weather."

Thotgol glanced at him. "I assume you explained to him it doesn't work like that?"

The other shrugged. "I couldn't. You're the one who knows how it works."

Thotgol gave him a steady look. "Seems to me you were at the fight last year, weren't you?"

"Yes, I was." The man was leaning forward a little, ready to leap on any word which sounded like an insult.

"So you heard me explain the use of the talisman before the battle. So I ask you again, why didn't you explain it to him?"

"Are you saying I'm a liar? Destroyer's Teeth, if you are, you won't hide behind the Lady Lusommi!"

"No, I won't call you a liar. Just dumb as a boot. Since you can't remember something which was said so recently. And something very important, at that."

The man was pulling his sword when Shanorio stepped forward. "No foolishness, either of you. Banorio, you're looking for a fight, and if you want, I'll call you stupid too. And will you call me out?

"And as for you, Thotgol, you're being stupid yourself. No matter how you explain something complicated and magical to a soldier, all he'll understand is that it's complicated and magical, and that you have your own selfish reasons for not doing what he wants.

"Now, there's to be no fighting on this march, save between us and the Wennz. You understand that?"

Banorio muttered an agreement, and Thotgol nodded sharply.

Lusommi said, "Shanorio's right. No fighting among ourselves. Now, are there any important reports to be made? If not, you're all dismissed."

And as they left, she felt very charitable towards Shanorio, for his quick thinking and action.

THE NEXT DAY, SHE BEGAN to feel less charitable toward him. The roads were becoming more solid, yet he refused to press the march any harder. "In this heat, Lady, we're already losing men. We push the march harder, we'll lose more men."

She glowered at him. "And the Wennzmen can gather another army to outnumber ours if we allow them to go at their own pace. Will we fight another murdering battle such as the last one, and what will be left of us after?"

"Or if we lose one in three of our own, and come up on them with half our men ready to drop, what good will it do? I won't give such orders, Lady."

Unspoken was the corollary she might, but it would be against his advice. Lusommi was tempted to go against that advice. But told herself Shanorio had the greater expertise in these matters.

However it went, the Wennzish Army was likely to get away from them.

After another four days, the weather ameliorated. It took considerable time, however, for the mood of the Army to ameliorate.

There was a storm, however, marching along well to the north of them, almost as if it were keeping pace with them.

After two days of good weather, a scout reported from the patrols keeping track of the Wennzish Army. "From all we can tell, Lady, they're getting more and more organized. We hear they've got parties of horsemen around rounding up all the deserters and stragglers. We still hear about one in three of them are armed."

"Are we overtaking them at all?"

He shook his head. "Not really, Lady. We've seen their rearguards from a distance, and occasionally exchanged arrows with their scouts. But as for coming up on the main body, no."

When the scout had been dismissed, she turned to Shanorio. "How much faster can we move?"

(One didn't ask Shanorio *'Can we move faster?'* The answer would be *'No.'*)

He frowned. It was a difficult thing, getting used to his dour pessimism after Aelkoriat's quiet confidence. "We can always move faster, Lady, but if they're determined not to let us come up to them, likely we won't."

"What about at least sending horsemen up to harass their rear guard?"

"We might do that," he admitted. "But it would be a risk to the horsemen."

"It's a risk we'll have to take, then. Not all our horsemen, for sure. But enough mounted archers to be able to protect themselves if the enemy suddenly turn on them. Will you give the orders?"

"If you wish, Lady."

DOCTOR GOBNASH LOOKED the man over, maintaining his usual lack of expression. Since joining Narnash, Dalthorio h'Anovoto had taken on Wennzish dress and customs. But on occasion, when he was unaware of being observed, there was a nervous, hunted, quality to his expression.

"What can I do for you, Doctor Gobnash?"

"It is more a matter of what I can do for you. The Army of Askos, with the Lady Lusommi at its head, is marching on us."

"You're certain?"

"I am quite certain bird-messengers from the frontier will be arriving by tomorrow, bearing news of the King's defeat and death."

"Destroyer's Teeth!"

"Yes, indeed. It is also certain a strong man must now take control, to save what remains of the Kingdom. The viceroy is not capable of taking the required actions. Even when he receives definite word of the circumstances, he will waste time fiddling with this and that until the Army of Askos is on us. At that time he will take little more decisive action than to ask what terms they will offer for surrender."

Doctor Gobnash could see Dalthorio took the point. Lusommi's terms would include the immediate surrender of Dalthorio.

"You have something in mind, Doctor Gobnash?"

"Yes. I propose you should take the throne. I will support you fully in this, and see to it your orders are obeyed. If the battle against her is not successful, you can at least demand the right to go into exile."

Dalthorio was not entirely stupid. "And what do you get out of this? Particularly if I am exiled?"

"Now, that is thinking of the worst possible circumstances. We may well be able to negotiate a peace which sees Wennz losing only a portion of territory. However, you know how I am regarded in Askos. If I am under your protection, the very worst which might happen is that I would be exiled along with you.

"But that, of course, is the worst of circumstances, and we shall plan on your being King of Wennz. Though it will be a Wennz with constricted borders."

"Are we not moving a little ahead of circumstances here? How will the Wennzish Lords take to having an Askos king?"

"I think I can assure you they will accept you, so long as I stand behind you. They may grumble, but after I make an example or two, they will fall in line.

He was just as pleased Dalthorio did not think to ask why choose him rather than any other Wennzish lord. For the answer to that was he could be more certain of his control over Dalthorio, who had no other base of support.

Chapter XX
The Border and Across

Yellow lamplight flickered in the tent as Shanorio reported to Lusommi. "We can't move faster, Lady. We began the march fully supplied from the magazines of Hellafriad. The delays we have encountered have forced us to use up those supplies, and to a great degree, we are now living off the land. This means that the march, of necessity, is slowed."

"And what are the Wennzmen living on? I doubt they brought many supply-carts away from the field."

"Lady, they have been foraging from the beginning. Which makes it all the more difficult for us to find food in their wake."

"So you are saying that we will not be able to bring them to battle before they have had a day or so to rearm, and quite possibly to bring in fresh troops?"

"We can only do what we can do, Lady."

She had always managed to avoid voicing comparisons between Shanorio and Aelkoriat. But sometimes it was difficult.

She finally said, "At the very least, we'll have the advantage of knowing that we've beaten them once already this year. And a good many of them will have that fact in their minds as well."

'Aelkoriat would have said that; why didn't you, Shanorio?

He only nodded. "Will there be anything else, Lady?"

"No. Thank you for your time."

She watched him leave, careful not to show by gesture or facial expression that she was displeased. Ordering this group of proud and temperamental hill-chiefs and lordlings for battle was difficult enough. She didn't need any of them taking into their heads that they could disobey Shanorio because he did not have the full confidence of the Lady Lusommi.

DOCTOR GOBNASH LOOKED around the room. The lords were all on edge. The doctor had summoned them, but had sent individual summonses to all of them. They clearly thought he'd wanted to see them individually. And as for the reason? Well, even the ones who had little in the way of royal aspirations would not want to risk the spite of Doctor Gobnash.

He spoke. "I thank you all for coming. As you will have heard by now, messenger birds have come in from the frontier announcing the defeat and death of King Narnash. It is necessary to choose someone to rule in his stead."

He paused. "I have decided to support the Lord Dalthorio."

As expected, there was a moment's silence, then uproar. Even the ones who had not had royal aspirations had bartered their support to one candidate or another. All were caught off guard. Certainly none of them were willing to accept an Askos turncoat.

Finally one stepped forward out of the crowd, shaking his fist and declaring, "No Wennzman will serve under the likes of that Askos scum! We—"

His voice broke off as Doctor Gobnash made a gesture with his hand. The Wennzish lord clutched at his throat as his face purpled, then a moment later he fell and lay still.

Sudden silence came over the room. "Are there any other objections? King Dalthorio is willing to be merciful to all who will swear to follow him.

"Now, who will be the first to swear fealty? Or who will be the next example?"

"THEY'RE WAITING FOR us, Lady."

Was she hearing a note of reproach in the scout's voice, or was it her imagination? Not that the scout, tired, dusty, and weatherbeaten, might feel cause for reproaching the Army of Askos for allowing the Wennzish Army the time to prepare itself, but he would not likely show that reproach before her.

"Have they managed to re-arm?"

"Not altogether, Lady, but they will likely manage that in the next day or so. They've got food, though, and they've got about five hundred fresh troops."

"Thank you. Find yourself some food and drink and a place to rest. I may wish you to take a message to your commander."

"Yes Lady."

Not for the first time, she exerted a good deal of self-control to prevent herself from publicly shouting at Shanorio. Who else could she have chosen in his place? All the others had their own faults: touchy temper, brash overconfidence, lack of experience. And indeed, it was too late now to take the command directly into her own hands. The eve of battle was not the time to disrupt the leadership entirely.

She spoke again. "Thotgol."

"Yes, Lady."

"Will you be ready to use the talisman again?" Lusi asked, *'Foolish question!'*

"Yes, Lady."

"Given the weather we have marched through to get here, you'd best do what you can to ameliorate the after-effects." She cautioned, *'I'm talking for the benefit of the rest, Thotgol; you know all this.'*

And he understood exactly what was going on, for he bowed slightly and said, without smile or grin, "Yes, Lady, I'll do my best."

THE WENNZISH ARMY WAS formed up in a line. The right flank anchored by a small knoll. The left protected by a force of light cavalry.

"We have to keep in mind, Lady, that from this distance we can only see the men themselves. Not the state of their arms and armour, and certainly not inside their heads. There will be no way, outside of actual battle, to discover how much or how little effect the previous lost battle and the loss of their king will have on them."

Now, with the enemy across the field from them, Shanorio had become decisive. He had issued brief but clear orders for the Askos line of battle. A line with one flank protected by a force of light troops, the other bearing the bulk of the cavalry.

Lusi was almost ready to forgive him for the lackadaisical pursuit, but not quite.

"Thotgol," Shanorio said, "Can you use the talisman against a section of the center of their line, just before the two forces meet? We might well be able to break through the line, and bring in a force of cavalry to make use of the breach."

Thotgol nodded. "Right."

"Rumour has it that three lords had cooperated to bring the Wennzish retreat to the frontier. And that two of them have agreed to accept the authority of the third during this battle. I suspect that this third, whoever he is, has plans for making this battle the beginning of his attempt to seize the crown of Wennz."

Shanorio swept his eye over the enemy line, and his own dispositions. "Order the advance. Thotgol, would you please make ready? I'll expect you to decide the time for yourself."

"Right."

Lusi wondered if it was only in the sight of the enemy that Shanorio could be so firm and decisive.

The army of Askos began to advance. The Wennzish army responded by beginning their own ragged and fitful advance. *'Maybe Shanorio was wrong about battle being the only way to assess the state of Wennzish morale.'*

But after a few paces, the commanders had brought order into the Wennzish line, and they came on steadily. Arrows and slung stones flew in both directions. Soldiers went down on both sides. Neither side wavered.

Then Thotgol called the full power of the North Wind on the center of the line. It was a little less effective than it had been against horsemen. But for all that, the center was completely disordered. Though commanders worked and swore, the formation was still ragged when the two forces came together.

As the battle joined, the section that had been hit by the wind struggled to hold its cohesion. Maybe it was the wind, the memory of the last battle. Or perhaps both. After a brief attempt at battle, that part of the army gave ground. Then it gave ground once more, until the arm finally turned to flee.

The calvary drove toward the gap. They bore down on the rear of the force to the left of the gap. While the infantry were already wheeling to the right to roll up the line in the other direction.

A Wennzish commander had seen the danger, at the time the wind had descended. He was leading a force of his own cavalry to retrieve the situation, if possible. (It was not known until afterward that he had led that force himself.)

For all his efforts, though, he was too late. Shanorio had held back another force of cavalry who were sent through the gap. This second force distracted the Wennzmen from the first cavalry force. The first cavalry force, after a brief difficulty negotiating the area where the North wind had struck, took the enemy in the rear. With this attack the Wennzish line began to unravel.

The second cavalry force delayed the Wennzish reinforcements just long enough. The Wennzish army was breaking up, more and more of them turned to flee.

In the end, after a great slaughter of Wennzish cavalry, much of the Wennzish phalanx still held. They formed into a rough square, with pikes presented on all sides.

"THEY OUGHT TO HAVE been destroyed!" raged Kwadahheron h'Nevis, his voice harsh in the crowded pavilion.

"To what purpose?" enquired Shanorio, calmly. Mutterings and murmurings of one to another of the lords around them rose and fell like the sound of the sea, as soft lamplight winked on polished gems and metal.

"To what purpose?" echoed Kwadahheron. Because they are armed, and they are Wennzmen! Is that not purpose enough?"

"We've had many years now when Wennzmen could oppress Askos simply because they were Askos. If we get to killing Wennzmen only because they're Wennzmen, we're starting down a rough path. And one that has an unsure ending. There are still more Wennzmen than Askos."

"All the more reason to finish them! And we've beaten them once, we'll beat them again!"

"And if they ambush patrols and cut off foraging parties, and wear us down bit by bit?"

"We burn their villages and slaughter their herds!" The young man was leaning forward slightly in his intensity, almost as though ready to spring like a cat.

"Thereby making ourselves even more beloved. No. It's done, the phalanx has surrendered, given up their arms, and are being allowed to return to their homes. Each of them knows that if they are taken in arms against us again, their lives are forfeit."

"Agreed." Lusommi spoke up. "Kwadahheron, the matter has already been decided. Arguing over what has been done is futile. What we need now is decide what to do next.

"The lord in charge of the Wennzish army died in the battle. Seems his name was Dungarash, a name I'm not familiar with. But at any rate, he left them pretty much leaderless. None of the other petty commanders is willing to take the responsibility of surrendering on behalf of Wennz. It would seem to me that we must march on Wennz until we reach their capital.

"Is there any argument on that?"

There was. Lord Vasario d'Goriat spoke. He was a man of loud opinions. He also had a following which, although small, was still large enough that his opinions required to be heard. "Lady, we have marched far and beaten two Wennzish armies. Wennz is no longer a threat to us. Let us go home."

Kwadahheron was quick to respond. "I don't agree with much of what Shanorio has said, but he is correct in one thing. The Wennzmen outnumber us. If we go home now, in a few years' time some new Wennzish king will have gathered a large enough army to send against us again. We must at least make an attempt to see that any Wennzish kingdom that is set up is less of a threat to us."

"Thank you, Kwadahheron, for your support," said Shanorio, "There is at least one more reason for us to march on Wennz. Doctor Gobnash is still alive."

There was more murmuring. "This is certain?" There was a touch of fear in Lord Vasario's voice. "He was on the battlefield where Narnash was slain, and Thotgol smote him with winds."

"This is true. However, his body was not found afterward. I for one, will assume he is still living until I know differently."

"Thank you, Shanorio," Lusommi said. "I agree. We will march as soon as possible."

THE WENNZISH LORDS came in sullen answer to the summons of their king. Most would have ignored the summons altogether, save for the knowledge that Doctor Gobnash stood behind King Dalthorio, as he had stood behind king Narnash.

Speaking in whispers and low mutters, they tried to guess at why they had been called together.

King Dalthorio sat on his throne before them, a nervous frown on his face. Doctor Gobnash stood behind him, and to his left.

Finally, Doctor Gobnash stepped forward. His plain sand-coloured robes standing in contrast to the mass of colours that were the lords.

"You have been called together for a particular purpose. Look, and learn!"

He snapped his fingers. The door behind the throne opened. Through the doorway floated the supine body of a man, floating on air, hands at his sides. It was followed by another and another, five in all.

There was little sign of the kind of death they had died. But they themselves were recognized by many in the audience. There was more than one murmur of "Dark Destroyer's teeth!"

"These five," announced Doctor Gobnash, "were found to be in conspiracy against their king. As such, they have died. Let all the rest of you take this lesson and learn from it. What you do in secret may not truly be secret."

The line of bodies continued to float through and amongst the gathered lords, so that all could see them. The lords themselves moved back from the corpses to avoid touching, or even being near them. They then floated back out the door through which they had come in, and the door closed softly behind them again.

Doctor Gobnash then said, "I am sure you will all understand the the King will suffer no treason. You are dismissed."

When the last of the lords had filed silently out, Doctor Gobnash turned to Dalthorio. "Now, this lesson has required such a concentration of my powers that many other things have had to be let slide. I think we can count on the lesson to hold, at least in the short term. During that time, there are certain measures I must take. I shall present a list of the materials I need, and you will sign the authority to purchase them. Is that agreeable, Highness?"

LUSOMMI AND THE ASKOS commanders were met in the main gate of the city by a tall, slim, and grey-haired man. He wore a long-sleeved robe of green as befit his station.

Lusommi acknowledged him. "Chief Magistrate of Gorron"

"There is no point, Lady." The Chief Magistrate's eyes, once defiant were now showing their weariness. "No point at all in all the traditional fiddle-faddle of requiring you to demand our surrender. Making you wait while we pretend to consult the matter. What troops we had were pulled away to fight in that useless battle. And while we might have manned the walls, that would merely have made our fate the worse. I can only ask that your terms be merciful."

Lusommi stood appraising him, "I see no point, nor any merit, in destroying your city, nor even in burdening it unduly. We will want ten pounds of gold from each of your chief citizens, and one for each citizen. According to your most recent census."

The Magistrate flinched. "Lady you speak of not burdening us unduly. Such a cost will bid fair to reducing the whole city to penury!"

"Magistrate, I have a fair understanding of how well-off your city is. Suppose I make you a bargain; you have three days. For each day before that day, you may may subtract twenty pounds of gold. For each day after, add one copper per citizen."

"Lady—-"

She cut him off with a wave of her hand. "I make no further bargains. Take this, or leave it."

"Yes Lady."

"If it is any comfort to you, Magistrate, your city is being treated the same as any other city in our line of march. All of whom have been in much the same state as yours."

The Magistrate's expression said that the situation of other cities was no comfort to him at all.

"INTERESTING NEWS," Shanorio said. "A week ago the Magistrate sent a bird to the capital, informing them that he could not possibly hold out if we advanced on him, and asking for more troops for the garrison.

"A bird has just come from the capital to the Magistrate carrying orders to hold the city at all costs. And it comes from none other than King Dalthorio h'Anovoto."

This caused an immediate uproar from those gathered in the room where Lusommi was conferring with her commanders.

"King Dalthorio! How does an Askos traitor come to be King of Wennz?"

"What else do we say, Kwadahheron," Lusommi responded, "when inexplicable things happen in Wennz? Doctor Gobnash is behind it."

"But why would an otherwise shrewd man such as Doctor Gobnash choose to elevate the likes of Dalthorio?"

"Because it gives Doctor Gobnash more power to do as he likes. Dalthorio is unlikely to have any other support. But Gobnash can terrorize the other lords into line. While Dalthorio sees to the day-to-day business of the kingdom, Doctor Gobnash takes care of his own affairs. Such as preparing his measures against our coming."

There was silence. A fly droned through the air.

"Don't be overly worried," Lusommi said. "We have beaten them before, and we have even triumphed against Doctor Gobnash's schemes. There is little reason why we should not do so again.

"Now, how are the preparations for our march?"

THERE WERE SEVERAL bales of pigskins, as well as several casks of what was claimed to be pig's blood. Though dark rumours circulates as to what kind of blood it might really be. There were several chests which were said to be pig's innards as well. Though no one could claim more accurate information than that which had been told to them by a butcher in a nearby town.

There were a number of other sealed chests. The rumours regarding their contents ranged from the eerie to the ridiculous.

The Doctor had all these moved into his workroom. But no one, not even the least knowledgeable regarding the Doctor's notions and temperament, asked any question. Nor did anyone make any speculation in the Doctor's presence regarding their contents or purpose. When the last of the deliveries were made, the Doctor called a man and said to him, "Go tell the King that I am making preparations for the approach of the Army of Askos. I will send to tell him when I am done."

He then went into his workroom and locked the door. As if even the most foolish had not the sense to avoid trespassing there.

"THIS IS A CHANGE! YOU asking me to accompany you on a risky enterprise."

Shapak-ailesh's face was grim. "If you'll think a bit, you'll understand that it's not something I'd suggest if I didn't see serious need."

"What's your plan, then?"

"We go into the capital, snoop around a bit."

"Maybe write on some walls?"

"Perhaps. But in main, I need to sniff out some magic."

"I'm not much good at sniffing magic; the only magic I can use is the talisman."

"But there are more dangers than Doctor Gobnash, and I need someone to watch my back while I sniff. And you always seem to have more luck than any man has a right to."

"Luck? Me? I only seem to have a knack for getting into trouble!"

"And for surviving those troubles."

"Mostly because someone else helped me out. Someone such as you."

"Which was a fortunate circumstance. That I was along, I mean. Look, if you're afraid to come, tell me. I'll find someone else."

"Well, in order to avoid putting you to the trouble of finding someone else, I'll overcome my terror and accompany you. But you know what my greatest terror is?"

"No, but it's undoubtedly something highly ridiculous."

"You think a scold from Lusi is ridiculous?"

Shapak-ailesh snorted. "I think you yourself have a great difficulty looking at life without laughing at it."

THEY PAUSED IN THE dimness of the evening. "Now, we have one more step to get into the city itself. When we get inside, I will be very busy, and will have not time to converse with you. The thing I have to do requires some time to complete, and that permits Doctor Gobnash a long time to become aware of my presence, and take his own countermeasures. The less interruptions I have, therefore, the less likely we are to be forced to deal with one of his nasty devices."

"And I keep watch."

"Yes, keep watch, make sure no one, such as the City Watch, interrupts me. You may find it necessary to use the talisman to save us. Keep in mind that the use of the talisman will send up a beacon bright as day for any who have magic sense."

In his right hand, Shapak-ailesh held a small blue sphere that seemed to have a faint light within it. He patted a small leather pouch at his belt. Apparently satisfied that all his necessary equipment was ready.

They then stepped into a rocky landscape where the earth was trembling. Cracks were opening in the ground, dust was rising, and the mule was shying wildly. "Sometimes the route through the Hidden Ways is a choice of insalubrious paths!" Shapak-ailesh shouted through the noise.

Then they were in a back alley, dark and smell-laden.

Shapak-ailesh put the small blue sphere against the wall at about the level of his waist, and left it there. It held by some force of its own.Taking his leather pouch, he went down on one knee.

From the pouch, he took a handful of stones in various colours, which showed up strangely in the light from the blue sphere. These he began to lay down in what looked like random order, one here, another there, and another way up here. By the time he had taken out the second handful of stones, it became clear that he was following a pattern. Though the random handfuls of stones made it necessary to lay them mostly in a scatter, or sometimes two or three close together.

Thotgol kept watch from inside the mouth of the alley, out of sight from the street. If the City Watch came, he reasoned that they would come marching, not stalking, and he would hear them.

While waiting for the Watch—or anyone else—he noted the pattern Shapak-ailesh was laying. Suddenly, he recognized the pattern. "That's the erss-pattern from the Dwarves' Bones!"

Shapak-ailesh glanced up at him briefly, then continued with his work. "It is indeed the erss-pattern. Which word is a corruption of *'erowis-pattern.'* Which in turn means *'power.'* Now, if you will hush, I hope to have this done before Doctor Gobnash stands over me, admiring me for my great fount of lore."

He continued to work with sure and steady fingers, laying the stones down in their proper configuration.

Finally he looked up and said, "The time-consuming part of this is done. Now comes the part which we will, figuratively, pound on Doctor Gobnash's door and shout, *'There is magic at work in the city!'*"

"And bring him trotting over with Spinners and Giggling Corpses following him, to ask politely *'What's going on?'*"

"Something of that sort. Now, once I have set this thing to working, it must continue its work. And no matter how rushed we might be in leaving here, I dare not leave any of these stones behind. Possession of even one of them will allow Doctor Gobnash to track me and attack me wherever I might be.

"So hold yourself ready. When the pattern is run, I want to be snatching up the stones and leaving."

He then spoke a low phrase in which Thotgol heard the word *'erowis,'* and the stones flickered to life. Lighting up in brief succession, a glow was running through the pattern, shining and ceasing to shine in succession. As Thotgol watched, however, there was a change. After it ran through the pattern, suddenly one red stone midway through the pattern did not flick out after its turn. Instead, it continued to shine a slightly duller red. Each time the flicker went over it, it shone. But each time the flicker passed, it merely shone a little less brightly.

Then a green one began to do the same, and a yellow one. After a time, there were six stones of various colours, at various points in the pattern, which continued to shine.

Perspiration shone on Shapak-ailesh's face, and he drummed a finger on his thigh. He was clearly concerned about the time it was taking. Thotgol, caught some nervousness from Shapak-ailesh. He could scarce prevent himself from peeking out of the alley-mouth to see if he could see any sign of Doctor Gobnash rushing up. Or perhaps flying up, or even a few of the Watch charging along the street.

'Or if Doctor Gobnash comes, will he do something like the Hidden Ways, and suddenly appear amongst us?'

Several things happened almost at once. The stones ceased their flickering. Except for the few that had been holding their light which flared briefly and went out. There was a faint sound like a faraway chime, and the blue light on the wall flared blood red.

Shapak-ailesh snatched up the stones in handfuls, stuffing them in the pouch. The mule, who had until then been standing calmly, whinnied. "Thotgol! Get over here! We're going now!"

The urgency in his voice brought Thotgol to his side in a jump. There was a brief snap of sound and light. A figure stood before them, visible only as a dark shape with the light from Shapak-ailesh's stone gone. "Wild-dancing whirlwind, come against this enemy here!"

'Fierce flying pig guts! Too close!'

The small man's hand touched his arm, and they were back in the land of the earthquakes. A crack in the ground was racing toward them. The mule reared in terror. Another step, and suddenly they were in a pine-scented forest, with a wind sighing through the trees.

"We have to go a little further. Doctor Gobnash will track us at least to the previous place, possibly here. But if we take another few steps we will be safe."

The next step took them to a battlefield where warriors in chariots wheeled back and forth. The warriors cast javelins and shot arrows at each other. Each of the chariots was driven by a younger man, often not much more than a boy, while an older man did the fighting.

The next step took them to a fair green plain, where large creatures grazed. Creatures with something the look of wild cattle about them.

Another step took them to a thick hot forest, where birds and animals screamed their harsh cries in the depths.

With a final step, they were outside the camp of the Army of Askos.

Chapter XXI
Fight For The City

"So, Thotgol, you've gone running off again?"

Thotgol spread his hands. "What can I say, Lady? Shapak-ailesh asked me along to watch his back. After what he's done for me, I could scarce turn him down."

She turned her gaze on the little man. "Shapak-ailesh, if you had asked me, I could have lent you a whole troop to guard you. Thotgol is still too important to us to be risked on casual ventures."

Shapak-ailesh bowed. "For true and certain you could have lent me guards, Lady. But if I had taken a half-dozen guards along, the chances were greater Doctor Gobnash would have noted our intrusion. Let alone the working of my little charm. Thotgol was as capable or more than a half-score of guards at watching. To say nothing of being able to throw a whirlwind into the face of Doctor Gobnash when he arrived."

"Put all that aside for a moment. I did learn Doctor Gobnash is up to something. If I'd had the time to run the pattern several more times, I would be able to tell you more exactly. But it seems he is building a force of special soldiers."

"Special soldiers? Magicians? Doesn't it take years of training to make a magician?"

"Lady, you leap ahead too quickly. There is magic involved, for certain, but they do not use magic. He has built a force of soldiers, built up out of various parts and components, and put a form of life into them. They will be, I believe, near invulnerable."

"How many?" demanded Shanorio.

"I fear that was not ascertainable in the time I had. At least fifty, possibly as many as a thousand. Certainly not more than that."

"A thousand invulnerable warriors?"

"I said '*near invulnerable*.' They can be slain, but with great difficulty. Please don't ask me for specifics, weak points, how many wounds, and the like. I can't help you there."

"You know," said Shanorio slowly, "there may be little difference, in effect, between '*near invulnerable*' and '*completely invulnerable*.' Once the men have seen the enemy take hard blows from the ranks in front of them, with little or no effect. Those men will be less likely to make the attempt, and soon your army will begin melting away like a mist in a hot sun."

"So, then, Shapak-ailesh," Lusommi asked, "is there anything you can do about these near-invulnerable warriors?"

"Regrettably, Lady, not much at all. Just as it requires time and preparation for Doctor Gobnash to make these warriors, so too do any countermeasures against them require time and preparation. And this time, I think, will not be granted us."

"So we will have to depend heavily on Thotgol and the talisman. Or are you going to tell us that will not be effective either?"

Shapak-ailesh bowed again. "No, Lady, I cannot see the talisman failing to be effective. I do wonder, though, if Doctor Gobnash has considered this in his plans."

THE MESSENGER KNOCKED diffidently on Doctor Gobnash's workroom door. He was a junior among the messengers. His compatriots had seen to it he had heard all the horror stories. All the tales of what Doctor Gobnash might do to a messenger who interrupted him when he didn't care to be interrupted.

On the other hand, one didn't disobey the king either. Narnash had been cruel and hard. But Dalthorio was vicious, punishing insults and threats which were discernible only to him. Not to knock on the wizard's door could well be construed as treason.

The door swung open, and Doctor Gobnash stood there. His beige robes were neat and tidy as usual. The only hint of haste was his skull cap was about a quarter-finger-breadth closer to his right ear than the left. He wore no expression, fierce or otherwise. "Yes?"

"The king has sent to tell you the Army of Askos is approaching."

"Yes. Inform the king that I am aware of this. My preparations will be done in time."

The door closed.

The messenger shivered. He was sure he would not be wanting to knock on that door without orders from the king. The Doctor was not a comfortable person to approach, not at all. He had made no threatening gestures, his expression had been calm, but still...

"HIGHNESS, I HAVE THE matter in hand." The wizard was showing a trace or weariness around his eyes. "If you would give the orders, I will send my force out to fight. Your commanders will have to see to it no one approaches them too closely. Be very certain that no one seems to threaten them."

"You have recruited soldiers?" Dalthorio sounded confused.

"Not recruited, but built, from various parts, and imbued with a sort of life. They have certain abilities that other soldiers do not."

"And you never produced them for Narnash?"

"No, Highness. For one thing, until recently, I had not achieved the requisite knowledge. For another, Narnash was never pressed so hard as we are. And for a third, the making of them is very difficult."

So soldiers were posted along the route between the workroom and the gate of the city, with special attention to the cross-streets. The guards were, in fact, mostly an assurance. There was no one in the city who would willingly look at any creation of Doctor Gobnash, let alone threaten them.

The soldiers, required to be on watch, observed the sight whether they wished to or not. They saw the workroom door open, and a man step out, followed by another and another and another. Once approximately fifty of them were in the street, they formed a column and marched away. More and more men kept coming out of the workroom.

The watching soldiers wondered how twenty of them could fit in the workroom, let alone fifty. As for the numbers which continued to come out, it was downright eerie.

And those strange marching soldiers merited attention themselves. At first they looked human, but soon differences became apparent. The faces were like a mix of man and pig. The pig-snout foreshortened into a broad nose, with boar-tusks protruding from the mouths. The ears, again, were like a mix of human and pig, and trimmed down to more human dimensions. The fact they all wore earrings, in a number of different fashions, only added to the weirdness.

The limbs were long, straight human-limbs, though they were well muscled. The hands were normal human-hands. The right hand of each held a spear slanted back over the shoulder. While the left hand carried a small shield.

Some of the soldiers guarding the route swore they could see faint seams in the flesh of Doctor Gobnash's army. A sort of patchwork effect. While others scoffed at that for a dreamer's tale.

OUTSIDE THE CITY, THE army of Askos saw the gates of the city open and a formation of fifty infantry march out and deploy into a line.

"Are these Doctor Gobnash's magic soldiers?"

"Yes, Lady, I can sniff the magic scent on them from here." Shapak-ailesh had become a part of Lusommi's war-council. A few had been angered at that, most shrugged and said, "If we have a Batan ox-driver with a wind-talisman, why not a little merchant with a knowledge of magic?"

"Only fifty?" demanded Kwadahheron "Are they that dangerous?"

Shapak-ailesh shook his head. "He has more available than he is showing here. He's playing a game of some kind."

"A game? I'll show him a game!" He urged his horse into motion.

"Come back here, Kwadahheron!" Shanorio shouted. The young man ignored him, riding toward a force of Askos horsemen some two hundred strong. "Destroyer's teeth!" the older man swore and rode after him.

The rest of them could see the two arguing for a moment in front of the horsemen. Then Kwadahheron rode toward the enemy. After a momentary hesitation, the horsemen followed after.

Shanorio returned, scowling, to the war-council.

The fifty infantry shifted formation, turning into a short, thin phalanx. Their spearpoints projected to hold off the horses. The horses shied away from those points, and the riders tried to strike at the infantry. Because they were being held at a distance of about a half-spearshaft, they had little effect.

They swept round the side of the phalanx. The men in the flanking files turned to face their spears toward this threat. Horses and men were down now. But none of Doctor Gobnash's men had fallen. The horses were all round the infantry now. It was no longer possible for the phalanx to maintain an impenetrable wall of spearpoints in all directions. This meant the cavalrymen were able to get a blow or two in. Though, with little affect.

Shortly thereafter, the cavalry began to pull back. A quarter of their number remained on the field. Their foe had lost no more than five, if that.

KWADAHHERON, CARRYING several minor wounds, was a chastened man. He sat his horse with bowed head as Shanorio scolded him. "Well-done, young man! With our whole army watching our effort, how easy will it be to attack these now? You were told '*near invulnerable.*' Did you not understand, or did you merely not believe? How many of them did you manage to kill?"

"Two, perhaps three." A murmur ran around the group; they understood the numbers. By the time they had killed all fifty, the morale of their army would be destroyed. And they had all heard Shapak-ailesh say there were more of these soldiers to fight.

Lusommi spoke, "Shapak-ailesh, is it possible Doctor Gobnash is hoping to have Thotgol use the talisman to the point where it is risky to use it again. Then have the rest of his soldiers attack us?"

"Lady, I believe you have guessed rightly. The life these soldiers have is not the kind of life you and I know. And such, free will as they possess is circumscribed by the necessity to do their maker's bidding. They will most likely do as they are ordered. Up to, and including offering themselves to be slain.

"It is just this sort of meddling with life which has brought Doctor Gobnash to the attention of The Lady of Praises who has asked me to help deal with him."

"Will you destroy him, then?"

He shook his head. "It is not so simple, Lady. I have certain abilities. But among them is not the ability to wave my hand and say *'Hangastaferaz,'* or some such, and will Doctor Gobnash not to be.

"I do have some little tricks and notions in my packs, things which can and will be of assistance. But I will require assistance as well. It will not be a simple matter, Lady."

"So. What will you require?"

"In the first instance, it will not be so much what I will require as who. I will need Thotgol to assist me."

"Why him specifically, and not another?"

"Because, Lady, it is possible we may find these," he gestured toward the enemy, "attacking us while we are doing what we must do. Another person would have nothing but edged metal to protect us. Thotgol has the talisman."

She considered that and nodded. "For my part, I agree,. But I will not command Thotgol to go into danger. Thotgol, the choice is yours."

He grinned. "Ah, then I have your permission to go running off, this time?"

"Yes, scoundrel, you have my permission. You also have my royal command to come back again."

"Without fail, Most Royal Lady of Askos. Come, Shapak-ailesh, quickly, before she changes her mind."

SHAPAK-AILESH LED THE three of them, including the mule, out toward the place where Doctor Gobnash's soldiers stood steady in their phalanx. Close to the city the grass was trampled down. A maze of paths and charred lumps showed where buildings outside the city walls had been destroyed. This was done to deny a besieging army either cover or building material for siege engines.

At somewhere close to a short bowshot, Shapak-ailesh stopped and began digging in the mule's pack. "Now where has it got to? It ought to be... Ah, here!"

He reached his arm into the pack so deeply, it seemed to Thotgol he must be reaching into the very belly of the mule herself. Shapak-ailesh then pulled out a large copper ring.

"Here, now, hold this end." The copper ring turned out to be a coil of copper wire, with a small blue ceramic bead at each end.

"Now, the idea is to stretch this out straight, so they have to cross it to get to us. Ideally, we'll avoid getting so close they divide to chase us down.

"Listen carefully; I'll call you when it's time to set this thing down. After that we go back here quickly, so even if they do chase after us, they'll have to cross the wire to do so. You understand?"

"Yes. Carry this wire down, drop it when you say drop, and run back here as though Morkerr Deathlord were on my heels."

So they carried the wire. Thotgol walking at a medium-quick pace, Shapak-ailesh moving at a near-run. After a bit, Thotgol began to wonder how close they were to come. The various features, broad flat noses, boar-tusks, and ears all became distinguishable. As did the fact some of the faces were turned toward him. Staring at him with an expression that could not quite be described as curiosity.

Shapak-ailesh's call came just as a pair of soldiers at this end broke ranks to stride toward Thotgol. While another pair went for Shapak-ailesh. Thotgol set the wire down, noting with a little surprise it lay straight. It didn't even attempt to return to its coil. He set out at a run toward the mule.

He arrived there and turned to see Shapak-ailesh still rushing in Thotgol's direction. His short legs moving quickly. The two warriors who had come after Thotgol were sprawled on the ground. About where the wire lay, although it was invisible at this distance. The other pair, who had been after Shapak-ailesh, were sprawled at the other end. They lay pretty much in direct line with the first two.

Shapak-ailesh came puffing up. "Some people," he gasped, "have an unreasonably unfair advantage in having legs long as trees."

"Now what? We hope they're stupid enough to charge across that wire, having seen what it's done to those four?"

"Well, if you'll give me a moment to catch my breath." Shapak-ailesh rooted in the mule's pack and pulled out his crossbow. "It's not so much a matter of their being stupid, as it is in overcoming what they possess in the way of good sense." He cocked the crossbow. "You see, they are made to attack and to fight. They might well even be pushed into an attack, where they ought not to attack."

He aimed the crossbow and squeezed the trigger. The bolt left the crossbow in a blur, and suddenly appeared in the chest of one of the soldiers. A human soldier would have dropped where he stood with such a wound, but not so here.

Several of them looked from the bolt in their companion's chest to where Thotgol and Shapak-ailesh stood. Straining as though trying to connect the two disparate elements.

"You're sure they're not completely stupid?"

Shapak-ailesh, cocking his crossbow, looked up at him and snorted. "They're not stupid. It's only their minds don't work the same way as yours or mine. We'll have to go closer."

"And if they can take a crossbow bolt and keep coming, I think I'd best be ready with the talisman."

"Just don't use it until they cross the wire."

"You mean some of them might?"

"It's possible. I think it's sufficiently powerful to be able to deal with this lot, but there are so many uncertainties."

"There are? How many are likely to cross? Twenty? Thirty?"

"No, not that many. I really have no way of knowing. Now hush."

He aimed the crossbow and shot again. The bolt zipped across the short distance and was suddenly stuck in the warrior's chest next to the first one. This time there was no doubt they realized what was happening. Thotgol heard a mutter of sound from the ranks. Next came a shout. Then they were coming, like a boulder rolling downhill. The warriors looked unstoppable.

He was just about to use the talisman when the first rank crossed the wire and sprawled without a sound. The second rank followed, stumbled, continued another pace, and dropped. The last rank followed and stumbled, though only a few fell immediately. The rest continued, converging on Thotgoal and Shapak-ailesh. More of them falling all the time. Until at last there was only one, coming on at a shambling run, as though partially stunned by the effect of the wire.

It seemed a little wasteful to Thotgol to use the talisman on one single soldier. Especially one staggering with the effect of Shapak-ailesh's magic wire. So he pulled his ox-goad free.

The spear thrust again. This time Thotgol moved aside and smashed a downward blow on the spearshaft with the ox-goad. The spearshaft cracked. The warrior, without hesitation, tossed it aside and drew his sword.

This evened matters out, as far as the comparative ranges of weapons was concerned. But the magic-built warrior was still quick. *'Fierce flying pig guts! I'd hate to be matched with him when he wasn't affected by magic!'*

Something whipped past Thotgol. A crossbow quarrel was sunk deep in the warrior's chest. The warrior glanced down. Thotgol lunged in and struck at the side of the man's neck. Then jumped back as the sword swung.

Without even a shake of the head, the warrior jumped. Thotgol parried. *'Fierce flying pig guts! That neck-blow would have dropped an ordinary man in his tracks! Near-invulnerable for sure!'*

The man stuck again and again. Thotgol had no time to do anything but dodge and parry. Another crossbow quarrel struck, this time in the man's right eye. The warrior grunted and paused. In that pause, Thotgol thrust for his throat.

The blow, which should have opened the vein in his neck, merely caused a sluggish flow of blood.

The warrior grunted again. Thotgol whipped in a blow to the side of his head. Which ought to have rattled the warrior's brain, even through the helmet. Thotgol jumped back to avoid a return blow of the sword.

Thotgol paused, inching a bit to the left, looking for an opening. The warrior having a little trouble seeing properly with only one eye, moved around cautiously himself. Without warning he jumped at Thotgol whipping his sword up for a quick downward slash.

Thotgol slipped aside and swung a stroke to the ribs. He saw his enemy's head jerk as another quarrel glanced off the helmet.

Thotgol was more than a little tired himself. Wary of this man who could shrug off deadly wounds, Thotgol moved too slow, and found himself guarding against a series of sword-thrusts.

The next crossbow bolt took the man in the left eye and he roared, not a sound of pain but of anger. Still he stood, whipping his sword back and forth in vicious slashes from one side to the other. Thotgol, feeling this ought to give him some advantage, approached carefully.

The man heard Thotgol, or sensed him by some other means, for he turned to face him, sword held ready. Thotgol, ox-goad up, moved in cautiously. A step this way. The sword followed. A step that way. The sword followed. Another quarrel struck into the man's chest, and he stumbled. Quick as he could, Thotgol lashed out with his ox-goad across the man's neck. He went down on one knee, then came surging up, driving the sword toward Thotgol.

Thotgol parried and thrust again at the throat. Having struck so many crippling blows only to see them have no effect, he jumped back again. The enemy turned to face him, then swung a vicious slash which missed by about the length of the sword and fell on his face.

Thotgol stamped a foot down on the back of the man's neck three times before he felt reasonably certain the magic-built warrior had ceased to move.

He turned to Shapak-ailesh. "One of them. And even with no eyes, still dangerous!"

"So now you know what *'near-invulnerable'* means."

"What a cheery thought! And what do we do now? Shout insults at the city until someone else comes out?"

"Oh, I think we needn't go to so much trouble. There's another batch coming now."

"How joyful! Do you have any other useful tricks in your mule's packs?"

"Not much of real use. I'm afraid it's up to you."

"You mean I get to be a hero all by myself?"

"Oh, yes. And if you survive the Lovely Lusi will fling herself on your neck and give you her heartfelt thanks."

"Huh! A heartfelt clout on the ear, more like. Any useful advice?"

"No, only that Doctor Gobnash hopes to have you use the talisman beyond what is safe. Keep that in mind."

"More cheerful thoughts. Well, let's see."

He looked at the band, another fifty of Doctor Gobnash's warriors, marching out the gate toward them.

He pointed. *"O North Wind from the frozen lands, blow, blow, blow!"*

The sudden, howling wind smashed into the soldiers, bearing a freight of freezing snow. The magic-built men slowed, falling in their tracks. By the time Thotgol felt it necessary to halt the wind, the last of them were down.

"It's never had such a deadly effect on people before."

Shapak-ailesh nodded. "I thought it possible they might be particularly sensitive to temperature. But it wasn't something I wanted you relying on. Besides that, this was only another fifty. How many more has he got in there."

"You're asking me? You're the one with the magical spying tricks. I'm just a blowhard with a talisman."

"Ever since our little excursion into the city, Doctor Gobnash has been holding a cloud over his works. That has an advantage for us, though."

"Your inability to spy on on him is an advantage for us?"

"No. His using power to shield his works and therefore having that much less power to work against us is an advantage. Now get yourself ready; here they come again."

Another fifty marched out of the gate. Not at all affected by the bodies of others of their fellows lying on the ground. nor by the swiftly melting snow.

Thotgol called the hot south wind on them. Partly, he was recalling Shapak-ailesh's advice about their sensitivity to temperature. Partly, considering the south wind to have an ameliorating effect on the north wind called previously. This might allow him a little extra use of the talisman.

The hot wind did have an effect, though not so drastic. Men began to fall, some of them rose again, others did not. Some did not fall at all. By the time Thotgol was required to lift the wind, there were some twelve or more still moving. The warriors were slightly unsteady, but they were still coming.

The picture in his mind of a boar-tusked warrior. Both eyes gone but still fighting, pressed Thotgol almost to the point of panic. Pointing at the remaining warriors, he called the whirlwind.

They were almost too near for that. The whirlwind started as a mere riffle in the grass in front of him. By the time it reached the soldiers it was a large dark funnel, picking them up and flinging them aside. It was close enough that he felt wind-eddies from it. He wondered how those cavalrymen had survived at the battle, and not only survived, but came on to attack him. Had the horses perhaps thrown them first, so they were missed by the wind?

But he realized he had no time for speculations. He turned to Shapak-ailesh. "Is there any way, any way at all, you can tell where Doctor Gobnash is? I can't keep using the north wind or the whirlwind."

"He's most likely standing on the walls, watching and directing. That takes no magic at all. On the other hand, the most precise position I can give for him is somewhere left of the gate."

"That'll have to do."

He pointed at the walls. "O wild dancing whirlwind, come against the magician on the walls before us!"

'Can it be directed so precisely?' he asked himself, *'No way of knowing, but it had to be tried. At least he might occupy Doctor Gobnash, keep him from sending his magic soldiers for a bit.'*

The whirlwind concentrated its force on part of the wall. Thotgol waited as long as he dared before calling it off. A dark figure came falling out of the sky where the whirlwind had been. It dropped heavily on the wall and rolled back inside. The gates remained shut.

Shapak-ailesh muttered something beside him.

"What?"

"A moment, please." He reached into the pouch at his waist and drew forth what seemed to be an ordinary coin. He flipped it into the air, caught it. Then slapped it down on his wrist, for all the world as though wagering on heads or tails. It was heads. Though Thotgol did not recognize the king shown thereon and the inscription was in some foreign writing.

"Hah!" There was victory in his grunt.

"What?"

"First of all, following your assault with the whirlwind, I felt the cloud over Doctor Gobnash's works begin to thin. I then used this," he held up the coin "as a rough-and-ready means of discovering if he were still there. Apparently, he is not. Though before we walk casually into the city, I would prefer to make some more complex tests."

"And his soldiers, if there are still any left in there?"

Shapak-ailesh scowled. "Now that is a difficult question. Unfortunately, without the Doctor to guide and direct them, they will not merely die. They may, however-—He broke off as sounds of fighting and shouting came from over the walls. "Well, there is the answer. Someone likely made a threatening motion. One or more of the warriors attacked, bringing in more soldiers to help the first ones. Which brought in more magical warriors. We'd best get back to the Lady."

Chapter XXII
Clearing The City

"From the look of it, Lady," Shapak-ailesh said, "without Doctor Gobnash to restrain them, the magical soldiers are attacking anyone and everyone in sight. This has caused fighting throughout the city, and likely also set into action those sorts of people who try to profit from any disturbance by looting and destruction. The end result is the city will suffer badly."

"And you can do nothing?"

He bowed, "Lady, I have some tricks and notions, and a bits of this sort of knowledge and that. Given some time, I can be of some help to you."

"You suggest we move into the city, then?"

"No, Lady, I suggest you send heralds to call to the people in the city, offering them safety if they come out. I suggest before you send people inside the walls, you permit me a bit of time to see what I can do for you."

LUSOMMI HAD GOOD REASON for talking to Thotgol privately. Though she realized it scandalized the more status-minded of her Lords, followers, and servants. But if she chose to offer him a seat and a glass of wine, that was up to her.

"So you met Shapak-ailesh in a strange fashion. And he spoke cryptic things about the "Lady of Praises" and the probability of having to help you. Other than that, you know nothing about him?"

"Lady, I know only what I've seen and heard. He knows a lot of things, he has limitations, and he has moral standards."

"Ah. Moral standards?"

"Yes, Lady. He—-"

"Call me Lusi. At least when we're alone."

"Ah. Lusi, then." There was a touch of diffidence in his voice. "I'm afraid the only nicknames ever attached to me were not the sort of thing suitable for a lady. At any rate, about Shapak-ailesh. He'd been given the job, as I understand it of seeing to the destruction of Doctor Gobnash.

"Now that Doctor Gobnash has been disposed of, he could simply have left us to deal with the magical warriors. But he will not. He will do his best to help us destroy them."

"Such as that magical wire?"

He shrugged. "I really can't say, Lusi. My impression is he has picked up various things in his travels, traded for some, and had teaching at others. I don't think I'd like to predict what he might do. You recall me telling you how he flipped that coin to determine if Doctor Gobnash were still there or not? Now, was that a trick he had learned, or was the coin an enchanted one he had gathered in his travels? And why does the mule always have to accompany him when he travels the Hidden Ways?"

"So if I want to know about him, I should ask him?"

"And like as not he would deflect your questions into some discussion of philosophy or poetics."

"LORD DISIKOMIN, I'D like you to take charge of finding food for the city refugees."

The grey brows lifted. "Me, Lady?"

"Yes. I think you'd be more sympathetic than many of my people."

"I think I understand," he said slowly, "but—-"

"I would not have you running your own men short. That was not my intention. Nor would I expect the refugees to be extremely well-fed. Enough to keep them from starving, particularly the children.

"And I'm sure some of the refugees have managed to bring a fair amount of money out with them. Extract what money you can from them, and use it to buy food for in the local farms and villages."

"And don't let the villagers overcharge us too badly either?" His smile was grim. "You'll lose some friends, Lady."

"You can promise them the Noble Lady will take their generosity into account come tax-time."

He laughed out loud. "Take with one hand, give with the other? You'll make a fine ruler, Lady."

"Thank you, Lord Disikomin."

SHAPAK-AILESH BOWED under the weight of a large leather sack over his shoulder. It chimed softly when he set it down. He looked up at Lusommi, his face worn and a bit pale.

"I believe I have what is needed, Lady."

"More magical wire?"

"In a sense, yes." He reached into the sack and pulled out a ring, slightly larger than would suit a man's finger.

"I have some thousand of these. Some are to fit around the shaft of an arrow, snug against the head. Some are to fit round a spearshaft, in much the same way. Finally, some are intended to fit round a sword-blade, next to the hilt. Each of them would have the capability of killing one magical warrior, perhaps more. Warn your soldiers not to go to the well too often.

"You will have to assign your commanders the task of handing out these things. I have no other advice, and I doubt your commanders would appreciate my interference in the ordering of their troops."

"And what do we owe you for this?"

"Lady, I plan to sleep for a week. When your soldiers have cleared the city of magical warriors, you can think what it might have been worth."

She smiled.

"And if I cheat you, it all rebounds on me?"

He returned the smile, somewhat wearily. "Ah, how good it is to know some still hold by the old standards. Good day, Lady."

"YOU REALLY THINK YOU should be with us, Thotgol?"

"Don't worry, Tahheron, I won't get in your way."

They were in one of the shabbier quarters of town. There stood single-story buildings made of rough lumber, sticks, and bricks. All held together with desperation. The streets were narrow and twisted, with an occasional alley which was more noisome than the street.

"I'm not worried about you getting in my way. I'm worried about what the Lady will say to me if you get in the way of some piece of sharp metal."

"Don't fret, Tahheron, I'll be very careful."

"I've seen you being careful, Skulking around cities full of enemies and scribbling on walls."

"You were never there!"

"I got reports from Moxatarum."

"Moxa's a nice fellow, but he tends to embellish."

"I did not! If anything, I downplayed it!"

"All right, enough nattering. Alley coming up. Let's watch out—-"

Thotgol considered the attackers had a fine sense of timing. There was a sound of footsteps in the alley, and the enemy was on them. The defenders had an advantage in that only one attacker could come out of the mouth of the alley at a time. There was also limited room in the street for them to spread out. On the other hand, there was only one man next to the alley with a weapon fitted for fighting the magical warriors.

"Bows!" Tahheron shouted. He'd arranged his force with just this sort of thing in mind. Bowmen, even using plain arrows, could have some effect on near-invulnerable warriors. This gave the men with the properly-fitted weapons an instant to change formation to meet the enemy.

There were only ten attackers. Though 'only ten', as applied to near-invulnerable opponents, had a meaning all its own. Arrows whipped through the air, thudding into wood. Sometimes making an uglier sound as they hit flesh. Weapons clashed, men grunted and shouted. Thotgol, having cadged one of the rings to put on his ox-goad next to the metal point, watched for a time or opportunity. He had no desire to disturb Tahheron's formation, having a fair degree of faith the Captain knew what he was doing. On the other hand, he was ready if matters came to that.

And suddenly the fight was done. "Mandoriat, are you all right?"

Mandoriat was staring at the carnage. "Just fine, Captain. Never saw anything like it. That one, I scratched him with my spear and he went down like he'd been hammered. And some of them were still fighting with a half-dozen arrows in 'em."

"So now you know what we're up against. They're tough, but they can be killed, particularly with the little man's magic.

"Now, anybody wounded? Take a minute for bandaging, everybody take a drink of water, then get ready to move again."

DALTHORIO SAT ON HIS throne and waited. One of those Wennzish servants had brought him the news of Doctor Gobnash's death, perhaps a little exultantly. And at that moment, he suddenly realized his position was beyond precarious, it was fatal. His status had been as an ally, and untrustworthy one, of Narnash. Then as a ruler supported only by Doctor Gobnash, and the fear of Doctor Gobnash among the Wennzish nobles.

He had not even had time to bring up his own Askos guards to replace the Wennzish guards. And there wasn't a one of those black-haired bastards who would put himself out to save Dalthorio from tripping over a doorsill. Much less put themselves in the way of a weapon for him.

There was a mutter of noise out in the hallway. No need to guess what it might be. He stood and drew his sword. No matter what they thought of him. He was not about to go running down half-familiar hallways to be trapped and cornered like some rat baring his teeth at last in a blind corner.

No, the gods had cursed him from the beginning. Bringing that Morkerr-eaten ox-driver with the talisman to replace him in Lusi's regard. He, who ought to have been king of Askos!

"Come on, you Wennzish louts, come on! Come in and see how a man dies!"

He wondered if there might just be some unwatched way out of the Palace. The sword was growing slippery in his hand.

LUSI PACED BACK AND forth in her pavilion. *'Showing my nerves,'* she sighed, *'Bad thing, but I'll have to live with it.'*

She'd thought it bad enough to watch an open battle. But this was worse. To wait out here. While here soldiers hunted, beyond her sight, through the streets and alleys of the city. Reports came to her, on an irregular basis. The last one said twenty-one of the magical soldiers had been confirmed dead, and the body of Dalthorio had been found. He'd been stabbed several times and left on the floor of the palace. Losses among the Askos were said to be light.

One of the unforeseen things in this operation was that some bands of looters had challenged the soldiers. Mostly with weapons from ambush. Even so, such unpredictable opponents could not be left in place. This meant attacking their positions. Usually defended houses. A task made only slightly less difficult by the lack of training and weapons on the part of the defenders.

She was fairly sure, short of having an actual report to the fact, Thotgol had attached himself to one of the hunting groups. She hadn't seen him recently, and where else would he be?

The only cheering thought in this was he would likely have managed to get hold of one of the magic rings for his ox-goad. *'Probably won it gambling.'*

With the war practically done and no Wennzish armies in the field. There was no longer a real reason to insist he stay safe. *'Wardesh guard and guide, Lusi if he were the kind of person who'd be willingly kept safe, would you be interested?'*

DISIKOMIN SMILED AT the citizens in front of him, gathered in front of the ragged and battered bits of shelter some of them had managed to make. The Army of Askos had steered them over to a relatively flat place away from the walls. But otherwise left them pretty much alone. "Now, it is necessary to find money to help pay for food for the refugees from the city. We require your assistance. In return, the Lady Lusommi will reward your generosity at tax-time."

One of the people in front of him shifted uncomfortably. "Lord, why am I brought here? I fled the city with nothing but the clothes I stand up in."

'And very expensive clothes they are, too.' Disikomin changed his smile to a look of disapproval. "You are all called here because we have it on very good authority you left the city with a fair sum of money. I would feel disappointed if any of you were to accuse me of untruth."

He knew well they had money. Most of them had been pointed out to his agents. As confirmation, most of them had been willing to bargain for a chicken, a bag of grain, a loaf of bread, or the like.

"Lord, what of our business within the city? Even now they are being plundered by the scum who remain inside. And indeed, if we pay our money to you we will be destitute. Even if the Most Powerful Lady does manage to destroy those unkillable ones!"

"If she does? Should I perhaps convey your lack of faith to the Lady Lusommi?"

The merchant paled, suddenly realizing what he had said.

Disikomin lost patience for further chatter. He waved away the profuse apologies before they were well underway. "Enough! There is no more to be said. You will be given a sheet of paper on which will be written a sum of money. You will report back here tomorrow noon, with the money in hand. The money ought to be in coin. Though some jewellery will be accepted, subject to agreed valuation by the Lady's people.

"Further, you will all report here at noon. There will be no excuses. If any of you die overnight, be prepared for me and my soldiers to be coming to Morkerr Deathlord to demand your presence. Understood?"

There were various mutters and mumbles, and they turned to go.

THOTGOL STRETCHED HIS legs out toward the campfire. They were bivouacking, rather than camping in some deserted house. A house might feel safe, with walls all around. But if someone tossed a torch in a window or door, it could be a deathtrap for people trying to get out through a limited number of exits. In the open, if it happened they were attacked at night, they'd have room to fight.

"Running out of tuskers," commented Moxatarum. "Haven't seen more than five all day, and this is what, the third day?"

"About that. Can't say I'm sorry to be running short."

"Me either. Captain, do we go after the looters, now?"

"No. Our orders are to attack if we run into 'em or if they attack us. Otherwise, just concentrate on the tuskers. Once they're done, the Lady'll probably send in more people to deal with the looters."

The fire crackled and spat in the silence, casting flickering light on the smudged faces, winking on the dully-shining metal of armour-harness and spearpoint.

"Moxa, it's time for you to spell Mandoriat on watch, and Griforio, you go spell Lanfatorum. Make sure you take a bit to get your eyes used to the dark before you send the other two back.

"Rest of you, get some sleep. No telling what we might run into tomorrow."

"LADY, ALL REPORTS SAY the magical warriors are no more. None have been seen anywhere in the last three days."

"It's time to deal with the looters, then?"

Shanorio nodded. "Yes, Lady. It's not the sort of fighting anyone looks forward to, but I suppose it has to be done."

"It's that difficult, then?"

"Well, usually they're no real fighters, Lady. But they tend to go to ground somewhere, and our men will have to go in and pry them out. It'd almost be easier to burn the city and start over again.

She was annoyed at herself for taking that notion seriously for a moment. "Yes, I suppose it might. But we haven't got the time to waste. We've got to rule this land, at least for long enough to set it up as a kingdom under someone we can trust."

She sighed. "Give the orders."

Chapter XXIII
Endings and Beginnings

"Dark Destroyer's Teeth! I don't want to be Lady of Wennz-Askos! I just want to go home and be Lady of Askos."

She strode across the tile-floored room, from one grey wall to the other.

"But you can't, Lusi. Shanorio's already told you. There's a snake-pit of lords here all ready to overthrow whoever you put in for King. In five years you'll have them ready to march to *'wipe out the stain of the defeat by Askos.'*"

"I know all that, Thotgol. How well do I know all that!" Lusommi looked over to a bright wallhanging, featuring Wardesh sending forth the birds. She stared at it as though it were to blame for everything. She whirled on him again. "But I don't like it! You know I'm going to have to be near as Bloody as Narnash was, at least for a few years?"

He nodded. "I wish I had something comforting to tell you."

"And I'm going to need an heir."

"Yes. It'll make more people feel safe, knowing that the succession is sure. Won't put an end to all the plotting, but it'll cut down on it some."

"I can't have an heir by myself."

"No, I imagine you'll have to look around and—-You're not considering me?"

"Ah, finally he sees it! Yes, you."

"That would put the lords in a fury. I'm not one of them, and they'd never forget."

"But you are one of them."

"What!"

"I've made a proclamation listing people whose services to me have entitled them to grants of land and favour and you're one of them. No, don't fuss. All the hereditary lords, if you look back in their family history, became lords in the same way. By giving service to the crown.

"And just in case you're thinking you were the only excuse for this latest proclamation, don't fuss. The reign and the maulings of Bloody Narnash have left us with a dearth of leaders.

"Besides, don't you think your efforts were worth something?"

"But you're paying me!"

"Nonsense! The one has nothing to do with the other!"

"And I'll spend most of my time fighting this lord and that because they insult me. Or will you make insulting your consort a capital offense?"

"You haven't thought it through. Most of my lords are in much the same situation as yourself. Men who've been rewarded by me, and with backgrounds not much more "noble" than your own.What you're likely to find is this lord or that coming to you to have you influence some decision of mine in their favour. Nobody will pick quarrels with someone they might someday have to ask a favour of."

"That's almost as bad. All that lot fawning over me, and me knowing it's only because of my position."

"So they come to you asking your favour, you suggest they toss the Dwarves' Bones with you for it."

"And if I lose, you pay my losses?" He rose, his voice going dangerous.

"Sit down, fool! If you lose, you do just what you said, mention their case to me. I make up my mind."

"And you'd be able to tell me a lot about what the lords are saying."

"Your pet spy? This is sounding worse and worse."

"You're the one who's making up all the excuses. I thought we knew each other a little. Is life with me such a terrible prospect, then?"

And suddenly, looking into the eyes becoming intense with annoyance, he realized what the answer was, despite all his objections.

"No, it isn't."

SHAPAK-AILESH LEFT before the wedding. "I regret, there are places I must be, little tasks for me to do. But I will surely come back from time to time, if only for a discussion of philosophy."

"And you'll be welcome. Will you come to the naming-feast of our first child?"

He smiled. "Lady, could I do any less for one who has such regard for the old ways? Yes, I will come indeed. And you, young Thotgol, if you find yourself in need, you know what to do."

"Sometime I am going to have to find a moment to discuss old epics with you."

"And as to that, I have a gift to you from me." He extended a leather case, worked with a motif of stars, trees, and flowers. "This contains two scrolls. One is a copy of the original of the epic in question. The other is a a translation of that same epic into the Common Language.

"And now, farewell, for I must be going."

DELFI CAME TEARING into the house, earning a mild reproof. "Delfi, you've got the whole outside for rushing around in."

"He's coming back, Ma! He's coming back!"

"Who's coming back, Delfi?"

He gave her a look full of small boy disgust. "Lord Disikomin, of course, Ma. Who else would it be?"

"Oh, that's nice. Don't go pestering him right away."

"Oh, Ma! I don't have to go anywhere! He's coming up the trail right now, wearing that shirt you made him!"

"Oh!" She touched a hand to her hair, then straightened, all trace of fluster gone. "He'll like something cool to drink. Go into the kitchen and ask Filoris to pour some cider. Go along, now, you can talk to the Lord in a bit."

Disikomin was, in fact, just coming into the yard when she stepped out to greet him.

He swung down off his horse, and turned to her.

"The war's over."

"So I'd heard. I'd have thought you'd go back to your homeland."

"There wasn't much there. The Lady had already promised me land hereabouts, and I believe I'll settle in Askos. In the Askos part of Wennz-Askos, I mean."

"How nice. And we'll see you from time to time?"

"Oh, for certain. I..." His voice trailed away.

"Come inside. Your scout announced your arrival, so there should be some cider ready."

"Oh, how is Delfi?"

"Doing fine. He's been expecting you, you know. He's a little young to understand about homelands, so he was quite sure you'd be back."

"And you weren't'

This destroyed her composure. "Well, I hoped-—I wished-—I wanted you to be happy, and it seemed more likely you'd be happy at home."

"But Junommi, my home is here."

Filoris, carrying a tray with pitcher and cups, stepped discreetly back into the house.

THE ARCHER STEPPED into the familiar clearing. She was over in front of the house. She was not one who would run to him with open arms, but as he approached, he noticed that her lips had quirked up into a smile. That was something he'd seldom seen over the last year.

"It's all over. I'm back."

"You're home," she corrected.

About the Author

J P Wagner was both a sci-fi/fantasy writer and journalist. While Jim's editorials and informative articles could be found in publications such as the Western Producer and the Saskatoon Star Phoenix, he made his debut as a novelist with the flint-lock fantasy, **Railway Rising** which was originally through Edge Publications in 2015. This was followed by the young adult fantasy novel **The Search for the Unicorns** (published posthumously in 2018).

A self-proclaimed curmudgeon but known to his family as a merry jokester, his words have brightened many lives.

You can visit his offical website at:

www.revjpwagner.com

Don't miss out!

Visit the website below and you can sign up to receive emails whenever J P Wagner publishes a new book. There's no charge and no obligation.

https://books2read.com/r/B-A-EKQG-CAHKB

BOOKS 2 READ

Connecting independent readers to independent writers.

www.ingramcontent.com/pod-product-compliance
Lightning Source LLC
Chambersburg PA
CBHW060425030726
47495CB00003B/736